Capta

Captain Pamphile

Alexandre Dumas

Translated by Andrew Brown

Hesperus Classics
Published by Hesperus Press Limited
4 Rickett Street, London SW6 1RU
www.hesperuspress.com

First published in 1839
First published by Hesperus Press Limited, 2006

Designed and typeset by Fraser Muggeridge studio
Printed in Jordan by Jordan National Press

ISBN: 1-84391-134-5
ISBN13: 978-1-84391-134-0

CONTENTS

FOREWORD

In 1968, at the age of twenty-two, I was made Director of the children's theatre company at the Midlands Art Centre in Edgbaston. It was an intoxicating time to live in Birmingham. Playwrights, novelists and painters had gravitated to the relatively cheap accommodation available in the area; the young Brian Cox and Michael Gambon were the stars of the Birmingham Rep; even our wisecracking security man had convinced himself he had talent, changed his name to Bob Carolgees[1] and was given his own television show.

Because both my girlfriend and I were holding down full-time jobs, we could afford a larger, slightly posher flat than any of our friends, so every night our sitting room was full of young hippies watching Monty Python, reading Hermann Hesse and Robert Crumb, listening to the Beatles, drinking pale ale and smoking fat cigarettes purchased from the dealers of Balsall Heath. We seldom went out in search of entertainment, preferring to bask in the company of our little circle, laughing at each other's witty anecdotes and observations. Others might find us cliquey, snobbish and feckless but, as far as we were concerned, if bees had knees we were those patellas.

Pets figured large in our lives at that time. My girlfriend had a miniature dachshund called Hermann who looked as cute as a Mabel Lucy Atwell drawing but was actually a greedy and ruthless food-processing machine. One Saturday night we shut him in our kitchen, and while we slept he managed to open the fridge door. Next morning he lay on the floor glassy-eyed and unable to move, with a stomach the size of a football, but our Sunday beef was nowhere to be seen. We also had a budgerigar named Trotsky,[2] a rabbit called Monty who could push a red ball round the room with his nose, and a cat, Eyebrows, to whom I was devoted. One day Trotsky was allowed out of his cage in a misguided gesture of liberation and Eyebrows ate him. I never felt quite the same about her after that.

1. Comedian and puppeteer. His best known puppet was Spit the Dog. Others included Cough the Cat and Plonky the Pink Lion. Now runs a candle shop in Cheshire.
2. Leading figure in the Russian Revolution. Opposed Stalin and was exiled from Russia. Murdered with an ice pick, probably by a Stalinist secret agent. Was a hero for many late-1960s student radicals.

I don't often think about that period of my life. This is partly because my memory of those days is decidedly hazy, but also because when I look at the photos I took in the late sixties, the kaftans, the miniskirts, the bells and beads and droopy moustaches seem to belong to an exotic, faraway time that bears little relation to the life I live now.

But it all came flooding back when I read *Captain Pamphile*. I think I understand Dumas's desire to celebrate his friends and their animals, even though the people he chose to surround himself with were as shallow and self-regarding as we were. I would love to imitate the book by peppering this preface with their names and their jobs (for instance Malcolm Smart was a Local Government Officer who lived at 175, Moseley Road and played acoustic guitar). Only my desire for brevity and my editor's reluctance to pay me for more than the stipulated one thousand words prevent me from sharing such details with you.

Of course had Dumas simply written a celebration of the lives of his mates and a description of their absurd fantasies, his book and the dustbin of history would have found themselves inextricably entwined. But what makes *Captain Pamphile* so readable is his overwhelming desire to amuse and entertain. I'm reluctant to tell you that this is a 'comic' novel, as there can be few experiences more likely to put the reader off literature for life than being immersed in the humour of yesteryear. By and large comedy has a short sell-by date. As a boy I revelled in P.G. Wodehouse, but my children find him plain silly. Which of us has not taken a sneaky glance at our watches during the so-called funny bits of a Shakespearean play, praying the misery will end soon. Even the majority of the Monty Python sketches we watched in such ecstasy a mere forty years ago now seem over-written and ponderous.

A few years after I left Birmingham, I got a lucky break in the children's BBC comedy series *Playaway* alongside Anita Dobson[3] and Brian Cant. Brian and I were given lengthy contracts not only as performers, but as writers too, creating a number of comedy sketches,

3. Actress and one-time recording star. Played Angie Watts in the popular television soap opera *Eastenders*. Married to Brian May, lead guitarist in the pop group Queen.

4. Estuary-side resort thirty miles east of London. Once popular with working-class holidaymakers, now principally inhabited by commuters and the elderly. Boasts the longest pleasure pier (1.33 miles) in the world.

which we filmed at Southend-on-Sea[4]. I knew exactly how I wanted them to look and sound when they were completed, but the editor didn't know me or my sense of humour, so how could he possibly put the raw film together in the way I wanted without my looking over his shoulder? To my amazement he did. The rhythms were just as I had imagined, the reveals of the visual gags were perfectly executed and the cuts from one shot to another were timed to perfection.

When I asked the editor how he had managed to do this, he mumbled something about the fact that we all had beating hearts and all breathed at roughly the same rate, so maybe there were internal rhythms we all shared and appreciated. This was not the answer I had expected from such a hardbitten, chain-smoking old pro, but I suspect he was right.

All of which is a rather tortuous way of saying that whereas so much comedy remains petrified in its own time like a fly in amber holding a tiny custard pie, Dumas has written a book that is still funny two hundred years down the line.

And his is not a trivial humour: it's about truth and fiction, the human qualities in animals, and the animal qualities in humans. It's about greed, slavery, and western imperialism... and it's also completely daft. Read it – it'll make you laugh!

– Tony Robinson, 2006

INTRODUCTION

Captain Pamphile is an oddly disconcerting text. It was composed in fits and starts, partly due to the exigencies of its original publication in serial form, partly because Dumas interrupted its composition to indulge in some of his other multifarious activities as a writer; as a result, it juxtaposes, in almost collage form at times, several different stories. The narrative strands can basically be reduced to three main types. First there is the evocation of the Bohemian milieu of artists and writers around 1830, the year of the revolution that toppled Charles X from his throne and replaced him with the July Monarchy of Louis-Philippe. These artists are fond of keeping extravagant pets, including the monkey James I and his 'successor' James II, the bear Tom, and the frog Mlle Camargo, and the first part of the novel tells of how these exotic creatures came to be living in Paris and the adventures that there befell them. Secondly we have the story of Captain Pamphile, a genial but ruthless buccaneer from Provence, whose 'trading' activities take him across half the globe, from the Indian Ocean via Africa to the wastes of North America. This section is very much in the style of a traditional boys' story of adventure and exploration, with mutinies on board ship, piratical encounters with merchant vessels, exploits among the American Indians (heavily indebted to James Fenimore Cooper), and a number of unlikely brushes with whales, bears, snakes, alligators and other denizens of ocean, jungle and forest. Some of these anecdotes are so surrealistic as to put Captain Pamphile in the same league as the Baron von Münchhausen. Finally, as a kind of coda to these entertainingly improbable exploits, there is one even more improbable than the rest: Captain Pamphile, feeling a little jaded by his activities as a trader and explorer, decides to become the ruler (cacique) of a country in Central America.

Perhaps because of its dancing bears, mischievous monkey and long-suffering frog (not to mention a host of other animals who play their various walk-on – or hop-on – parts in the story), *Captain Pamphile* has often been categorised as a children's story. But there is nothing saccharine in Dumas's animals. On one occasion he refers to the *Fables* of La Fontaine, and if there is an anthropomorphism in his view of animals, it is of this darker kind in which the qualities animals share with humans are often those that least redound to the honour of the latter: cruelty (of an often sadistic kind), cunning, egotism, jealousy and spite. Perhaps, of course, this makes it suitably realistic fare for children, who are often more at home with the bracing amoralism of animal (and human) life than their elders imagine. On the other hand, the fantasy and exaggeration of the story, its 'fabulous' (or 'confabular', given Pamphile's typically Provençal confabulations) dimension, is constantly being firmly rooted into the concrete details of Dumas's own France: although he mainly confines his own role to that of narrator, he brings in many of his own friends and acquaintances, sometimes including their real addresses and telling us which shops they use with a Joycean relish for the real. He also peppers his text with references, often quite recondite, to science, history, geography, myth and legend. Admittedly there is a deadpan quality to these references, as if Dumas were parodying the very same realism that he is exploiting: since his text is so securely anchored in fact (he seems to be suggesting), we are more likely to give credence to the more incredible aspects of the tales he has to tell. Hence the footnotes (sometimes personal, sometimes more objective) and the learned allusions to scientific taxonomy (albeit in a work that claims, without turning a hair, that tigers are common in Africa). But this poker-faced demeanour infects areas of the text in ways that are deeply disturbing – all the more so for being narrated with an absence of any but the most arch moral comment. Indeed, in one footnote, Dumas refers to his preference for telling the story straight and letting the reader draw his or her own moral conclusions:

> The different moral lessons of our story can be drawn perfectly simply, so we do not feel it is necessary to spell them out to our readers, relying rather on the pure and simple narrative of events; for this would mean depriving them of an opportunity to meditate on the punishment that egotism and greed always bring down on themselves.

This Flaubertian absence of authorial comment is particularly perplexing in the latter quarter of the story: we have seen Pamphile is an amiable rogue, no doubt as cruel and merciless when his authority is questioned (as in the mutiny aboard the *Roxelane*) as any other buccaneer, but still entertainingly amoral rather than villainous. But when he indulges in the slave trade, and packs the slaves he has recently won by conquest aboard his vessel (Dumas gives us, drily, what are doubtless all-too-accurate facts and figures for the terrifying way the slaves would have been crammed into the cramped and claustrophobic ship), we can no longer take him as just a lovable pirate; he becomes a colonialist, an exploiter, a racist, a cynical murderer. The slave trading episode in his career is the book's heart of darkness, and Dumas's absence of comment, which deliberately places Pamphile's participation in the slave trade on the same narrative and stylistic level as his encounter with a dancing bear or his drily effective duping of an Indian chief, is haunting.

There is, indeed, an irony in the narrative as well as the style. The most striking irony is that it is just at the moment the story becomes most incredible that it becomes most 'realistic', since it concurs with something that actually happened in history. The stories of Pamphile battling (usually alone) with boa constrictors and bears all rely on his own unreliable witness, and are clearly part of the topos of the solitary hero confabulating fantastic stories to a receptive audience of people who have pleasantly suspended their disbelief, as they can in any case rarely check the veracity of his account. The story of Pamphile becoming head of a sovereign state in Latin America and persuading British financiers to invest in it, British citizens to emigrate to it, and the British authorities to recognise his claims to rule over it, involves too great a degree of public credulity for us to take it seriously. It is an act of Pamphilesque braggadocio too far. And yet it is true.

Or rather, it is based on well-attested historical events that occurred in the decade or so before 1830. In 1820, an impressive figure in a uniform sailed into harbour in Britain – a certain Gregor MacGregor, a relative of Rob Roy. Like Pamphile, he had a colourful past (which he carefully embroidered). He had indeed served with the troops of the Allies in Spain, fighting against Napoleon, and subsequently in the armies fighting the Spanish during the wars of independence in South America, where he had become a close associate of Simón Bolívar, the Liberator (he even married Bolívar's glamorous niece). But his real, if not always very important military achievements (including a particularly gruelling retreat through swamp and jungle) did not sate his desire for fame and wealth, and from 1817 onwards he lived the life of a pirate along the Spanish Main. In 1820 he sailed to the Mosquito Coast (it is at this point that the parallels with the career of Pamphile himself become most striking, and it would be an interesting exercise to study exactly how closely Dumas drew on the details of MacGregor's career to crown that of his own rascally protagonist). Here he forged a friendship with a local leader, the resoundingly named George Frederic, known as the 'King of the Mosquitos'. He contrived to get the King addicted to whisky, and then extracted from him a document proclaiming MacGregor to be Gregor I, Cacique of Poyais, a domain that extended to some eight million acres of land. Whereupon MacGregor set sail for Britain, where he put into effect his plan: to inveigle local speculators into investing in Poyais, a land that was in fact largely uncharted jungle, but that he described as a kind of utopia, with towns and cities and even a flourishing opera house. Poyais, he claimed, was 'full of large rivers, that run some hundred miles up into a fine, healthful and fruitful country', salubrious in climate, rich in varied kinds of timber, plants and minerals, with (and this is a detail that will appeal to readers of *Captain Pamphile*) a seashore filled with 'Turtle, especially the species denominated Hawksbill, which is particularly desirable on account of its shell, so much prized in Europe, under the name of *Tortoise-shell*'. In the feverish atmosphere of Britain under its new king George IV, emerging from the years of austerity that had followed the Napoleonic Wars, Poyais seemed well worth a flutter, and many speculators sank their money into this enticing country. Indeed, by the beginning of 1823, two ships were ready to leave for Poyais with some 240 emigrants on board.

Readers who want to find out what happened to those who embarked for this far-away and exotic land that seemed to promise so much are invited to read the excellent account by David Sinclair, *Sir Gregor MacGregor and the Land that Never Was*, which shows how closely Dumas drew on MacGregor's career for the details of the zenith of his own Captain Pamphile's career. (I have not found any reference to these parallels between Pamphile and MacGregor in the secondary literature on Dumas: I am sure they must have been noted, since Dumas lets the cat out of the bag once he provides us with the 'Constitution' of a country called 'Poyais' in his documentary appendix: Gregor MacGregor himself in 1836 published a 'Plan of a Constitution for the inhabitants of the Indian coast in Central America, commonly called the Mosquito shore'.) This tall story, in MacGregor's case as in that of Captain Pamphile, 'worked', at least for a while – with tragic results. People love a tall story, and are prepared to sacrifice every security and comfort once they are in thrall to the charisma of a determined and inventive hoaxer, whether Captain Pamphile or Gregor MacGregor. Thus Dumas's story is a celebration of the art of storytelling, of travel and adventure – but also, between the lines, it alludes to the dubious consequences that can ensue when stories are used to beguile and entrap, travel leads to traumatic uprooting and the loss of all home (or to the founding of colonies and the expropriation of native peoples), and an otherwise laudable sense of adventure is inseparable from an alarming indifference to others. But of course, Dumas never bothers to make this moralising conclusion explicit: bad men, like eccentric animals, make good stories, even when the stories sail just a little close to the shores of hard fact.

– *Andrew Brown, 2006*

Note on the text:
I have used the excellent edition by Claude Schopp (*Le Capitaine Pamphile*, Paris: Gallimard, 'Folio Classique', 2003), and I am indebted to its wealth of notes and background information.

My quotations above, on the description of Poyais put into circulation by MacGregor, are taken from pp. 12 and 66 respectively of David Sinclair's fascinating account in *Sir Gregor MacGregor and the Land that Never Was: The Extraordinary Story of the Most Audacious Fraud in History* (London: Hodder Headline, 2003).

Captain Pamphile

1

Introduction, with the help of which the reader will become acquainted with the main characters in this story, and also with its author.

In 1830, I was just walking past the door of Chevet's shop,[1] when I spotted inside an Englishman who was carefully examining a turtle over which he was haggling with the obvious intention of converting it, once it had become his property, into turtle soup.I was touched by the air of profound resignation with which the poor animal was allowing itself to be examined, not trying to retire within its shell and thus evade the cruelly gastronomic gaze of its enemy. I was filled with a sudden desire to save it from the pot into which its rear legs were already dangling; I went into the shop, where, in those days, I was a very well-known customer, winked at Mme Beauvais, and asked her if she had saved for me the turtle I had reserved when I dropped in the day before.

Mme Beauvais divined my intentions with the quickness of uptake that distinguishes the class of Parisian shopkeepers, and, politely scooping the creature from the hands of the haggler, she placed it in mine. At the same time she turned to our friend from beyond the Channel, who was watching open-mouthed, and told him, with a pronounced English accent, 'I am vairry sorry, your Lordship: ze little turtle, 'e already sold to Monsieur zis morning.'

'Oh?' the suddenly ennobled gentleman said to me in perfectly good French. 'So this charming creature belongs to you, Monsieur?'

'Yes, yes, your Lordship,' replied Mme Beauvais, still in English.

'Well, Monsieur,' he continued, 'you have there a little animal that will make an excellent soup; I have only one regret – it is the only one of its species that Madame happens to possess just now.'

'We are 'oping to 'ave more of zem tomorrow morning,' replied Mme Beauvais.

'Tomorrow will be too late,' the Englishmen said coldly. 'I have made arrangements to blow out my brains this evening, and I really wished to eat a turtle soup before I did so.'

And with these words, he bowed to me and left.

'Good heavens!' I said after a moment's reflection, 'such a gallant gentleman deserves to be indulged in his last whim.'

And I rushed out of the shop, shouting, like Mme Beauvais, 'Your Lordship! Your Lordship!'

But I did not know which way his Lordship had gone; I was quite unable to trace his steps.

I returned home in a thoughtful frame of mind; my humanity towards a beast had become inhumanity towards a man. What a singular machine is this world, where you cannot do good to one without doing harm to the other!

I reached the rue de l'Université, climbed up to the third floor where I lived, and set my acquisition down on the carpet.

It was quite simply a turtle of the commonest kind: *Testudo lutaria, sive aquarum dulcium* – meaning, according to Linnaeus (of the older authorities), and according to Ray (of the moderns), European pond turtle or freshwater turtle.*[2]

Now the European pond turtle or freshwater turtle occupies more or less the same rank, in the social order of Chelonians, as that occupied among us by grocers (in the civilian order) and by the National Guard[3] (in the military order).

It was, furthermore, the strangest body of a turtle that ever stuck its four legs, head and tail through the openings of a shell. No sooner did it sense that it was on the ground than it gave me a demonstration of its eccentric character by heading straight for the mantelpiece with a swiftness that immediately earned it the name *Gazelle*, and by doing its level best to get through the slits of the fender and into the fire, whose light attracted it. Eventually, after a good hour, it saw that its desires were impossible to fulfil, so it decided to go to sleep, having first stuck its head and its legs through one of the openings closest to the hearth, thus choosing, for its particular pleasure, a temperature of fifty to fifty-five degrees (approximately) of heat, which led me to believe that, by either vocation or destiny, it was fated to be roasted one day or another, and that

* It is well known that reptiles are divided into four categories: the Chelonians or turtles, which occupy the first rank; the Saurians or lizards, which occupy the second; the Ophidians or snakes, which occupy the third; and finally the Batrachians or frogs, which occupy the fourth.

I had merely changed the way it would be cooked, rescuing it from my Englishman's pot only to transport it to my room. But let's not get ahead of our story. The rest of this narrative will prove that I was not mistaken.

As I was obliged to go out, and was afraid that Gazelle might meet with an accident, I called my servant.

'Joseph,' I said, when he appeared, 'you must look after this creature.'

He came over and looked at it curiously.

'Ah!' he said, 'It's a turtle… It can support a whole carriage.'

'Yes, I know, but I hope you never feel the urge to prove it.'

'Oh, it wouldn't hurt it,' replied Joseph, who was eager to show off to me his knowledge of natural history. 'Even if the Paris–Laon coach drove over its back, it wouldn't crush it.'

Joseph mentioned this particular coach as he himself came from Soissons.

'Yes,' I told him, 'I'm sure the green sea turtle, *Testudo mydas*, could support such a weight, but I doubt whether this one, which is a smaller species…'

'It makes no difference,' replied Joseph, 'those little creatures are as strong as Turks; and, you know, a wagoner's cart could pass…'

'All right, all right; you can buy some lettuce and snails for it.'

'What – snails?… Does it have lung problems? The gentlemen for whom I worked before I entered Monsieur's service used to eat a broth of snails as he was *tubular*… Still, that didn't stop him…'

I left without hearing the rest of the story; halfway down the stairs, I realised that I'd forgotten to bring a pocket handkerchief: I went straight back upstairs. I found Joseph, who hadn't heard me re-enter, standing in the pose of the Apollo Belvedere,[4] one foot placed on Gazelle's back and the other suspended in mid-air, so that not the tiniest ounce of the 130 pounds that the old fool weighed would be lost on the poor creature.

'What do you think you're doing, you idiot?'

'I had told you it would work, Monsieur,' replied Joseph, proud to have proved at least in part his hypothesis.

'Get me a handkerchief, and don't ever touch that creature again.'

'Here you are, Monsieur,' said Joseph, bringing me what I had asked for… 'But you need have no fears for the turtle… A wagon could roll over it…'

I fled, but I hadn't gone down twenty steps before I heard Joseph closing my door, muttering between clenched teeth: 'Good heavens! I know what I'm talking about… Anyway, it's easy to see, from the way those animals are built, that a cannon loaded with grapeshot could…'

Luckily, the street noises prevented me from hearing the end of the wretched sentence.

That evening I came home rather late, as is my custom. At the first steps I took into my room, I felt something cracking under my boot. I quickly lifted my foot, putting all my weight onto the other leg: the same cracking noise was heard once more. I imagined for a moment that I must be treading on eggs. I lowered my candle… My carpet was covered by snails.

Joseph had straight away obeyed my instructions: he had bought some lettuce and some snails, and had placed the whole lot in a basket in the middle of my room; ten minutes later, either because the temperature of my apartment had taken the numb chill off them, or because the fear of being gobbled up had filled them with panic, the whole caravan had started to move off, and had already covered a fair distance, as was easy to tell from the silvery trails they had left on the carpet and the furniture.

As for Gazelle, she had stayed at the bottom of the basket, being unable to climb up against its walls. But several empty shells proved that the flight of the Israelites had not been so swift as to prevent her swallowing quite a few of them before they had time to cross the Red Sea.

I immediately undertook a precise review of the battalion manoeuvring in my room, as I did not much care for the idea that I might have to take charge of it in the middle of the night; then, carefully picking up all of the stragglers in my right hand, I replaced them, one by one, in their guardroom, which I was holding in my left hand, and closed the lid on them.

After five minutes, I realised that, if I left that entire menagerie in my room, I ran the risk of not getting a minute's sleep; they were making the same noise as if a dozen mice had been tied up in a bag of hazelnuts, so I decided to take the whole lot into the kitchen.

On my way there, I reflected that, if Gazelle went on at this rate, and if I left her in such a well-supplied food store, I'd find her dead of indigestion the next morning; at the very same moment, as if by inspiration, I suddenly remembered a certain tub placed in the yard, in which the restaurant owner on the ground floor purged his fish: this struck me as such a marvellous lodging for a *Testudo aquarum dulcium* that I decided there was absolutely no point in racking my brains trying to find another one for her. So, removing her from her refectory, I bore her, there and then, to the said destination.

I quickly climbed back upstairs and went off to sleep, convinced that I was the most ingenious and quick-witted man in France.

The next day, Joseph woke me as soon as it was light.

'Oh, Monsieur!' he said, planting himself squarely in front of my bed. 'What a game!'

'What game?'

'What a game your turtle's played on me!'

'Pardon?'

'Well, would you believe it, she's got out of your apartment, I don't know how… she's climbed down the three floors, and she's cooling her heels in the restaurant fish-tank!'

'You idiot! Didn't you realise it was I who put her there?'

'Ah… I see!… Well I must say that was a fine idea of yours!'

'Why?'

'Why? Because she's eaten the tench, a superb tench weighing three pounds.'

'Go and get Gazelle, and bring me some scales.'

While Joseph was carrying out my orders, I went into my library, and opened my copy of Buffon[5] at the article 'turtle'; I was eager to reassure myself that this Chelonian was indeed an ichthyophage, and I read the following words:

'This freshwater turtle, *Testudo aquarum dulcium*' (for this is what she was) 'has a preference for swamps and stagnant waters; when it is in a river or a pond, it attacks all fish without distinction, even the biggest; it bites them under their bellies, inflicting serious wounds on them, and when they are exhausted by loss of blood, it avidly devours them and leaves little more than the fish bones and heads, and even their air bladder, which sometimes floats to the surface of the water.'

'Damn it!' I said, 'the restaurant owner has M. de Buffon on his side: what he's saying might well be true.'

I was brooding over the probability that such an accident had occurred, when Joseph returned, holding the accused party in one hand and the scales in the other.

'You see,' said Joseph to me, 'these kinds of creature eat a great deal, to keep their strength up – fish in particular, since they're very nourishing; do you think that they'd be able to support a whole carriage otherwise?... After all, in seaports, think how sturdy the sailors are: it's because they only ever eat fish.'

I interrupted Joseph.

'How much did the tench weigh?'

'Three pounds: the waiter's demanding nine francs for it.'

'And did Gazelle eat it all up?'

'Oh, all except the bones, head and bladder.'

'That's it! M. de Buffon is a great naturalist.* All the same,' I added in an undertone, 'three pounds... that does seem an awful lot.'

I placed Gazelle on the scales; she weighed only two and a half pounds, shell included.

The result of this experiment was not that Gazelle was innocent of the misdeed of which she stood accused, but that she must have committed the crime on a cetacean of smaller volume.

This seems to have been the opinion of the waiter, too, as he seemed perfectly pleased with the five francs' compensation I gave him.

The adventure with the snails and the incident with the tench made me feel less enthusiastic about my new acquisition, and as I happened to meet, that very same day, one of my friends, an eccentric fellow and a painter of genius, who at that time had turned his studio into a menagerie, I warned him that, the next day, I would be adding a new item to his collection, one that belonged to the worthy category of Chelonians; this seemed to give him great pleasure.

That night, Gazelle slept in my room, where everything passed off in peace and quiet, given the absence of snails.

* As we must render to each his due, this praise really belongs to the man who continued M. de Buffon's work, M. Daudin. [François Marie Daudin (1774–1804), French zoologist, who composed an eight-volume work on reptiles – *Tr.*]

The next day, Joseph came into my room as usual, rolled up my bed rug, opened the window, and started to shake the dust out of it, but all of a sudden he uttered a loud cry and leaned right out of the window as if he were about to fling himself down.

'Whatever's the matter, Joseph?' I said, drowsily.

'Ah, Monsieur, your turtle was lying on the rug, and I didn't see her!…'

'And…?'

'And, oh dear, I didn't mean to, but I've gone and shaken her out of the window!'

'You idiot!…'

I jumped out of bed.

'Oh look!' said Joseph, whose face and voice were reassuming a most welcome expression of serenity, 'look! She's eating a cabbage!'

And indeed the creature, who had instinctively pulled her whole body back inside her suit of armour, had by chance fallen onto a pile of oyster shells, which, slipping and sliding about, had deadened her fall, and finding a suitable vegetable within reach, she had quietly stuck her head out of her shell, and was busying herself with her breakfast every bit as calmly as if she hadn't just fallen from a third-floor room.

'I told you so, Monsieur, I told you so!' Joseph kept saying in the joy of his heart. 'Nothing can hurt those animals! – And while she's eating, as you can see, a carriage could roll over her…'

'Never mind that, run down and get her for me.'

Joseph obeyed. In the mean while, I got dressed – a task that I had already completed before the time Joseph reappeared; so I went down to meet him and found him holding forth in the midst of a circle of curious onlookers, to whom he was explaining what had just happened.

I took Gazelle from his hands, and jumped into a cabriolet that dropped me off at 109, Faubourg Saint-Denis; I climbed up five floors and went into my friend's studio. He was painting.

Around him were a bear lying on its back, playing with a log of wood; a monkey sitting on a chair pulling out the bristles from a paintbrush one by one; and, in a goldfish bowl, a frog squatting on the third rung of a little ladder, by which it was able to climb right up to the surface of the water.

My friend's name was Decamps, the bear's name was Tom, the monkey's name was James I,* and the frog's name was Mlle Camargo.[6]

2

How James I conceived a fierce hatred for Gazelle, all thanks to a carrot.

My entry caused a real commotion.

Decamps lifted his eyes from the wonderful little painting, the *Clever Dogs*,[7] that is already known to you all; he was just completing it.

Tom dropped the log he had been playing with onto his nose, and fled back to his den between the two windows, groaning.

James I quickly threw down his paintbrush and picked up a straw that he innocently brought up to his mouth in his right hand, while scratching his thigh with his left and raising a blissful gaze to the skies.

Lastly, Mlle Camargo languidly climbed one more rung on her ladder – which in any other circumstances might have been taken for a sign of rain.

As for me, I placed Gazelle down at the threshold, where I had halted, saying: 'My dear friend, here is the creature. As you can see, I'm a man of my word.'

This wasn't the best of times for Gazelle; the motion of the cabriolet had so shaken her that, no doubt to gather her thoughts and reflect on her situation while we were en route, she had withdrawn her whole person inside her shell, so what I placed on the ground looked quite simply like an empty shell.

Nonetheless, when Gazelle sensed, through the restoration of her centre of gravity, that she was back on terra firma, she ventured to poke her nose out through the upper opening in her shell; just to be sure, however, this part of her body was cautiously accompanied by her two front legs; at the same time, and as if all her limbs had unanimously obeyed the uncoiling of some inner spring, her two hind legs and tail

* Thus named to distinguish him from James II, a fellow of the same species, who belonged to Tony Johannot. [Tony Johannot (1803–1852), another friend of Dumas's, was an engraver and a highly distinguished illustrator from the Romantic period – *Tr.*]

appeared at the lower extremity of the shell. Five minutes later, Gazelle was in full sail.

However, she remained stationary for just another moment, swaying her head right and left as if to gain her bearings; then all at once her gazed steadied – and she moved forward, as swiftly as if she had been racing against La Fontaine's hare,[8] towards a carrot lying at the foot of the chair that served James I as a pedestal.

Initially, the latter watched the new arrival advancing towards him with a somewhat indifferent air, but as soon as he realised to what goal she seemed to be heading, he gave signs of real disquiet, manifested in the form of a low growl that degenerated, as she gained ground, into an uninterrupted series of harsh cries interrupted by a grinding of teeth. Finally, when she was only a foot away from the precious vegetable, James's agitation assumed the character of real despair; he seized the back of his chair in one hand, and the straw seat in another, and – doubtless in the hope of scaring off the parasitical beast who was on her way to nibble at his dinner – he shook the chair with all the strength in his wrists, flinging both feet back like a kicking horse, and accompanying his twistings and turnings with all the gestures and grimaces that he thought would suffice to ruffle the automaton-like impassivity of his enemy. But it was all in vain; in spite of all his efforts, Gazelle's pace did not slacken in the slightest. James did not know which way to turn.

Luckily for James, help was at hand. Tom, who on my arrival had withdrawn to his den, had finally grown used to my presence and, like all of us, was paying a certain attention to the scene before him; at first astonished to see signs of movement in this unknown animal that, thanks to me, had come to share his apartment, he had watched with increasing curiosity as she raced towards the carrot. Now as Tom was not one to look down his nose at a nice carrot, when he saw Gazelle about to reach the precious vegetable, he trotted over in a hop, skip and jump and, raising his mighty paw, placed it heavily on the back of the poor beast who, striking the ground with the flat bottom of her shell, withdrew forthwith into her carapace and remained immobile, two inches from the food that, at this moment, was the object of the ambition of three creatures.

Tom seemed most surprised to see head, legs and tail disappearing, as if by enchantment. He brought his nose up to the shell and blew noisily into every aperture; finally, and as if to gain a better idea of the strange way the object in front of his eyes was fashioned, he took it and turned it this way and that in his two paws; then, as if convinced that he had been wrong to conceive the absurd idea that such a thing could ever walk, he negligently dropped it, took the carrot in his teeth, and set about returning to his den.

James was not best pleased at this turn of events; he had not expected that the favour his friend Tom was performing for him would be ruined by such an outburst of selfishness, but since he did not feel the same healthy respect for his comrade as for the newcomer, he quickly jumped off the chair where he had cautiously remained during the scene we have just described and, seizing in one hand by its green top the carrot that Tom was holding by its tail, he stiffened with all his might, grimacing, swearing, chattering away, while with his free paw he administered slap after slap to the nose of his pacific antagonist who, without responding (but also without dropping the object of their dispute), contented himself with lowering his ears on his neck and shutting his little black eyes each time that James's agile hand came into contact with his big round face. Eventually, as usually happens, the victory fell not to the strongest but to the most brazen. Tom unclenched his teeth, and James, the possessor of the blessed carrot, dashed up a ladder bearing his trophy, which he hid behind a plaster cast of Malaguti,[9] on a shelf that had been set up six feet above the ground. Once this operation had been completed, he came down more calmly, certain that neither bear nor turtle would be able to climb up there to get their claws on his prize.

When he had come down as far as the bottom-most rung, and was about to set foot on the ground, he cautiously halted and, glancing at Gazelle, whom in the heat of his dispute with Tom he had forgotten, realised that her posture was far from aggressive.

Indeed, Tom, instead of carefully setting her back as she had been when he picked her up, had – as we have said – negligently dropped her, quite carelessly, so that when she came to her senses, the unfortunate creature, instead of finding herself in her normal position, viz., on her belly, had found herself lying on her back, a position (as everyone knows) that is in the highest degree displeasing to any individual belonging to the race of Chelonians.

It was easy to see, from the confident expression with which James approached Gazelle, that he had deduced straight away that her accident meant she was in no state to defend herself. However, having advanced to within six inches of the *monstrum horrendum*, he halted for a moment, gazed into the aperture that was turned his way, and began, with an air of ostentatious negligence, to examine her, cautiously moving round her like a general inspecting a city he is about to besiege. Having completed his reconnaissance, he carefully stretched out his hand, and touched with his fingertip the extremity of the shell; then, swiftly retreating, he immediately began, without taking his eyes off the object of his attentions, to dance for joy on hands and feet, accompanying this movement with a kind of victory song that he habitually uttered each time that, through some difficulty overcome or some peril confronted, he felt able to congratulate himself on his skill or his courage.

However, this song and dance suddenly stopped; a new idea flickered through James's brain, and seemed to absorb all of his thinking faculties. He gazed attentively at the turtle, which his hand had set swinging, all the more vigorously as the spherical shape of her shell prolonged her period of oscillation. He sidled crabwise up to her and then, once he was close, stood on his hind legs, and straddled her the way a horseman straddles his horse, gazing at her for a moment as she moved between his two legs; finally, apparently completely reassured by his detailed examination, he sat on this moving chair and, making her rock rapidly to and fro – without her legs even leaving the ground – he merrily swayed atop her, scratching his haunches and screwing up his eyes, gestures that – for those who know him – were the expression of an indescribable joy.

All at once, James uttered a shrill cry, leapt three feet up into the air, fell on his haunches and, dashing up his ladder, went to seek refuge behind the head of Malaguti. This sudden new development was caused by Gazelle who, wearying of a game in which she evidently took little pleasure, had finally given a sign of life, scratching James's mangy thighs with her cold, sharp claws. He was all the more taken aback by this act of aggression as he had been expecting nothing less than an attack from that quarter.

Just then, a buyer came in, and Decamps signalled to me that he wished to remain alone with him. I picked up my hat and walking stick, and started to leave.

I was still on the landing when Decamps called me back.

'By the way,' he said, 'do come along tomorrow and spend the evening with us.'

'So what are you up to tomorrow?'

'We'll be having supper and a reading.'

'Hmph!'

'Yes: Mlle Camargo is going to eat a hundred flies, and Jadin[10] is going to read a manuscript.'

3

How Mlle Camargo came into the possession of M. Decamps.

Despite the verbal invitation Decamps had extended to me, the next day I received a printed letter. This additional invitation was to remind me of the dress code: guests would be admitted only in dressing gown and slippers. I arrived on the dot, and scrupulously observed the dress code.

A painter's studio is a curious thing to see, when, in order to honour his guests, he has daintily hung on his four walls his prize possessions, the products of the four corners of the world. You think you're walking into an artist's lodgings, and you find yourself inside a museum that would do honour to more than one county town in France. Those suits of armour representing Europe in the Middle Ages date from various different reigns, and their shape reveals the period in which they were made. This one, burnished on both sides of the breastplate, with its sharp, shining crest and its engraved crucifix, at the feet of which is a Virgin in prayer with this motto: *Mater Dei, ora pro nobis*,[11] was forged in France and given to King Louis XI, who had it hung on the walls of his old castle in Plessiz-les-Tours. That one, whose convex breastplate still bears the mark of the mace blows from which it protected its master, was dented in the jousts of the Emperor Maximilian, and comes from Germany. This other one, with its relief of the dauntless labours of Hercules, may have been borne by King François I, and certainly comes from the Florentine studios of Benvenuto Cellini. This Canadian tomahawk and this scalping knife come from America: the former broke French heads and the latter sliced off powdered scalps. These arrows and this kris are Indian; the heads of the former and the blade of the latter are deadly, as they have been dipped in the poisonous juice of herbs from Java. This curved sabre was tempered in Damascus. This yatagan,[12] which bears on its blade a number of notches, one for each head it has cut off, was torn from the dying hands of a Bedouin. Lastly, this long rifle with silver butt and bands was brought back from the kasbah, maybe by Isabey, who may have given it to Youssef in exchange for a sketch of the bay of Algiers or a drawing of Fort-l'Empereur.[13]

Now that we have examined in turn these trophies, each of which represents a whole world, turn your eyes to those tables on which are scattered pell-mell countless different objects, all of them most surprised to find themselves next to one another. Here are porcelain objects from Japan, Egyptian figures, Spanish knives, Turkish daggers, Italian stilettos, Algerian slippers, Circassian skullcaps, idols of the Ganges, and crystals from the Alps. Look: enough to keep you busy for the day.

Under your feet you find the skins of tigers, lions and leopards, taken from Asia and Africa; over your heads are wings spread out and seemingly endowed with life – here is the seagull that, just as the breaker is curling, sweeps under the wave's crest as if it were an arch; the *margat*[14] that, when it sees a fish appear at the surface, folds its wings and plummets down onto it like a stone; the guillemot that, just as the hunter's rifle is taking aim at it, dives down and resurfaces only when it is out of range; finally the kingfisher, the halcyon of the Ancients, whose plumage sparkles with the most vivid colours, aquamarine and lapis lazuli.

But what is most worth the attention of an amateur attending an evening reception at a painter's is the heterogeneous collection of pipes, all of them filled, waiting there (like the man to whom Prometheus brought his aid) for fire from heaven to be stolen for them. Nothing, after all, is more fantastical and whimsical than the workings of a smoker's mind. One smoker prefers a simple clay pipe, to which our old grumblers gave the expressive name *brûle-gueule*;[15] this is only ever filled with tobacco from the state tobacco industry, called 'caporal'. The other will bring his delicate lips only to the amber tip of an Arab chibouk, and this is filled with the black tobacco of Algiers or the green tobacco of Tunis. One smoker, as solemn as an Indian chief in Fenimore Cooper, takes methodical Maryland puffs from his calumet; another, more sensuous than a nabob, winds the flexible tube of his Indian hookah like a serpent around his arm – and by the time the vapour of the *latakieh* reaches his mouth, it is already cold, and imbued with the odour of rose and benzoin. There are those who, in their smoking habits, prefer the meerschaum of the German student, or the strong Belgian cigar, with its fine-chopped tobacco, to the Turkish hookah, whose praises have been sung by Lamartine,[16] and the tobacco of Sinai, whose reputation, good or bad, depends on whether it was harvested on the mountains or in the plain. There are, lastly, others who, out of some eccentricity or whim, crick their necks in the effort to keep the hubble-bubble pipe of the Negroes in a perpendicular position, while a helpful friend stands on a chair and tries – with all the aid he can get from a live coal and plenty of lungpower – first to dry and then to light the clayey herb of Madagascar.

When I entered mine host's lodgings, everyone had already chosen their place and taken their seat, but they all squeezed up together when they saw me, and, in a movement whose precision would have done honour to a company of the National Guard, all the pipes – whether of wood or clay, horn or ivory, jasmine or amber – came out of the lips that held them in an amorous clench, and presented themselves to me. I waved my hand in sign of thanks, pulled out of my pocket some liquorice paper, and started to roll in my fingers an Andalusian *cigarrito*, with all the patience and skill of an old Spaniard.

Five minutes later, we were swimming in an atmosphere thick enough to power a twenty-horsepower steamboat.

As far as this fug allowed, you could just make out the guests, as well as the habitual table companions of the house with whom the reader is already acquainted. There was Gazelle who, this evening, had suddenly been seized by a strange obsession: that of climbing along the marble mantelpiece to warm herself by the lamp, and who relentlessly devoted her efforts to this incredible exercise. There was Tom, of whom Alexandre Decamps had made a support for himself, rather like a sofa cushion, and who, from time to time, mournfully raised his friendly face from under his master's arm, breathing noisily so as to blow away the smoke that was getting in his nostrils, then lying down again, heaving a huge sigh. There was James I, sitting on a stool next to his old friend Fau,[17] who, making frequent use of his whip, had brought his training to its present level of perfection, and to whom he felt the greatest gratitude (and, above all, to whom he showed the most unquestioning obedience). Lastly, there was, in the middle of the circle of people, and in the middle of her goldfish bowl, Mlle Camargo, whose gymnastic and gastronomic exercises were to be the main attraction of the party.

Now that we have reached this point, it is essential for us to look backwards and inform our readers of the bizarre concatenation of circumstances by which Mlle Camargo, born in the Saint-Denis plain, now found herself living with Tom, who came from Canada, with James, who had seen the light of day on the coasts of Angola, and with Gazelle, who had been fished out of the swamps of Holland.

Everyone knows what excitement fills Paris, in the Saint-Martin and Saint-Denis districts, when the hunting season returns with the month of September; the streets are crowded with middle-class gentlemen returning from the canal, where they have been *getting their eye in* by shooting swallows, dragging their dogs along on leashes, carrying rifles on their shoulders, and promising themselves that this year they will be less *clumsy oafs* than last year, and stopping everyone they know to ask them, 'Do you like quails, partridges...?'

'Yes.'

'Good! I'll send you some next month, on the 2nd or the 3rd...'

'Thank you.'

'By the way, I killed five swallows with eight shots.'

'Well done.'

'Not a bad shot, am I?'

'Not bad at all.'

'Goodbye.'

'Good evening.'

Now, towards the end of August 1829, one of these hunters came in by the main door of the house at 109, Faubourg Saint-Denis, asked the concierge if Decamps was at home, and, when he replied in the affirmative, went up, pulling his dog behind him, step by step, and banging the barrel of his rifle on every corner of the wall, climbing the five storeys that lead to the studio of our famous painter.

The only man he found there was the latter's brother, Alexandre[18].

Alexandre is one of those witty, eccentric men who can be recognised as artists just by the way they walk; who would be good at everything, if only they weren't too profoundly lazy ever to busy themselves seriously with any one activity; having in all things an instinct for the true and the beautiful, and recognising it wherever they find it, without worrying whether the work that occasions their enthusiasm is acknowledged by a coterie or signed by a well-known name; in other respects, a good chap in every sense of the term, always ready to dig deep into his pockets for his friends, and, like all those who are preoccupied by an idea of some worth, easily led, not out of any weakness of character, but because they are bored by argument and dislike exerting themselves.

Given this cast of mind, Alexandre was easily persuaded by the newcomer that he would really enjoy inaugurating the hunting season with him on the Saint-Denis plain, where this year there were, it was reported, bevies of quail, coveys of partridges and downs of hare.

As a consequence of this conversation, Alexandre ordered a hunting jacket from Chevreuil, a rifle from Lepage and leggings from Boivin: the whole lot cost him 660 francs, not including his permit to bear arms, which was delivered to him at the Prefecture of Police, on presentation of a certificate of good moral character, which the police superintendent granted him without demur.

On 31st August, Alexandre suddenly realised that only one thing was missing before he could be a consummate hunter: a dog. He immediately dashed to the man who had posed with his pack of hounds for his brother when the latter was painting the *Clever Dogs*, and asked him whether he had what he needed.

The man replied that he had just the thing: animals who had a real flair for the hunt. And, moving from his room to the kennel, which adjoined it on the same floor, he whisked off the three-pointed hat and suit adorning a kind of black and white beagle,* came back with him straight away, and presented him to Alexandre as a thoroughbred. The latter pointed out that a thoroughbred had straight, pointed ears, which was quite contrary to all received habits, but to this the man replied that Love was English, and that it was in the best possible taste for English dogs to have ears like that. Since, all things considered, this might well be true, Alexandre accepted the explanation and took Love home with him.

The next day, at five in the morning, our hunter came to wake up Alexandre who was sleeping like a lamb, tore him off a strip for not being ready, and blamed him for the fact they would be late since by the time they arrived they would find the whole plain had already been *wiped clean.*

And indeed, as they came towards the city limits, the detonations grew louder and livelier. Our hunters stepped out, crossed the customs barrier, headed down the first alleyway leading to the plain, plunged into a cabbage patch and fell into the thick of a real vanguard action.

You need to have seen the Saint-Denis plain on the first day of the hunting season to have any idea of the absurd sight it presents. Not a lark goes by, nor a house sparrow, without its appearance being greeted by a volley of innumerable rifle shots. If it falls, thirty hunters quarrel over it, and thirty dogs sink their teeth into one another; if it flies on its way, all eyes are fixed on it; if it lands, everyone runs up; if it takes wing again, everyone takes a pot shot. Of course, now and again there are a few scattered lead shots that are aimed at the beasts of the air but actually hit other people: you don't have to worry too much about that; in any case, there's an old proverb, tailor-made for Parisian hunters, according to which 'lead is a man's friend'. If that is so, I myself have three friends in my thigh, lodged there by a fourth.

The smell of gunpowder and the sound of rifle-fire produced their usual effect. Hardly had our hunter sniffed the former and heard the latter than he plunged into the thick of the fray and immediately started to play his part in the witches' sabbath that had just enfolded him in its alluring force field.

* Cross-breed.

Alexandre, less impressionable than he, advanced at a more moderate step, religiously followed by Love, whose nose was glued to his master's heels. Now everyone knows that it's the job of a hunting dog to scour the plain, and not to see if any nails have dropped out of his master's boots: this is the thought that naturally occurred to Alexandre after half an hour. Consequently, he waved at Love and said to him, 'Seek!'

Love immediately rose on his hide legs and started to dance.

'I say!' said Alexandre.

And, resting the butt of his rifle on the ground and gazing at his dog, he added, 'Apparently Love possesses not only a university education, but talents as an entertainer as well. I think he was an excellent buy.'

However, as he had bought Love to hunt and not to dance, as soon as the dog had fallen back onto his four legs, he waved to him again, this time more expressively, and said more loudly, 'Seek!'

Love stretched out full length, closed his eyes and played dead.

Alexandre raised his pince-nez to his eyes and stared at Love. The clever creature was perfectly motionless; not a hair on his body was moving; he looked as if he had been dead for twenty-four hours.

'That's really nice,' resumed Alexandre; 'but, my dear friend, this really isn't the time to indulge in this kind of jollity; we've come to hunt, so let's hunt. Come on, be a good dog!'

Love didn't move.

'Just you wait!' said Alexandre, pulling out of the ground a cane that had been used to stake out peas, and he walked over to Love with the intention of giving him a taste of it about the shoulders. 'Just you wait!'

No sooner had Love seen the stick in his master's hands than he jumped to his feet and followed his every movement with a remarkable expression of understanding. Alexandre, who had noticed this, decided to postpone the intended good hiding, and thinking that, this time, the dog would at last obey him, he pointed the cane in front of Love, and told him for the third time:

'Seek!'

Love ran up and leapt over the cane.

Love was extremely good at three things: he could dance on his hind legs, play dead, and jump over a stick for his master.

Alexandre who, right now, did not really appreciate this last talent any more than he had the others, smashed the cane over Love's back. The dog ran off howling towards our hunter.

Now, as Love dashed up, our hunter was just taking a shot, and, as luck would have it, an unfortunate lark, which had happened to be in the line of fire, fell into Love's jaws. Love thanked Providence for sending him such a blessing, and, not pausing to ask whether it was roasted or not, swallowed it in a single mouthful.

Our hunter flung himself onto the wretched dog uttering the direst imprecations, seized him by the throat and squeezed it so grimly that he forced Love to open his jaws, despite feeling a strong urge to do nothing of the sort. The hunter frenziedly plunged his hand down his gullet, and pulled out three of the lark's tail-feathers. As for the body, he could just as well forget it.

The lark's rightful owner felt in his pocket for a knife with which to disembowel Love, and by this means gain possession of his prey, but unluckily for him, and luckily for Love, he'd lent his knife to his wife the evening before so that she could trim the skewers all ready for him to string his partridges on them, and she had forgotten to give it back. Forced, in consequence, to resort to less violent means of punishment, he gave Love a kick strong enough to break down a big front gate, carefully placed the three feathers he had saved in his game bag and shouted to Alexandre at the top of his voice:

'You can rest assured, my dear friend, that I will never in future go hunting with you. Your rascal Love has just gobbled down a superb quail! Oh, just you come back here, you scamp!...'

Love was in no mood to 'come here'. Quite the contrary: he was dashing as fast as his legs would carry him towards his master, which proved that, all things considered, he preferred being given a drubbing with a cane to being given a good kick.

However, the lark had given Love an appetite and, as from time to time he observed various creatures fluttering up before him who all appeared to belong to the same species, he started to run every which way, doubtless in the hope that he would end up encountering a second windfall as good as the first.

Alexandre was laboriously following, cursing himself as he did so: the fact is that Love was seeking his prey in a way totally different from that adopted by other dogs, namely with his nose in the air and his tail down. This proved that his sight was better than his smell, but this displacement of his physical faculties was intolerable for his master. Love continued to scour the plain a hundred paces ahead of him, raising the game at a distance that was twice as great as a rifle's range, and chasing it to its covert, barking loudly.

This merry-go-round lasted all day long.

By around five in the evening, Alexandre had covered some fifteen leagues, and Love more than fifty: the former was exhausted from shouting and the latter from barking; as for the hunter, he had accomplished his mission and taken his leave of both of them to go and shoot snipe in the marshlands of Pantin.

Suddenly Love started pointing.

He was pointing in such a clear and motionless way that he looked as if, like Cephalus' dog, he had been changed to stone.[19] At this altogether novel sight, Alexandre forgot how tired he was and ran like crazy, trembling all the time lest Love run down his prey before it was in rifle range. But there was no danger of this: Love's four paws were glued to the ground.

Alexandre caught up with him, attentively followed the direction his eyes were looking in, saw that they were fixed on a tuft of grass and, beneath this tuft of grass, spotted a greyish shape. He thought it must be a young partridge separated from its covey, and, trusting more in his hunter's cap than in his rifle, he laid his rifle on the ground, held his cap in his hand and, creeping up as stealthily as a child trying to catch a butterfly, brought the aforementioned cap down on the unknown object, plunged his hand under it, and brought out a frog.

Anyone else would have flung the frog a good thirty feet away: Alexandre, on the contrary, decided that, since Providence had sent him this beguiling beast in such a miraculous manner, she must have secret plans for the creature and was saving it for great things.

And so, he carefully placed the frog in his game bag, and devoutly brought her home, where he immediately decanted her into a bowl out of which, the day before, we had eaten the last cherries, and poured over her head all the remaining water in the carafe.

The pains he took for a frog might have appeared extraordinary on the part of any man who had obtained her in a less complicated way than had Alexandre, but Alexandre knew what this frog had cost him, and he treated her accordingly.

She had cost him 660 francs, not including his licence to bear arms.

4

How Captain Pamphile, commanding the trading brig the Roxelane, *found better hunting on the banks of the River Bengo than Alexandre Decamps had in the Saint-Denis plain.*

'Ah ha!' said Dr Thierry[20] as he came into the studio the following day, 'you have a new lodger.'

And, paying no attention to Tom's friendly grunt and James's welcoming grimaces, he walked over to the bowl containing Mlle Camargo and dipped his hand in.

Mlle Camargo, who didn't recognise Thierry as a highly skilful doctor and a man of great wit, started to paddle round and round as fast as she could, but this could not stop her being seized, a moment later, by the tip of her left foot, and pulled out of her dwelling place upside down.

'Well!' said Thierry, turning her rather like a shepherdess turns a spindle, 'just look, it's *Rana temporaria*, thus named because of these two black patches that extend from the eye to the tympanum; it lives both in running water and in marshes; some writers have called it the "mute frog" because it croaks under water, while the green frog can croak only when out of water. If you have 200 of this sort, my advice is to cut off their hind legs, season them in a chicken fricassee, send to Corcelet's[21] for two bottles of Bordeaux Mouton, and invite me round to dinner, but since we have only one, we will simply (with your permission) use it to clear up a scientific point that is still obscure, though the claim has been made by several naturalists: this frog can go for six months without eating.'

With these words, he dropped Mlle Camargo back into her bowl, which she immediately swam round two or three times, with all the joyful suppleness of which her limbs were capable; after which, spotting a fly that had fallen into her domain, she darted up to the surface of the water and gulped it down.

'I'll let you have that one,' said Thierry; 'but just remember that it's the last you'll have for 183 days'.

For, unluckily for Mlle Camargo, the year 1830 was a leap year: thanks to this solar phenomenon, science gained twelve hours.

Mlle Camargo did not seem in the least bit worried by this threat and cheerfully stayed with her head out of water and her four feet nonchalantly extended and quite immobile, with the same aplomb as if she had been resting on solid ground.

'Now,' said Thierry, opening a drawer, 'let's take care of the prisoner's furnishings.'

He took out two cartridges, a gimlet, a penknife, two paintbrushes and four matches. Decamps watched him in silence; he understood nothing of this manoeuvre, which the doctor performed with as much care as if he were preparing for a surgical operation; then he emptied the powder into a handkerchief container and kept the bullets, throwing the pen and the bristle over to James and keeping the handle.

'What the hell do you think you're up to?' exclaimed Decamps, tearing his two best paintbrushes from James's hands. 'You're ruining my business!'

'I'm making a ladder,' said Thierry solemnly.

And he had indeed just used the gimlet to pierce holes in the two lead bullets, fitted the paintbrush handles into the holes, and, into these handles, forming the uprights on the ladder, he placed crossways the matches that were to act as rungs. Within five minutes the ladder was finished and lowered into the bowl, standing upright on the bottom, thanks to the weight of the two bullets. No sooner had Mlle Camargo come into possession of this piece of furniture than she tried it out, as if to assure herself of its solidity, by climbing up to the topmost rung.

'We're going to get some rain,' said Thierry.

'Damn!' said Decamps, 'do you think so? And there was my brother hoping he'd be able to do another spot of hunting today!'

'That's not the advice Mlle Camargo would give him,' replied the doctor.

'What?'

'I've just saved you the expense of having to buy a barometer, my dear friend. Each and every time Mlle Camargo climbs up her ladder, it's a sign of rain; when she comes down it, you can be sure that you're in for fine weather; and when she stays in the middle, don't venture out without an umbrella or coat: changeable weather! Changeable!'

'Well, well, well!' said Decamps.

'Now,' continued Thierry, 'we're going to seal the bowl with a piece of parchment, as if it still had all those cherries in it.'

'Here you are,' said Thierry, handing some over.

'We'll fasten it with some string.'

'There!'

'Then if I might ask you for some wax! Fine… a light! There we are… and to make sure of my experiment' (he lit the wax, sealed the knot of string and imprinted the stone of his ring onto the seal), 'there, that's that for six months. And now,' he continued, piercing a few holes in the parchment with his penknife, 'now, do you have a pen and ink?'

Have you ever asked a painter for pen and ink? No? Well, just don't ask; he'd only do what Decamps did: he'd offer you a pencil.

Thierry took the pencil and wrote on the parchment:

2nd September 1829

Now, on the evening of the gathering of which we have been attempting to give our readers some idea, it had been precisely 183 days, in other words six months and twelve hours, since Mlle Camargo had been invariably indicating, without a moment's reflection, rain, fine weather and changeable weather. This regularity was all the more remarkable because, during this lapse of time, she hadn't ingested a single atom of food.

And so, when Thierry had pulled out his watch and announced that the last second of the sixtieth minute of the twelfth hour had gone by, and the bowl had been brought over, a general feeling of pity overcame the assembly when they saw the wretched state to which the poor animal had been reduced, especially as she had just, to the detriment of her stomach, shed such great and significant light on an obscure point in science.

'You see,' said Thierry triumphantly, 'Schneider and Roësel were right!'[22]

'Right, were they?' said Jadin, picking up the bowl and holding it up to his eyes. 'There's nothing to prove that Mlle Camargo isn't actually dead.'

'Don't listen to Jadin,' said Flers;[23] 'he's always had it in for Mlle Camargo.'

Thierry took a lamp and held it behind the bowl.

'Look,' he said. 'You'll see that her heart is beating.'

Mlle Camargo had indeed become so thin that she was as transparent as glass, and you could make out her entire circulatory system; you could even tell that the heart had only one ventricle and one auricle, but these organs were performing their tasks so feebly, and Jadin was so close to the truth, that it was hardly worth telling him he was wrong, as you wouldn't have given the poor animal ten minutes more to live. Her legs had become all thin and spindly, and her hind parts were attached to the front of her body only by the bones that form the spring that helps frogs to jump instead of walking. Furthermore, on her back there had grown a kind of moss that, when looked at through the microscope, turned into a veritable display of marine vegetation, with its reeds and its flora. As a botanist, Thierry even claimed that this imperceptible growth belonged to the same family as lentiscs and cress. Nobody felt like arguing.

'Now,' said Thierry, when everyone had examined Mlle Camargo in turn, 'we need to let her enjoy a quiet bit of supper.'

'And what will she eat?' said Flers.

'I've got her meal here in this box.'

And Thierry, lifting the parchment, slipped into the space reserved for air such a great number of flies, all of them with one wing missing, that it was obvious he had spent his morning catching them, and his afternoon mutilating them. We had the impression that Mlle Camargo had enough there for another six months: one of us went so far as to express this opinion.

'You're wrong,' replied Thierry. 'In a quarter of an hour's time, there won't be a single one left.'

Even the least sceptical of us shrugged doubtfully. Thierry, buoyed up by this first success, carried Mlle Camargo back to her usual place, without even deigning to reply.

No sooner had he sat down in his seat again than the door opened and the manager of the café next door came in, carrying a tray on which were a teapot, a sugar bowl and some cups. Hot on his heels came two waiters carrying, in a wicker basket, a loaf of munition bread,[24] a brioche, a lettuce and a host of little cakes of every shape and kind.

The munition bread was for Tom, the brioche for James, the lettuce for Gazelle, and the little cakes for us. The animals were served first, and then those present were told they were free to help themselves to whatever they wanted. And this seems to me, with all due deference, the best way of doing the honours when one is playing the host.

There was a moment of apparent disorder as everyone yielded to the promptings of his appetite and helped himself as he saw fit. Tom growled as he carried his loaf back to his den; James took refuge, with his brioche, behind the busts of Malaguti and Ratta; Gazelle slowly pulled the lettuce under the table; as for us, we did what people quite generally do, and took a cup in our left hands and a cake in our right, or vice versa.

Ten minutes later, there were no tea or cakes left.

And so they rang for the café manager, who reappeared with his acolytes.

'More!' said Decamps.

And the café manager bowed his way out backwards in obedience to this injunction.

'Now, gentlemen,' said Flers with a sly glance at Thierry and a respectful glance at Decamps, 'while we await for Mlle Camargo to finish her supper, and some more cakes are brought for us, I think it would be nice to fill the interval by reading one of Jadin's manuscripts. It's all about the first years of James I, whom we all have the honour of knowing on an individual basis, and in whom we take too cordial an interest for the slightest details garnered about him not to acquire great importance in our eyes. *Dixi*[25].' Everyone bowed in sign of agreement; one or two people even applauded.

'James, my friend,' said Fau who, in his role as tutor, was of all of us the one closest to the hero of this tale, 'you can see everyone's talking about you: come over here.'

And immediately after these few words, he uttered a particular whistle so familiar to James that the clever animal immediately leapt from his plank onto the shoulder of the man addressing him.

'Well done, James; it's good to be obedient, especially when your cheeks are stuffed with brioche. Say hello to these gentlemen.'

James brought his hand up to his brow in a military-style salute.

'And if your friend Jadin, who's going to read your story, happens to utter any slanderous remarks about you, just tell him he's a liar.'

James nodded to show he understood perfectly.

In fact, James and Fau were really and truly linked by an intimate friendship. On the animal's part in particular, there was a depth of affection that is no longer found among men. Where did it spring from? It has to be confessed, to the shame of the simian race, that the tutor had acquired this deplorable influence over his pupil not by educating his mind, as Fénelon had done for the Grand Dauphin, but by flattering his vices, as Catherine had done for Henri III.[26] For instance, when James had first come to Paris, he had merely been a lover of fine wine: Fau had turned him into a drunkard; he had initially merely been a sybarite like Alcibiades: Fau had turned him into a cynic of the school of Diogenes; he had merely been a gourmet, like Lucullus: Fau had made him greedy like Grimod de la Reynière.[27] Admittedly, he had gained from this moral corruption a host of physical accomplishments that made him an animal of the greatest distinction. He could tell his right hand from his left, play dead for ten minutes, dance on a tightrope like Mme Saqui,[28] go hunting with a rifle under his arm and a game bag slung across his back, and show his weapons permit to the gamekeeper and his backside to the police. In short, he was a charming bad boy, whose only mistake had been to be born under the Restoration instead of under the Regency.

And so, whenever Fau knocked on the front door, James quivered; if he started climbing up the stairs, James could hear him coming. Then he would utter little shrieks of joy, jumping up and down on his rear legs like a kangaroo, and when Fau opened the door, he would fling himself into his arms, as still happens in the Théâtre-Français in the play *The Two Brothers*[29]. In short, all that was James's was also Fau's, and the former would have taken the brioche out of his own mouth to offer it to the latter.

'Gentlemen,' said Jadin, 'if you would like to take a seat and light up your pipes and cigars, I'm ready.'

Everyone obeyed. Jadin coughed, opened the manuscript, and read out the following narrative:

5

How James I was torn from the arms of his dying mother and taken on board the trading brig the Roxelane *(captained by Pamphile).*

On 24th July 1827 (he began), the brig the *Roxelane* set sail from Marseilles to load up with coffee in Moka, spices in Bombay and tea in Canton. To replenish its food supplies, it dropped anchor in the bay of Saint Paul de Loanda, situated, as everyone knows, halfway along the coast of Lower Guinea.

While the goods were being brought aboard and paid for, Captain Pamphile, who was travelling to India for the tenth time, took his rifle and, in a heat of seventy degrees, amused himself by going up the banks of the River Bengo. Captain Pamphile was, after Nimrod, the mightiest hunter before the Lord who had ever appeared on the earth.[30]

He had no sooner taken twenty steps through the thick grass that grows along the riverside than he felt his foot twisting on an object as round and slippery as the trunk of a young tree. At the same moment he heard a sibilant hiss, and, ten steps in front of him, he saw the head of an enormous boa constrictor looming up; he had just trodden on its tail.

Anyone other than Captain Pamphile would of course have felt some anxiety on seeing himself threatened by this monstrous head whose bloodshot eyes gleamed like two carbuncles as they surveyed him, but the boa didn't know what kind of a man Captain Pamphile was.

'Shiver me timbers, reptile, d'you think you frighten me, eh?' said the Captain.[31] And just as the snake was opening its jaws, he fired a bullet that went right through its palate and out through the top of its head. The snake dropped dead.

The Captain's initial action was to reload his rifle calmly; then, pulling his knife out of his pocket, he went over to the animal, slit open its stomach, and separated the liver from the entrails, as the angel of Tobias had done;[32] after a few moments of careful investigation, he found in it a small blue stone the size of a hazelnut.

'Good!' he said.

And he placed the stone in a wallet in which there were already a dozen similar ones. Captain Pamphile was as well-read as a mandarin: he had read the *Thousand and One Nights* and was seeking the magic bezoar of Prince Camaralzaman.[33]

As soon as he thought he had found it, he set off hunting again.

After a quarter of an hour, he saw the grass rustling forty steps in front of him and heard a terrible roar. At that noise, every animal seemed to recognise the lord of creation. The birds, who had been singing, fell silent; two gazelles, filled with panic, leapt up and bounded across the plain; a wild elephant, visible a quarter of a league away on a hill, raised his trunk and prepared to do battle.

'Prrrrou! Prrrrrou!' said Captain Pamphile, as if it were a matter of making a covey of partridges take wing.

At this sound, the tiger, who until then had been lying down, rose up, swishing its sides with its tail: it was a royal tiger of the biggest size. In one bound it was twenty feet closer to our hunter.[34]

'You must be joking!' said Captain Pamphile. 'Damme, d'you think I'm going to shoot at you from this distance and ruin your fine skin? Prrrrrou! Prrrrrou!'

The tiger took a second leap that brought it another twenty feet closer, but just as it was landing, a shot rang out and the bullet struck it in the left eye. The tiger curled up like a hare and expired there and then.

Captain Pamphile calmly reloaded his rifle, pulled his knife out of his pocket, rolled the tiger onto its back, slit its skin under the belly, and skinned it just as a cook does a rabbit. Then he draped himself in the fur of his victim, just as the Nemean Hercules had done 4,000 years before – and as an inhabitant of Marseilles, the Captain claimed to be a descendant of Hercules.[35] Then he set off hunting again.

Not half an hour had elapsed before he heard a loud commotion in the waters of the river whose banks he was following. He quickly ran to the edge and realised it was a hippopotamus making its way up river and rising every now and again to the surface to breathe.

'Blow me!' said Captain Pamphile. 'That'll save me having to lay out six francs on glass jewellery!'

This was the current price of oxen in Saint Paul de Loanda, and Captain Pamphile was considered to be careful with his money.

And so, guided by the bubbles that betrayed the position of the hippo as they rose and burst on the river surface, he followed the animal's progress, and when it raised its huge head, the hunter, selecting the only vulnerable point, sent a bullet through its ear. Captain Pamphile could have shot Achilles in the heel at a distance of 500 paces.

The monster twisted and turned for a few seconds, bellowing horribly and lashing the water with its feet. For a moment it looked as if it were going to sink in the deep whirlpool created by its death agony, but soon its strength was exhausted, and it rolled over like some great bundle; then, little by little, the smooth whitish skin of its belly appeared, instead of the black wrinkled skin on its back, and in one final effort, it ran aground, its four legs in the air, amid the grass growing at the riverside.

Captain Pamphile calmly reloaded his rifle, pulled his knife from his pocket, cut down a small tree the thickness of a broomstick, sharpened it at one end, split it at the other, planted the sharpened end into the belly of the hippopotamus, and inserted into the split end a piece of paper torn from his notebook, on which he wrote in pencil: 'To the cook of the trading brig the *Roxelane*, from Captain Pamphile, hunting on the banks of the River Bengo.'

Then he pushed the animal away with his foot. The hippo got caught up in the current and quietly floated down the river, labelled like a travelling salesman's portmanteau.

'Ah!' said Captain Pamphile, when he saw his provisions safely on their way to his boat, 'By gum, I rather think I've earned meself a spot of lunch!'

And since this was a truth that he alone needed to recognise for all its consequences to be immediately deduced, he stretched his tiger skin out on the ground, sat on it, pulled out of his left pocket a flask of rum and placed it to his right, from his right pocket a superb guava that he placed to his left, and from his game bag a piece of biscuit that he placed between his legs; then he started to stuff his pipe so he wouldn't have anything too tiring to do after his meal.

I'm sure you have seen the way Deburau takes such care over the preparations for his lunch, only for Harlequin to eat it?[36] I'm sure you'll remember the look on his face when he turns round and sees his glass empty and his apple swiped? Yes? Well, just look at Captain Pamphile, when he discovers that his flask of rum has been knocked over and his guava has vanished!

Captain Pamphile, who has never been silenced by a decree of the Minister of the Interior,[37] uttered the most wonderful 'Shiver me timbers!' ever uttered by Provençal lips since the foundation of Marseilles, but, as he was more sceptical than Deburau, as he had read the ancient and modern philosophers, and as he had learned from Diogenes Laertius and M. de Voltaire that there is no effect without a cause,[38] he immediately set out to seek the cause whose effect was so prejudicial to him – but seemingly without doing anything, not moving from where he was, and apparently just nibbling on his dry bread. Only his head turned round, five minutes or so later, like that of a Chinese magot,[39] giving quite a start when all of a sudden a nondescript object fell onto his head and remained entangled in his hair. The Captain raised his hand to the place that had been struck, and found the peel of his guava. Captain Pamphile lifted his nose into the air and spotted, directly above him, a monkey pulling faces in the branches of a tree.

Captain Pamphile stretched his hand towards his rifle without taking his eyes off the thief; then, propping the rifle butt against his shoulder, he fired. The female fell to his side.

'Damn and blast it!' said Captain Pamphile examining his new prey. 'I've killed a two-headed monkey.'

And indeed, the animal lying at Captain Pamphile's feet had two quite separate and distinct heads, and the phenomenon was all the more remarkable as one of the two heads was dead and its eyes were closed, while the other was alive and its eyes were open.

Captain Pamphile, who wanted to shed light on this bizarre phenomenon of natural history, picked up the monster by the tail and examined it attentively, but on his first inspection, all his astonishment vanished. The monkey was a female, and the second head was that of her baby, whom she had been carrying on her back when she was shot; the baby had accompanied her in her fall without leaving the maternal breast.

Captain Pamphile, from whom not even the devotion of Cleobis and Biton would have wrung a tear,[40] took the little monkey by the scruff of its neck, tore it away from the corpse to which it was still clinging, examined it for a moment as closely as M. de Buffon could have done, and, pursing his lips with an expression of inward satisfaction, exclaimed: 'Blow me! It's a marmoset; it's worth fifty francs if it's worth anything – that's what I'd get in the harbour at Marseilles.'

And he placed it in his game bag.

Then, as Captain Pamphile had not eaten, thanks to the incident we have related, he decided to head back to the bay. In any case, although he had been hunting for only about two hours, he had in that space of time killed a boa constrictor, a tiger, and a hippopotamus, and brought back a marmoset alive. There are many Parisian hunters who would be happy to bag a tally like that in a whole day.

When he arrived on the deck of the brig, he saw the whole crew gathered round the hippopotamus, which had fortunately reached the right address. The ship's surgeon was pulling out his teeth, so as to turn them into knife handles for Villenave and dentures for Désirabode;[41] the foreman was removing his leather and cutting it into strips to make whips to beat the dogs with and cats-o'-nine-tails to dust off the flies; lastly, the cook was carving beefsteaks from his haunches and entrecôtes from his ribs for Captain Pamphile's table: the rest of the animal was to be cut up into quarters and salted down for the crew.

Captain Pamphile was so satisfied with this activity that he ordered an extraordinary ration of rum to be served, and reduced the seventy lashes of the cat that a cabin boy had been sentenced to receive down to five.

That evening, they set sail.

Seeing this excess of provisions, Captain Pamphile decided there was no point in dropping anchor at the Cape of Good Hope, and leaving Prince Edward's Isles to the right, and the land of Madagascar to the left, he swept out into the Indian Ocean.

So the *Roxelane* was running with the wind in her sails, skimming along at a speed of eight knots per hour, which, sailors say, is rather a good rate for a trading vessel, when a sailor keeping watch cried down from the topsails: 'Sail for'ard!'

Captain Pamphile took his telescope, trained it on the ship indicated, looked with his naked eye, and pointed his telescope at it again; then, after a moment's attentive examination, he called over his mate and silently placed the instrument in his hands. The mate raised it straight away to his eye.

'Well, Policar,' said the Captain, when he thought the other had had plenty of time to examine the object in question, 'what do you think of that leaky old hulk?'

'My word, Captain, I think it has a distinctly odd look about it. As for its flag' – he raised the telescope to his eye again – 'devil take me if I know what power it represents: it's a green and yellow dragon on a white field.'

'Well, you must bow down to the ground, my friend, for you have before you a ship belonging to the Son of Heaven,[42] the father and mother of the human race, the king of kings, the sublime emperor of China and Cochin China, and what's more, I can see from its rounded crown work and its tortoise-like progress that it's not returning to Peking with its belly empty.'

'Good Lord! Good Lord' said Policar, scratching his ear.

'What do you think of this encounter?'

'I think it would be odd...'

'I quite agree... I think so too, my boy.'

'So we should...?'

'Bring the ironmongery up on deck and put out every last inch of sail.'

'Ah! Now he's noticed us too.'

'Very well, let's wait for nightfall and, until then, nicely pay out our cable, so he won't suspect a thing. As far as I can judge from the rate he's going, we'll be in his waters by five o'clock; all night, we'll sail side by side, and tomorrow, as soon as day breaks, we'll say hello.'

Captain Pamphile had developed his own system. Instead of ballasting his vessel with cobbles or pigs,[43] he loaded the hold with half a dozen swivel guns, four or five twelve-pounder carronades and a long eight-pounder; then, just in case, he added several thousands of cartridges, fifty or so rifles, and some twenty boarding sabres. On occasions similar to the one in which he now found himself, he would bring all these bits and pieces up on deck, fit the swivel guns and carronades onto their pivots, drag the eight-pounder to the stern, hand out the rifles to his men, and start to draw up what he called his system of exchange. So, the next day, the Chinese vessel found him quite ready to do business.

Great was the stupefaction on board the imperial ship. The day before, its captain had recognised a merchant vessel, and had thereupon gone straight off to sleep, smoking his opium pipe, but overnight, lo and behold, the cat had become a tiger, and was now showing its iron claws and its bronze teeth.

Captain Kao-Kiou-Koan was soon informed of the situation in which the Chinese vessel now found itself. He was just coming to the end of a delightful dream: the Son of Heaven had just given him one of his own sisters in marriage, so that he was now brother-in-law to the moon.

He thus found it remarkably difficult to understand what Captain Pamphile wanted from him. Admittedly, the latter was talking to him in Provençal and the bridegroom was replying in Chinese. Eventually they found a Provençal on board the *Roxelane* who could speak a little Chinese, and on board the vessel of the Sublime Emperor a Chinese sailor who could get by quite well in Provençal, so the two captains finally managed to understand one another.

The result of the dialogue was that half the cargo of the imperial vessel (captained by Kao-Kiou-Koan) was immediately brought on board the trading brig the *Roxelane* (captained by Pamphile).

And as this cargo just happened to be composed of coffee, rice and tea, the result was that Captain Pamphile did not need to put in either at Moka, or Bombay, or Peking, and this saved him a great amount of time and money.

This put him in such a good humour that, stopping off at Rodrigues Island, he bought a parrot.

When the ship reached the tip of Madagascar, the crew realised they were about to run out of water, but since Cape Saint-Marie afforded no sure anchorage for a vessel that was as heavily laden as was the *Roxelane*, the Captain put everyone on half rations, and decided he would press on to the bay of Algoa. As he was proceeding to load up the barrels of water, he saw advancing towards him a chief of the Gonaquas, followed by two men carrying on their shoulders, rather as the envoys of the Hebrews had carried a bunch of grapes from the Promised Land,[44] a magnificent elephant's tooth: this was a sample that Chief Outavari (whose name in the Gonaquas language means *Son of the East*) was bringing to the coast, hoping that the party would put in an order.

Captain Pamphile examined the ivory, found it to be of first-rate quality, and asked the Gonaquas chief how much 2,000 elephants' teeth similar to the one on display would cost. Outavari replied that it would cost him exactly 3,000 bottles of brandy. The Captain wished to haggle; but the Son of the East held firm, and maintained that he hadn't named too high a price. So the Captain was reluctantly obliged to accept the terms the Negro was asking – which did not cost him all that much, in fact, since at this price there was about ten thousand per cent to be gained. The Captain asked when the order could be delivered: Outavari demanded two years; this length of time fitted in admirably with Captain Pamphile's schedule, so the two worthy merchants shook hands and went their ways, each charmed and delighted by the other.

However, this deal, however advantageous it was, nagged at the worthy Captain's mercantile conscience; he reflected, in private, that if he'd managed to pick up the ivory so cheaply on the eastern side of Africa, he must be able to find it at half the price on the western side, since it was on that side in particular that elephants were to be found in such great numbers that they had given their name to a river. So he decided to find out for sure, and once the ship reached the 30th degree of latitude, he ordered the sailors to head for land; unfortunately, he was out in his reckoning by four or five degrees, and landed at the mouth of the Orange river, instead of the Olifants river.

Captain Pamphile was not overly disquieted by this; the two places were so close that they would not lead to any variation in price, and so he had the rowing boat lowered and took it upstream as far as the capital city of the Little Namaquois, situated two days' journey away in the interior. He found Chief Outavaro returning from a great hunting expedition in which he had killed fifteen elephants. So there was no lack of samples, and the Captain deemed them to be even better than those of Outavari.

As a result, Outavaro and the Captain came to a business arrangement that was even more to the latter's advantage than the deal he had struck with Outavari. The Son of the West gave Captain Pamphile 2,000 tusks in return for fifteen hundred bottles of brandy; this deal was a third as good again as his colleague's, but, like him, he required two years to gather his supply. Captain Pamphile did not argue over the length of time; on the contrary, he found it made good economic sense, as he would need to make just one journey to pick up the two cargoes. Outavaro and the Captain shook hands to conclude their deal, and went their ways, the best friends in the world. And the brig the *Roxelane* resumed its course for Europe.

At this point in Jadin's story the clock struck midnight, the curfew for practically all those whose lodgings are higher than the fifth floor. So everyone was getting up to leave, when Flers reminded Dr Thierry that there was one last check that still needed to be made. The Doctor took the bowl, and held it up for all to see. Not a single fly was left in it; Mlle Camargo, however, had swollen to the size of a turkey's egg, and looked as if she had just emerged from a tin of shoe polish. As everyone departed, they each congratulated Thierry on his immense erudition.

The following day, we received a latter conceived in the following terms:

MM. Eugène and Alexandre Decamps have the melancholy honour of informing you of the sad loss of Mlle Camargo, who died of indigestion on the night of 2nd/3rd March. You are invited to the funeral repast that will take place at the home of the departed, on the 6th inst., at five o'clock in the evening precisely.

6

How James I started by plucking the chickens and ended by plucking a parrot.

Immediately after the funeral dinner, which ended at seven or eight in the evening, Jadin, whose story at the previous session had aroused the most lively interest, was invited to continue. Mlle Camargo, however interesting a creature, had not been able – given the cloistered existence she had led during the six months and a day that she had lived in Decamps's studio – to leave any particularly vivid memories in either the minds or the hearts of the habitual guests. Of all of us, Thierry was the one to whom she had been closest, and yet her relations with him had been purely scientific. As a result, the sorrow caused by her death was short-lived, and was soon blotted out by the huge advantages that science had derived from it. So the reader will easily understand how our curiosity was rapidly rekindled by the adventures of our friend James, as told by such a faithful, conscientious and skilful narrator as Jadin, whose reputation as a painter had already been made by his fine painting *Cows*, and as a historian by his *The History of Prince Henry*, a work he wrote in collaboration with M. Dauzas*: even before it has been published, it is enjoying the full reputation it deserves. So Jadin did not need to be asked before pulling his manuscript out of his pocket, and resuming the story where he had left off…

The parrot bought by Captain Pamphile was a cockatoo of the finest species, with a body as white as snow, a beak as black as ebony, and a crest as yellow as saffron – a crest that rose and sank depending on whether the bird was in a good or a bad mood, and that sometimes gave it the paternal appearance of a grocer wearing his cap, and at other times the formidable aspect of a member of the National Guard adorned with his bearskin. Over and above these physical advantages,

* Forthcoming: it will very shortly be in all the bookshops in the capital: *The History of Prince Henry whose Heart was Encircled by Three Hoops of Iron*, with his portrait showing him the moment after he has torn out his eye, and a facsimile of his handwriting. Readers may subscribe without advance payment: M. Amaury Duval, 36, Rue d'Anjou-Saint-Honoré.

Cotackoo[45] had a host of entertaining talents; he could speak equally well English, Spanish and French, sing 'God Save the King' like Lord Wellington, '*Pensativo estaba el Cid*' like Don Carlos and the *Marseillaise* like General La Fayette. One can readily understand that, with philological aptitudes of this kind, he lost no time, now that he had fallen into the hands of the crew of the *Roxelane*, in rapidly extending the circle of his acquaintances. As a result, no sooner had the ship, after a week's sailing, come within sight of Cape Sainte-Marie, than he started to swear in the very best Provençal, to the great jubilation of Captain Pamphile, who, like the troubadours of old, spoke nothing but the *langue d'oc*[46].

Thus, when Captain Pamphile had awoken and inspected his vessel, checking that every man was at his post and everything in its place; when he had ordered the sailors to be given their rations of brandy and the cabin boys to be given their taste of the cat-o'-nine-tails; when he had examined the sky, studied the sea and whistled up the wind; when he had finally attained that serenity of soul that comes with the certainty of having fulfilled one's duties, he would go over to Cotackoo – followed by James, who was visibly growing plumper, and who shared Captain Pamphile's entire affection with his feathered rival – and give him his Provençal lesson; then, if he was pleased with his pupil, he would stick a sugar lump between the bars of the cage, a reward that Cotackoo gratefully received and of which James was obviously extremely jealous. And so the minute an unexpected incident took Captain Pamphile elsewhere, James would come over to the cage, and so contrive matters that the sugar lump would habitually end up at a quite different destination, to the utter despair of Cotackoo, who, with his claw hovering in mid-air and his crest erect, would fill the air with his most formidable songs or his most terrible oaths; as for James, he would hang around the prison in which the bird of the air was dancing with rage, and, when he didn't have time to gobble down the *corpus delicti*,[47] stuffed it into his cheek pouches where it slowly melted while he scratched his haunches, blinking ecstatically, since his only punishment was being forced to drink his sugar instead of eating it.

As you will realise, this assault on property rights was as disagreeable as can be imagined to Cotackoo, and as soon as Captain Pamphile came over to him, he would deploy his entire repertoire. Unfortunately, none of his tutors had taught him to cry 'Thief!', so his master took this sortie, which was nothing other than a formal accusation, as a sign of the pleasure occasioned by his presence, and – convinced that the bird had eaten his dessert – contented himself with delicately scratching his head. Cotackoo appreciated this up to a certain point, but he certainly appreciated it far less than he would have appreciated the sugar lump in question. So Cotackoo realised that he had only himself to count on when it came to taking his revenge, and when, a day after stealing the sugar lump, James again stuck his hand into the cage to pick up the remaining fragments, Cotackoo dangled from one claw and, apparently quite absorbed in his gymnastic exercise, caught James's thumb and bit it fiercely. James uttered a piercing yell, leapt onto the rigging, climbed up until rope and wood ran out, and then, coming to a halt at the highest spot on the boat, remained there clinging pitifully to the mast with three of his paws and shaking the fourth as if he had been holding a holy water sprinkler.

At dinner time, Captain Pamphile whistled for James, but James didn't reply; this silence was so contrary to his habits of hygiene that Captain Pamphile started to grow worried; he whistled once again, and this time heard in reply a kind of angry murmur that seemed to come from the clouds; he looked up and spotted James, who was giving his blessing *urbi et orbi*[48]. Then there was an exchange of signals between James and Captain Pamphile, and the result of this was that James obstinately refused to come down. Captain Pamphile, who had trained his crew to unquestioning obedience, and was quite unwilling to allow his strict rules to be contravened by a monkey, picked up his loudhailer and called for Two-Mouths. The individual thus summoned appeared straight away, climbing back up the ladder that led down to the galley, and came up to the Captain rather in the same way that a dog who is being trained will come up to the guard who is about to chastise him; Captain Pamphile, who wasted no words on his inferiors, showed the cabin boy the recalcitrant creature who was pulling faces from the tip of his spar; Two-Mouths immediately grasped what was being asked of him, gripped the ladder that led to the shrouds, and started to climb up with an agility indicating that

Captain Pamphile, by honouring Two-Mouths with this hazardous mission, had made an extremely judicious choice.

One other point that rested entirely on, I won't say the study of the heart, but a knowledge of the stomach, had also influenced Captain Pamphile's determination: Two-Mouths was employed above all in the galley, an honourable function that was appreciated by the whole crew, in particular James, who was especially fond of this part of the vessel; so he had struck up a close friendship with the new character we have just brought onstage, who owed the expressive nickname that had replaced his patronymic appellation to the fact that his position made it easier for him to dine before the others – which did not prevent him from also dining *after* the others. So James understood Two-Mouths' character, just as Two-Mouths understood James's, and the result of this mutual appreciation was that, instead of trying to escape (which he would not have hesitated to do if anyone other than Two-Mouths had been sent to him), James met him halfway, and the two friends met on the tiller crosstree of the main topgallant sail, and came down at once, one carrying the other, to the deck, where Captain Pamphile was awaiting them.

Captain Pamphile knew only one remedy for wounds of every kind whatsoever: a compress of brandy, tafia, or rum, so he soaked a piece of cloth in the aforesaid liquid and wound it round the wounded creature's finger; when the alcohol came into contact with his raw wound, James at first made a terrible face, but when he saw how, the minute Captain Pamphile's back was turned, Two-Mouths quickly swallowed the liquid still remaining in the glass where the cloth had been soaked, he realised that the liquor, though painful when used as a medicine, could be beneficent when taken as a drink, and so he extended his tongue out towards the dressing, delicately licked the compress, and, gradually starting to get a taste for it, ended up quite simply sucking his thumb. As Captain Pamphile had commanded that the bandage be soaked afresh every ten minutes, and his orders were executed promptly, the result of this was that, within two hours, James's eyes were starting to blink and his head to nod, and as the treatment continued to be administered, and James appreciated his treatment more and more, he finally fell dead drunk into the arms of his friend

Two-Mouths, who took the wounded creature down into the cabin and laid him on his own bed.

James slept uninterruptedly for twelve hours, and when he woke up, the first thing that met his eyes was his friend Two-Mouths busy plucking a chicken. This was not a new sight for James, and yet on this occasion he seemed to pay particularly close attention to it; he quietly got up, went over, fixed his eyes on the scene, examined the mechanism by the aid of which the work was proceeding, and remained motionless and absorbed all the time the operation lasted; once the chicken had been plucked, James, who still felt rather heavy-headed, went up on deck to take the air.

The wind continued favourable the next day, with the result that Captain Pamphile, seeing that everything was going as he wished, and deciding that there was no point in transporting to Marseilles the chickens still on board – which he had in any case not purchased with any financial speculations in mind – gave orders, on the pretext that his health was starting to give cause for concern, that every day he should be served, in addition to his slice of hippopotamus and his bouillabaisse, some fresh poultry, either boiled or roast. Five minutes after these orders had been given, the squealing of a duck having its neck wrung were heard.

At this noise, James came down so quickly from the main yard that anyone less acquainted with his selfish nature would have thought he was hurrying to rescue the victim. He dashed into his cabin, where he found Two-Mouths, who was conscientiously fulfilling his tasks as chef's assistant, plucking the bird until not the tiniest shred of down was left on its body; this time, just as before, James seemed to take the greatest interest in the whole business; then, when it was all over, he went back up on deck, wandered over to Cotackoo's cage for the first time since the incident, sauntered several times round it, taking care to keep out of range of its beak, and finally, seizing the right moment, he caught one of the bird's tail feathers and pulled it so hard that, for all Cotackoo's oaths and fluttering of wings, it finally came off in his hand. This experiment, although it initially seemed rather insignificant, seemed to give James great pleasure; he started dancing round on his four feet, jumping up and down on the spot, which was his way of showing the greatest contentment.

In the mean time, the ship had lost sight of land and was moving full sail ahead across the Atlantic; everywhere was the sea and the sky and, beyond the horizon, a sense of vast expanses. From time to time, far-flying seabirds – but no others – flew across the sky for as far as the eye could see, passing from one continent to another; Captain Pamphile, trusting the animal instinct that was to teach Cotackoo that his wings were too weak for him to venture on a long journey, opened his lodger's prison and gave him complete liberty to fly around the rigging. Cotackoo immediately took advantage of this to fly up to the topgallant sail, and once he was there, almost out of his mind with joy, and to the great satisfaction of the crew, he began to spin out his entire repertoire, making as much noise all by himself as did the twenty-five sailors watching him.

While this parade was taking place on the deck, a scene of quite a different kind was happening in the cabin. James, as was his wont, had gone over to Two-Mouths when it was time for some poultry to be plucked, but this time, the cabin boy, who had noted the attention his friend paid to his activities, had decided that he had discovered in him a hitherto quite unsuspected vocation for the office he was performing. As a result, a particularly bright idea came to Two-Mouths' mind: from now on, he would give James the job of plucking his chickens and his ducks, while, changing roles, he would fold his arms and watch him at it. Two-Mouths was one of those resolute characters who leave as little time as possible between the idea and the execution of a thing, and so he quietly moved towards the door and closed it, armed himself – just in case – with a whip that he slipped under the belt of his breeches, making sure he had left the handle perfectly visible, and, returning immediately to James, placed in his hands the duck that his own hands were supposed to be plucking, and pointed at the handle of the whip that, should there be any argument, he fully intended to call upon as a referee.

But James did not even force him to resort to this extremity. Either because Two-Mouths had guessed correctly, or because the new talent that he was enabling James to acquire seemed to the latter to put the final necessary gloss on any education, James took the duck between his two knees, as he had seen his tutor do, and settled down to his task with an ardour that dispensed Two-Mouths from any act of violence against him; indeed, towards the end, seeing that the feathers were disappearing and giving way to down, and the down to flesh, the feeling that filled him grew into real enthusiasm; as a result, when the task was completely finished, James started to dance, as he had done the day before, next to Cotackoo's cage.

Two-Mouths was, for his part, overjoyed; the only thing he regretted was that he hadn't been quick enough to take advantage earlier of his acolyte's inclinations, but he promised himself that he wouldn't let these inclinations grow cold. And so, the next day, at the same time, in the same circumstances, and having taken the same precautions, he began the second performance of the previous day's play; it was just as successful as the first, and as a result, on the third day, Two-Mouths, recognising James as his equal, tied his kitchen apron round his loins and entrusted him with all the turkeys, chickens and ducks. James showed himself to be worthy of his trust and, within a week, he had left his teacher far behind him in skill and quickness of execution.

Meanwhile the brig sailed on like an enchanted ship: it had passed James's homeland, and, on the left, out of sight, the islands of Saint Helena and Ascension, and was moving full sail ahead towards the equator. It was one of those days you get in the tropics when the sky weighs heavily on the earth: there was only the pilot at the helm, the watchman in the shrouds, and Cotackoo on his spar; as for the rest of the crew, they were seeking shade wherever they thought they might find it, while Captain Pamphile himself, lying in his hammock, and smoking his hubble-bubble pipe, was being fanned by Two-Mouths with a peacock's tail. This time, quite unusually, James, instead of plucking his chicken, had placed it back intact on a chair and taken off his kitchen apron, and looked just like everyone else, either overwhelmed by the heat or absorbed in his own thoughts. However, this torpor was of short duration; he glanced around quickly and alertly, and then, as if frightened by his own boldness, picked up a feather, brought it up to his mouth, dropped it with an expression of indifference, and scratched his haunch, blinking, and, with a bound that the most meticulous observer would have seen as nothing more than the effect of a sudden whim, he jumped onto the first rung of the ladder leading up on deck: there, he stopped for another few seconds, gazing at the sun through the hatches, then started to climb nonchalantly up, like someone out for a stroll who can't find anything to do and goes looking for something to entertain him on the Boulevard des Italiens.

Once he was on the last rung, James saw that the deck was deserted: the ship looked like an abandoned vessel drifting along aimlessly. This solitude seemed to give James the greatest satisfaction; he scratched his haunches, his teeth chattered, his eyes blinked, and he performed two perpendicular little leaps, while his eyes carefully sought out Cotackoo, whom he finally discovered in his usual place, fluttering his wings and singing 'God Save the King'. Then James seemed to lose interest in him; he climbed onto the ship's rails furthest from the mizzenmast, on the top of which his enemy was perched, reached the yards, stopped for a moment in the topsails, climped up the foremast, and ventured onto the single rope that leads to the mizzenmast; halfway across this tremulous bridge, he hung from his tail, let go with his four paws and swayed upside down, as if he merely wanted to play at swinging. Then, convinced that Cotackoo wasn't paying him any attention, he crept towards him, apparently thinking of something completely different, and just when his rival was giving full throat to his song of joy, crying at the top of his lungs and beating the air with his feathered arms, like a coachman trying to keep warm while he waits for his fare, James interrupted his *arietta* and his jubilation and gripped him firmly in his left hand, just where the wings are fixed to the body. Cotackoo uttered a cry of distress, but nobody paid the least attention, since the entire crew was overcome by the stifling heat pouring down from the sun at its zenith.

'Hurricanes and hawsers!' Captain Pamphile suddenly said, 'now that's a phenomenon, snow beneath the equator!…'

'Ah no!' said Two-Mouths, 'that's not snow; it's… ah, blow me down!'

And he darted to the steps.

'Well, what is it?' asked Captain Pamphile, rising in his hammock.

'What it is,' cried Two-Mouths from the top of his ladder, 'is James plucking Cotackoo!'

Captain Pamphile sent one of the most magnificent oaths ever to have been heard beneath the equator echoing round his vessel, and also darted up on deck, while the whole crew, waking with a start as if by the sound of the powder store exploding, rushed up in turn through every opening in the brig's frame.

'So, you useless boy!' cried Captain Pamphile seizing a marlinspike, and addressing Two-Mouths, 'what are you going to do about it, eh? Emergency, emergency!'

Two-Mouths gripped the rigging and shinned up like a squirrel, but the faster he climbed, the quicker James worked; Cotackoo's feathers were forming a veritable cloud and falling as thick and fast as snow in December; for his part, Cotackoo, seeing Two-Mouths drawing near, squawked louder and louder, but just as his saviour was holding his arm out to him, James, who so far hadn't seemed to be paying any attention to what was happening on board, decided that his habitual task was now sufficiently complete, and dropped his enemy, who by this time had feathers only on his wings. Cotackoo, greatly distressed by pain and alarm, forgot that he could no longer rely on his tail for a counterweight, fluttered around quite grotesquely for a moment, and finally fell into the sea, where he drowned, not having webbed feet.

'Flers,' said Decamps, interrupting the reader of this tale, 'you've got a big fine voice, go and shout to the concierge's little girl to bring us up some cream – we've run out.'

7

How Tom hugged the concierge's daughter as she brought the cream up, and the decision that was taken in regard to this event.

Flers opened the door and went onto the stairs to make the request as he had been asked; then he came back in without noticing that Tom, who had followed him, was still outside; then Jadin, who had come to a pause at the death of Cotackoo, was invited to continue his reading…

Here, gentlemen (he said, showing the completed manuscript), a simple narrative will replace the written memoirs, because of the relative unimportance of the events we still have to relate: the offering made by James to the gods of the sea made them favourable to Captain Pamphile's vessel, so the rest of the crossing was completed without any adventures other than the ones we have related; there was just one day when they feared that James had met with a fatal accident. It was on the following occasion.

Captain Pamphile, passing off the Cape of Palms, in sight of Upper Guinea, had caught in his cabin a magnificent butterfly, a veritable flying flower of the tropics, its wings as iridescent and dazzling as the breast of a hummingbird. The Captain, as we have seen, neglected nothing that might have any value on his return to Europe, and so he had taken the greatest precautions in capturing his imprudent guest, so as not to blur the down on its wings, and had nailed it with a pin to the wainscoting of his quarters. There is not one of you who has not seen the death agony of a butterfly and who, impelled by the desire to preserve, in a box or under glass, that graceful child of the summer, has not allowed that desire to stifle his heart's more tender promptings. So you know how long the poor victim will struggle, twisting on the pivot that has transfixed its body, and dying of its own beauty. Captain Pamphile's victim lived in this state for several days, beating its wings as if it had been sucking the juice from a flower; this movement drew the attention of James, who looked at it out of the corner of his eye, pretending not to see anything, but taking advantage of the first moment when Captain Pamphile's back was turned to jump up against the woodwork where, judging from the brilliance of its colours that it would be good to eat, he devoured it with his usual greediness. Captain Pamphile turned round when he heard James leaping and somersaulting about; when James had swallowed the butterfly, he had also swallowed the pin: its copper crest had got stuck in his throat; the poor wretch was choking.

The Captain, who had no idea of the reason for his grimaces and contortions, thought he was jumping for joy, and enjoyed watching his mad antics for a while, but when he saw they were going on indefinitely, that the voice of the jumping creature was starting to mimic more and more the shrill tones of Punchinello, and that instead of sucking his thumb as he had been in the habit of doing ever since his treatment, he was stuffing his whole hand down his throat, right up to the elbow, he started to suspect that in these gambols there was something more pressing than the desire to entertain him, and went over to James. The poor devil's eyes were rolling in a way that left no doubt as to the nature of the sensations he was experiencing, and Captain Pamphile, seeing that his beloved monkey was definitely on the point of passing from life to death, bellowed for the doctor with all the strength in his lungs: not that he placed much trust in medicine, but so that he would have nothing to regret.

Because of his concern for James, Captain Pamphile's voice had assumed a character of such distress that not only the doctor, but all others who heard it, immediately came running up; among the swiftest was Two-Mouths, who, busy with his usual jobs, was torn away from them by the Captain's cry for help, and ran over holding a leek and a carrot that he had been peeling. The Captain had no need to explain the reason for his cries; he had merely to point at James, who continued to display, in the middle of the cabin, the same signs of agitation and pain. Everyone fussed round the patient: the doctor declared that he was suffering a stroke, an illness to which the species of green monkeys was particularly prone, since they have picked up the habit of hanging by their tails and are thus naturally exposed to the risk of a sudden rush of blood to the head. In consequence, James needed to be bled without delay, but in any case, as the doctor hadn't been summoned as soon as the first symptoms declared themselves, he wouldn't promise he could save him; after this preamble, he pulled out his doctor's bag, sharpened his lancet, and ordered Two-Mouths to hold the patient still, so that he wouldn't open an artery instead of a vein.

The Captain and crew had every confidence in the doctor, so they listened with the deepest respect to the scientific argument of which we have related the main trend; only Two-Mouths shook his head doubtfully. Two-Mouths harboured an ancient hatred for the doctor: one day when some sugared plums of which Captain Pamphile thought very highly, seeing that they came from his wife – one day when these plums, shut away in his own private cupboard, had visibly diminished in number, he had assembled his crew to find out which thieves were capable of laying hands (not to say teeth) on the private provisions of the supreme head of the *Roxelane*: everyone had denied the charge, Two-Mouths as well as the others; however, as this would not be the first time the cabin boy had done such a thing, the Captain had taken his denial with a pinch of salt, and asked the doctor if there wasn't some means of reaching the truth of the matter. The doctor, whose motto was that of Jean-Jacques, *vitam impendere vero*,[49] had replied that there was nothing easier, and two infallible methods presented themselves: the first and quickest would be to slit open Two-Mouths' stomach, an operation that could be performed in seven seconds; the second was to give him an emetic that, depending on its strength, would entail a greater or lesser delay, but one which in any case would not extend beyond an hour. Captain Pamphile, who preferred gentle persuasion, opted for the emetic; his medicine was administered immediately and forcibly, then the delinquent was handed over to two sailors, with strict orders to keep a close eye on him.

Thirty-nine minutes later, his watch in his hand, the doctor came in with five plum stones that, for greater security, Two-Mouths had thought best to swallow along with the rest, and which he had just with the greatest reluctance brought up. The proof of the crime was patent, as Two-Mouths declared he had eaten nothing for the past week but bananas and Indian figs, so his punishment was not long in coming: the guilty party was sentenced to a fortnight on bread and water and, after every meal, as dessert, twenty-five lashes of the cat, administered to him, in accordance with regulations, by the boatswain's mate. The result of this incident had been that Two-Mouths, as we have seen, cordially detested the doctor, and since that time had never lost an opportunity to be disagreeable to him.

So Two-Mouths was the only person who didn't believe a word of what the doctor was saying to him; in James's illness there were symptoms that Two-Mouths knew perfectly well, having experienced them himself when, caught just at the moment he was tasting the Captain's bouillabaisse, he had swallowed a piece of fish without having had time to take out the bones. So his eyes instinctively roamed around to find, by analogy, what it was that had tempted James's greed. The butterfly and the pin had disappeared; this was all Two-Mouths needed to reveal the whole truth to him. James had a butterfly in his tummy, and a pin in his throat.

So when the doctor, lancet in hand, went over to James, whom Two-Mouths was holding in his arms, the latter declared, to the great stupefaction and the great scandal of the Captain and crew, that the doctor was mistaken; that James didn't run the slightest risk of apoplexy, but of choking, and that for the time being he wasn't suffering from the least haemorrhage in the brain, but from a pin obstructing his oesophagus. With these words, Two-Mouths, employing on James the remedy to which he himself usually resorted in similar circumstances, repeatedly plunged into his throat the leek that he had by chance been holding when he had come running up in response to the Captain's cries, so as to divert into broader channels the foreign body that had got stuck in narrow ones. Then, certain that the operation had redounded to his honour, he placed the moribund in the middle of the room. Instead of continuing to indulge in the frantic gambols that the whole crew had observed him performing five minutes earlier, James sat for a while in a state of perfect calm, as if to assure himself that the pain had indeed disappeared; then he blinked, then started to scratch his belly with one hand, then began to dance on his rear legs, and this, as you know, was James's way of showing that he was perfectly happy. But this was still not all. To deal one final blow to the doctor's reputation, Two-Mouths handed the convalescent the carrot that he had brought. James, who was as fond of this vegetable as is possible to imagine, grabbed it straight away, and demonstrated, by starting to nibble it uninterruptedly forthwith, that his channels of nutrition were perfectly unblocked, and were asking for nothing better than to resume their normal service. The author of the operation was triumphant. As for the doctor, he swore he would take his revenge if Two-Mouths ever fell ill, but unfortunately, throughout the rest of the journey, Two-Mouths suffered from nothing worse than a slight bout of indigestion when off the Azores, and this he treated himself in the same fashion as the Ancient Romans – by putting his fingers in his mouth.

The brig the *Roxelane*, under Captain Pamphile, after a tranquil crossing, thus arrived in the port of Marseilles on 30th September, where it unloaded, to its profit, the coffee, tea and spices that it had exchanged, in the Indian archipelago, with Captain Kao-Kiou-Koan; as for James I, he was sold, for the sum of seventy-five francs, to Eugène Isabey, who gave him to Flers in exchange for a Turkish pipe, and Flers then gave him to Decamps in exchange for a Greek rifle.

And this is how James came from the banks of the River Bengo to 109, rue du Faubourg Saint-Denis, where, thanks to the paternal care of Fau, his education attained the degree of perfection that you see in him now.

Jadin was bowing modestly to the applause of all present when a scream was heard from the door: we rushed out onto the landing, and found the concierge's young daughter half fainting in Tom's arms. Startled by our unexpected appearance, he started to bound down the stairs at top speed. At the same moment, we heard a second cry even more piercing than the first: an old marquise, who for thirty-five years had lived on the third storey, had come out, holding a candle, to investigate the noise, had found herself face to face with the fugitive and had fainted away completely. Tom climbed back fifteen steps, saw that the door on the fourth floor was open, went in as if it were his own apartment, and found himself in the middle of a wedding meal. There was an immediate uproar; the guests, bride and groom at their head, rushed out onto the stairs. The whole house, from the cellar to the attic rooms, found itself in an instant ranged on every landing, with everyone talking at once, and, as happens in circumstances such as this, nobody could hear what anyone else was saying. Eventually, they tracked the ruckus down to its source: the young girl who had raised the alarm told them that she had been climbing the stairs without any light, holding the cream that she had been asked to bring, when she felt someone grabbing her round the waist; thinking it was some impudent lodger who was making so bold, she had replied to his declaration of intent with a hearty slap. Tom had responded to the slap with a low growl that had immediately betrayed his incognito; the girl, terrified to find herself in the claws of a bear, when she had thought it had been a man's arms seizing her, had uttered the scream that had brought us all out; our sudden appearance, as we have said, had startled Tom, and Tom's alarm had led to the subsequent events: the fainting of the marquise and the flight of the wedding party.

Alexandre Decamps, who was closest to Tom, assumed responsibility for apologising for him to all those present and, as a demonstration of his good neighbourliness, he offered to go and find Tom wherever he might be and bring him back just as Saint Martha had brought back the Tarasque with a simple blue or pink ribbon:[50] whereupon, a little rascal of twelve to fifteen came forward and held out the bride's garter, which he had taken from under the table; he had been just about to decorate the guests with it when the alarm had been given. Alexandre took the ribbon, went into the dining room, and found Tom walking with the most marvellous skill on the table, laden as it was with food: he was on his third rum baba.

This latest misdemeanour proved his downfall: unfortunately, the groom had the same tastes as Tom; he appealed to all who were fond of rum babas; violent murmurs immediately arose, and the docility with which poor Tom followed Alexandre could not quell them. At the door, he met the proprietor, whom the marquise had just informed that she was giving in her notice; for his part, the groom declared that he wouldn't stay another quarter of an hour in the house, unless his just demands were met; the remaining lodgers all joined in the chorus. The proprietor turned pale as he saw that he would soon have an empty house, and so he informed Decamps that, however greatly he desired to keep him on as a lodger, this would prove impossible if he did not straight away get rid of an animal who was giving, at such a time of day and in a decent household, such grave cause for scandal. For his part, Decamps, who was starting to get thoroughly fed up with Tom, put up only as much resistance as was needed for his final surrender to be accepted with gratitude. He gave his word of honour that, the next day, Tom would leave the apartment, and so as to reassure the lodgers who were requesting that the expropriation be carried out there and then (declaring that, if there were any delay, they would not sleep at home), he went down into the yard, forced Tom, willy-nilly, into a dog kennel, turned the opening to the wall, and loaded it down with cobblestones.

This promise, which had just been given such a dazzlingly effective start, seemed quite adequate to the plaintiffs; the concierge's young daughter wiped her eyes, the marquise was satisfied with just one more tantrum (her third), and the groom magnanimously declared that, if he couldn't have his rum baba, he would make do with brioche. They all went back into their apartments and, two hours later, calm was completely restored.

As for Tom, he initially attempted, like Enceladus,[51] to remove the mountain that was weighing down on him; but seeing that he had no chance of succeeding, he made a hole in the wall, and escaped into the garden of the house next door.

8

How Tom dislocated the wrist of a municipal guard,[52] and the source of the alarm with which this respectable militia filled him.

The lodger at no. 111 on the ground floor was really quite surprised when, the following morning, he saw a bear wandering around his flower beds; he quickly shut his back door, which he had opened so as to indulge in the same exercise, and tried to discover, staring through the windowpanes, by what means this new lover of things horticultural had managed to get into his garden; unfortunately, his view was blocked by a clump of lilacs, so the inspection, despite being quite lengthy, produced no very satisfactory result. So, as the lodger at no. 111 on the ground floor had the great good fortune to be a subscriber to the *Constitutionnel*,[53] he remembered reading, a few days earlier, in the Valenciennes section, that this town had been the setting for a most peculiar phenomenon: a rain of toads had fallen, to the accompaniment of thunder and lightning, and in such great quantities that the streets of the town and the roofs of the houses had been covered with them. Immediately after this, the sky – which, two hours before, had been ashen grey – had turned indigo blue. The subscriber to the *Constitutionnel* lifted his eyes and, seeing the sky as black as ink and Tom in his garden, and being unable to account for the way the creature had managed to get there, started to think that a phenomenon similar to what had occurred in Valenciennes was about to happen all over again, with the one difference that, instead of toads, it was about to rain bears. Both phenomena were equally improbable; a hail of bears would be heavier and more dangerous, that was all. Absorbed in this idea, he went back to his barometer, whose needle was pointing to rain and storm; at just this minute, a clap of thunder was heard. A bluish flash of lightning lit up the apartment; the subscriber to the *Constitutionnel* decided there wasn't an instant to be lost, and, thinking there might be competition, he sent his valet to fetch the police inspector and his cook to fetch a corporal and nine men, so that in every eventuality he would be fully protected by the civil authorities and guarded by the strength of the military.

Meanwhile, the passers-by, who had seen the cook and the valet leaving no. 111 in a great panic, had gathered outside the main door and were indulging in the most incoherent conjectures; they cross-questioned the porter, but the porter, to his great disappointment, knew no more than anyone else; all he could tell them was that the alert, of whatever kind, came from the body of the dwelling situated between the inside yard and the garden. Just then, the subscriber to the *Constitutionnel* appeared at his back door, pale, trembling, and calling for help; Tom had noticed him through the windowpanes and, being used to the society of men, had come trotting over to make his acquaintance, but the subscriber to the *Constitutionnel,* mistaking his intentions, had read as a declaration of war what was merely an act of politeness, and had beaten a prudent retreat. Once he was at the door to the inner yard, he had heard the windowpanes of the back door cracking; then retreat had changed into a veritable flight, and the fugitive had appeared, as we have said, before the curious onlookers, giving signs of the greatest distress and calling for help at the top of his lungs.

What usually happened on occasions such as this then happened: instead of responding to the appeal addressed to it, the crowd scattered; just one municipal guard who happened to find himself among their ranks stayed at his post and, advancing towards the subscriber to the *Constitutionnel*, brought his hand up to his shako in a salute, and asked him whether he could be of any assistance to him, but the man he was addressing had lost all powers of speech; he pointed to the door he had just opened and the flight of steps he had just come tumbling down. The municipal guard realised that the danger came from there, doughtily drew his sabre, walked up the steps and through the door, and found himself in the apartment.

The first thing he noticed on entering the living room was the meek expression on the face of Tom who, rearing up on his hind legs, had pushed his head and forepaws through a window, and, leaning on a wooden crosspiece, was gazing in curiosity at the interior of this mysterious apartment.

The municipal guard stopped suddenly, not knowing – however doughty he might be – whether to advance or to retreat, but no sooner had Tom seen him than, fixing on him a haggard stare, and breathing as heavily as a panic-stricken buffalo, he hurriedly withdrew his head from the opening window and started to flee as fast as his four legs would carry him, to the most distant corner of the garden, showing the most obvious signs of terror at the sight of the municipal uniform.

Now, up until now, we have presented our friend Tom to our readers as being an animal full of reason and commonsense, so they will have to allow us to pause for a moment, in spite of the interest of the situation, to tell them what lay behind this panic, which might be thought premature, since it had not yet been provoked by any demonstration of hostility, and might, in consequence, damage the irreproachable reputation that he has left behind.

It was one evening during carnival in the year of grace 1830. Tom had been living in Paris for hardly six months, yet the artistic society among which he was living had civilised him to such a point that he was one of the most amiable bears one could dream of seeing: he would go and open the door when anyone rang, he would stand guard for hours on end on his hind feet, holding a halberd, and he would dance Exaudet's minuet[54] while holding – with incomparable grace – a broomstick behind his head. He had spent the day indulging in these innocent pursuits, to the great satisfaction of everyone in the studio, and had just been sleeping the sleep of the just in the cupboard that he used as a den, when there came a knock at the front door. At that moment, James gave signs of such evident joy that Decamps guessed it was his beloved tutor who was coming to pay him a visit.

Indeed, the door opened; Fau appeared, dressed as a clown, and James, as was his wont, flung himself into his arms.

'There there, there there!…' said Fau, placing James on the table and handing him his walking stick. 'what a charming beast you are! Shoulder arms! Present arms! Take aim! Fire! Marvellous! I'll have a complete grenadier's uniform made up for you, and you can stand guard instead of me. But you're not the person I need to talk to right now; it's your friend Tom. Where is that animal?'

'He's in his den, I imagine,' replied Decamps.

'Tom, here, Tom!' shouted Fau.

Tom uttered a low growl indicating that he had understood perfectly well that it was he who was being summoned, but that he was in no hurry to follow up the invitation.

'Well now,' said Fau, 'is that the way people obey me when I'm talking? Tom, my friend, don't force me to use violence.'

Tom held out a paw, which emerged from his cupboard without any other part of his person becoming visible, and started to yawn in a prolonged and plaintive fashion, like a child being awoken who cannot find any other way of protesting against the tyranny of his teacher.

'Where's the broomstick?' said Fau, with a hint of menace in his voice, and noisily banged around among the savages' bows, the blow-pipes, and the fishing rods piled behind the door.

'Here!' called Alexandre, showing Tom, who, at this well-known noise, had quickly got up and was waddling over to Fau in an innocent and paternal way.

'Well done!' said Fau; 'you might be a bit friendly, when we make a point of coming all this way to see you from the Café Procope[55] to the Faubourg Saint-Denis.' Tom slowly nodded his head.

'That's the style! Now, a handshake for your friends! Marvellous!'

'Are you taking him with you?' said Decamps.

'For a while,' replied Fau, 'and we're going to find something that will amuse him, too.'

'So where are you off to together?'

'Oh, just the masked ball. Come along, Tom, off we go, my friend. We've got a fiacre already waiting.'

And as if Tom had grasped the value of this last argument, he went down the stairs four at a time, followed by his usher. When he reached the fiacre, the coach driver opened the door and lowered the step, and

Tom, guided by Fau, climbed into the coach as if he'd done nothing else all his life long.

'Blimey, that's a funny disguise and no mistake!' said the coachman. 'You really would say it's a proper bear, y'know. Anyway, where would you gents like me to take you?'

'To the Odéon,' replied Fau.

'Grooonnn!' said Tom.

'All right, all right, keep yer 'air on,' replied the coachman. 'It's a bit of a jaunt, but we'll get there all right.'

And indeed, half an hour later, the fiacre was pulling up at the theatre entrance. Fau got out first and paid the coachman, then he gave his hand to Tom, bought two tickets from the ticket office, and entered the dance hall without the man at the door making the least comment.

The second time they did the rounds of the foyer, people started following Tom. The accuracy with which the newcomer could mimic the demeanour of the animal whose skin he was wearing had impressed several lovers of natural history. The curious were thus drawn to take a closer and closer look, and, wishing to assure themselves that his talent for observation extended to his voice, they pulled hairs out of his tail or pinched the skin of his ear.

'Grrroooon!' said Tom.

A cry of admiration rose from those assembled: you could easily have thought it was a real bear.

Fau led Tom to the buffet and offered him a few little cakes, to which he was very partial and which he ingested with such well-mimicked voracity that the gallery burst out laughing; then he poured him a glass of water that Tom picked up delicately between his paws, as he was wont to do when Decamps happened to grant him the honour of allowing him to sit at his table, and swallowed it in a single gulp: the enthusiasm of all present reached a new peak.

Indeed, when Fau tried to leave the buffet, he found himself so closely hemmed in on all sides that he started to fear lest Tom, in order to escape the crush, might feel it was time to resort to his teeth or claws, which would have complicated matters, so he led him into a corner, propped him up and ordered him to stand there quietly until further notice. This was, as we have said, a kind of exercise quite familiar to

Tom – standing guard, that is: after all, it was perfectly well suited to the indolence of his character. And so, more obedient to instructions than many National Guards of my acquaintance, he performed his guard duty in this instance until he was relieved. Then a harlequin offered him his bat[56] to complete the parody, and Tom solemnly placed his heavy paw on his wooden rifle.

'Do you know,' said Fau to the obliging son of Bergamo, 'to whom you have just lent your bat?'

'No,' replied the harlequin.

'You can't guess?'

'Not in the slightest.'

'Come now, look more closely. From the grace of his movements, from the systematic way he leans his neck on his left shoulder, like Alexander the Great, from the way he perfectly imitates the whole physiology...[57] what!... don't you recognise him?'

'My word of honour, I really don't!'

'Odry,' said Fau, mysteriously; 'Odry, wearing the same costume as in *The Bear and the Pasha*.'[58]

'No – he plays the white she-bear!'

'Precisely! He has taken Vernet's skin to disguise himself in.'[59]

'Oh, what a wonderful joke!' said the harlequin.

'Grrrooon!' said Tom.

'Now I recognise his voice,' said the man talking to Fau. 'Oh, it's surprising I didn't guess earlier. Tell him to disguise it a bit more.'

'Yes, yes,' said Fau, heading towards the dance hall; 'but you shouldn't bother him too much if you want him to act funny. I'll try and get him to dance a minuet.'

'Oh! Really?'

'He promised me. Tell your friends, so they won't play silly tricks on him.'

'Don't worry.'

Fau crossed the circle of party-goers, and the harlequin went off delightedly to tell each masquerader in turn the news and to repeat the advice he had been given, whereupon everyone moved discreetly away. Just then, the signal for the galop was given, and everyone in the foyer rushed into the dance hall, but before he followed his companions, the facetious harlequin tiptoed over to Tom and, leaning towards him, murmured in his ear:

'I know who you are, you fine masquerader.'

'Grooonnn!' said Tom.

'Oh, you can go *grr grr* as much as you like, you're still going to dance the minuet; you *are* going to dance the minuet, aren't you, my darling Marécot?'[60]

Tom slowly nodded his head, as was his wont when people asked him questions, and the harlequin, satisfied with this affirmative reply, set off in search of a Colombine[61] to dance the galop himself.

All this time, Tom had continued to stand right next to the girl selling lemonade, motionless at his post, but with his eyes unwaveringly fixed on the counter where piles of cakes rose in pyramids. The lemonade seller noticed this unswerving attention, and, seeing a sure way of selling some of her wares, she took a plate and held out her hand: Tom extended his paw, delicately picked up one cake, then a second, then a third; the lemonade seller was happy to go on offering him cakes, and Tom was happy to go on accepting them, and the result of this exchange was that he was just starting on his second dozen when the galop finished and the dancers returned to the foyer. Harlequin had recruited a shepherdess and a Pierrette, and he was bringing these ladies to dance the minuet.

Then, being an old acquaintance, he went up to Tom, and said a few words in his ear; Tom, who had been put into a very good mood by the cakes, replied with one of his most amiable growls. The harlequin turned round to the gallery and announced that Lord Marécot was most happy to agree to the request of those present. At these words, applause broke out, and cries of 'Into the dance hall! Into the dance hall!' were heard. The Pierrette and the shepherdess led Tom along, each taking one paw; Tom, for his part, allowed himself to be led alike like any gallant dancing partner, gazing in surprise at his two ladies in turn. He soon found himself with them in the middle of the dance floor. Everyone took their places, some in the boxes, the others in the galleries, most in a circle; the orchestra struck up the music.

The minuet was a triumph for Tom, and one of Fau's choreographic masterpieces. So success was assured from the first turns, and it continued to increase: by the time they reached the last figures, the applause was delirious. Tom was carried off in triumph into a stage-box, then the shepherdess loosed her crown of roses and placed it on his head; the whole dance hall clapped, and one voice went so far as to shout in enthusiasm: 'Long live Marécot I!'

Tom leaned on the balustrade of his box with considerable grace; at the same moment, the first bars of the *contredanse* were heard, and everyone rushed onto the dance floor, with the exception of several of the new king's courtiers, who stayed near him, in the hope of extracting from him a ticket for the show, but Tom's only answer to every request was his eternal *grooonnn.*

As the joke was starting to become a bit monotonous, people gradually began to move away from the obstinate minister of the great Shahabaham,[62] admitting that he was a talented tightrope walker but declaring that his conversation was really rather dull. Soon there were hardly three or four people paying him any attention; an hour later, he had been completely forgotten: thus passes the glory of the world.

Meanwhile, the time to leave had come; the stalls were emptying, the boxes were already deserted. The wan gleam of daylight was starting to trickle into the dance hall through the windows of the foyer when the usherette, as she did her rounds, heard emerging from the stage-box in the first row a snoring that betrayed the presence of some belated masquerader; she opened the door and found Tom who, wearied by the tempestuous night he had just passed, had retired to the back of his box and yielded to a sweet sleep. Regulations on this point are strict and an usherette is a slave to regulations, so she went in and, with all the politeness characteristic of the estimable class of the society to which she had the honour to belong, she pointed out to Tom that it was nearly six o'clock in the morning, a sensible time to think about going home.

'Grooonnn!' said Tom.

'Yes, I know,' replied the usherette: 'you're fast asleep, old chap, but you'll be even more comfortable in your own bed. Come along now. Your wife must be worried. My word, he can't hear! He's as fast as a rock!'

She tapped him on the shoulder.

'Grooonnn!'

'All right, all right. It's gone past the time to keep people guessing; anyway, we know who you are, you fine masquerader. Look, they're lowering the footlights and putting out the chandelier. Would you like us to go and get a fiacre for you?'

'Grooonnn!'

'Come on, come on now, the dancehall of the Odéon isn't a cheap hotel; on your way! Oh, so that's how you're going to take it, is it? Shame on you, Monsieur Odry! Treating an old artiste like that! Well, Monsieur Odry, I'm going to call the police; the superintendent won't have gone to bed yet. Ah, so you won't obey the regulations? Lay into me with your fists, would you?... Hitting a woman? We'll see about that. Superintendent! Superintendent!'

'What's the problem?' replied the fireman on duty.

'Help, fireman, help!' shouted the usherette.

'Hey! Police!...'

'What's up?' said the voice of the sergeant in charge of the patrol.

'It's old mother So-and-So shouting for help, in the stage-box in the front rows.'

'We're on our way.'

'Over here, sergeant, over here!' shouted the usherette.

'All right, all right, we're coming. Where are you, love?'

'You needn't worry, there aren't any steps. Over here, this way! He's in the corner, against the theatre side door. Oh, what a bandit! He's as strong as a Turk!'

'Grooonnn!' said Tom.

'D'you hear him, then? I ask you, is that any way for decent folks to talk?'

'Now then, my friend,' said the sergeant, whose eyes, being used to darkness, were starting to make Tom out in the gloom. 'We all know what it's like to be young... me as much as anyone else, I like a laugh, don't I, Mum? But I have to obey the regulations. It's time to return to the paternal or conjugal guardroom; on the double, forward march! And put your best foot forward.'

'Grooonnn!'

'Yes, very nice, we can imitate the cry of animals so well, can't we? But now it's time for a different kind of exercise; come on now, old fellow, let's leave nice and quietly. Oh, so we don't want to? Going to be nasty about it, are we? Fine, fine, fine, let's have a laugh. Grab that sly customer for me, and throw him out.'

'He's refusing to walk, Sarge.'

'Very well! That's what we've got butts on the end of our rifles for! Let him have it, in the small of his back and on his thighs and calves.'

'Grooonnn! Grooonnn! Grooonnn!'

'Go on, land him one!'

'D'you know what, Sarge,' said one of the police officers, 'if you want my opinion, he's a real bear: I just grabbed him by the collar and his skin is firmly attached to his flesh.'

'Oh, if it's a bear, then treat him with a bit of respect: his owner might make us pay for him. Go and get the fireman's lantern.'

'Grooonnn!'

'It don't make no difference whether he's a bear or not,' said one of the soldiers, 'he's been given a good thwacking, and if he's got any memory, he won't forget the municipal guard.'

'Here's what you asked for,' said a member of the patrol, bringing over the lamp.

'Bring the light up to the suspect's face.'

The soldier obeyed.

'That's a bear's muzzle,' said the sergeant.

'Jesus! My God!' said the usherette and took to her heels. 'A real bear!'

'Well, now, so it is, a real bear! We need to see if he's got any papers, and take him back to his lodgings; there'll probably be a reward; the creature must have got lost, and since he's fond of society, that's why he'll have wandered into the Odéon ball.'

'Grooonnn!'

'Look, he's answering!'

'Well, well, well,' said one of the soldiers.

'What's the matter?'

'He's got a little bag hanging round his neck.'

'Open the bag.'

'A card!'

'Read the card.'

The soldier took it and read:

'My name is Tom; I live at 109, rue du Faubourg-Saint-Denis; I have a hundred sous in my wallet, forty sous for the fiacre and three francs for those who bring me home.'

'Good God, it's quite true, here are the hundred sous!' exclaimed the municipal guard.

'This citizen is perfectly in order,' said the sergeant. 'Two volunteers eager and willing to take him back to his official domicile.'

'I'll do it!' chorused the municipals.

'No preferential treatment! Age before beauty! The two most seasoned troopers can enjoy the benefit of the thing. Come along, boys.'

Two municipal guards went up to Tom, and wrapped round his neck a rope, making sure (better safe than sorry!) that they wound it three times round his muzzle. Tom didn't put up any resistance: the blows from the rifle butts had made him as supple as a glove. Thirty yards or so from the Odéon, one of the guards suddenly said, 'Look, it's a nice morning; if we don't take the fiacre, the walk will do the old fellow good.'

'And that way, we'd each have forty sous instead of thirty!'

'Carried unanimously!'

Half an hour later, they were at the door of no. 109. At the third knock, the concierge in person, still half asleep, came to open up.

'Say, old Sleepyhead,' said one of the municipal guards, 'here's one of your lodgers. Do you recognise this individual as a member of your menagerie?'

'Indeed I do,' said the concierge; 'it's M. Decamps's bear.'

That same day, a bill for little cakes was brought to Odry's address: seven francs fifty centimes in total. But the minister of Shahabaham I was easily able to prove his alibi: he had been on guard at the Tuileries.

As for Tom, from that day forth he was filled with fear for that respectable body of men that had laid into the small of his back with their rifle butts and made him walk home even though he'd paid for a fiacre.

So it will come as no surprise that when he saw the face of the municipal guard appearing at the door into the living room, he immediately beat a retreat to the very bottom of the garden.

There is nothing so heartening to a man as the sight of his enemy retreating. Moreover, as we have said, the municipal guard was not lacking in courage, so he set off in pursuit of Tom, who, finding himself cornered, first tried to climb up the wall and then, after two or three attempts, seeing that he had no chance of escape, rose up on his hind-quarters and prepared to put up a stout defence, drawing for the nonce on the boxing lessons that his friend Fau had given him.

For his part, the police officer put himself on guard and attacked his adversary according to all the rules of the art. At the third pass, he feinted a lunge at the head, but in fact aimed his blow at the thigh; Tom parried with a *seconde*. The municipal threatened Tom with a straight lunge; Tom returned to the on-guard position, made a coupé on the weapons and, swiping at his enemy's sabre guard with all the strength of his clenched paws, so violently knocked back his hand that he dislocated his wrist. The municipal dropped his sabre, and found himself at the mercy of his adversary.

Fortunately for him and unfortunately for Tom, the superintendent arrived at just that moment; he saw the act of rebellion that had just been committed against armed force, pulled from his pocket a scarf, rolled it three times around his belly, and, sensing he had the support of the guard behind him, motioned the corporal and the nine men down into the garden, commanded them to draw up in battle array, and stood on the steps to give the order to fire. Tom, his attention fixed on these manoeuvres, allowed the municipal to beat a retreat, holding his right hand in his left, and stayed upright and motionless against the wall.

Then the cross-questioning began. Tom stood accused of breaking into a dwelling by night and attempted murder on the person of an agent of the authorities, an attempt that had failed only due to circumstances beyond his control. As he could produce no witness for the defence, he was sentenced to death, and so the corporal was requested to proceed with the execution, and gave the soldiers the order to prepare their weapons.

Then a great silence fell among the crowd that had come running up after the patrol, and the only voice to be heard was that of the corporal: he ordered each move of the twelve-step manoeuvre. However, after the words 'take aim!', he thought it best to turn one last time to the superintendent; at this point, a murmur of compassion ran through the assembled crowd, but the police superintendent, who had been disturbed in the middle of his breakfast, was inexorable: he held out his hand in sign of command.

'Fire!' said the corporal.

The soldiers obeyed, and the unhappy Tom fell, pierced by eight bullets.

At this very moment, Alexandre Decamps was returning home with a letter from M. Cuvier, saying that the doors of the Botanical Gardens were now open to Tom, and assuring him that Martin[63] was still alive.

9

How Captain Pamphile quelled an uprising on board the brig the Roxelane, *and what ensued.*

Tom had been born in Canada; he belonged to that herbivorous race that is habitually circumscribed by the mountains situated between New York and Lake Ontario, and which in winter, when the snow drives it away from its icy peaks, sometimes ventures to come down in famished groups as far as the outskirts of Portland and Boston.

Now, if our readers would really like to know how Tom had come from the banks of the Saint Lawrence River to the banks of the River Seine, they need only be so kind as to go back to the end of the year 1828 and follow us to the furthest reaches of the Atlantic Ocean, between Iceland and the point of Cape Farewell. There we will show them, sailing along at the steady rate they will all recognise, the brig of our old friend Captain Pamphile who (breaking for once with his taste for the Orient) has sailed up towards the North Pole, not in the hope of seeking, as had Ross or Banks, a passage between Melville Island and Banks's Land, but with a more useful and above all more lucrative aim in mind. Captain Pamphile still had two years to wait before his ivory would be ready, and he had taken advantage of this to try and introduce into the northern seas the system of exchange we have seen him practising with such success on the way to the archipelago of the Indian Ocean. This last theatre of his old exploits was starting to be less productive as a result of his frequent bandying of words with ships cruising along at that latitude, and in any case, he needed a change of air. But this time, instead of seeking spices or tea, Captain Pamphile was really after whale oil.

Given the personality of our intrepid freebooter, it will be easily understood that he had not spent his days recruiting a crew of whaling sailors, nor had he bothered to overload his vessel with rowing boats, coils of rope and harpoons. When the time came to put to sea, he had merely checked over the swivel guns, the carronades and the eight-pounders that, as we have said, he used as ballast; he had inspected the rifles and had ordered the landing sabres to be sharpened, had replenished his provisions for six weeks, had passed through the straits of Gibraltar and, towards the month of September (in other words at the peak of the fishing season) he had reached the 60th degree of latitude and immediately begun to practise his industry.

As we have seen, Captain Pamphile was a trifle work-shy. So he addressed himself in particular to the vessels that he could tell, from their gait in the water, were suitably heavily laden. We know what manner he adopted when trading in a delicate situation; he had made no change in this manner despite the difference in locality, so there is no need to remind our readers – we will merely inform them that his tactic succeeded perfectly well. So it was that he was returning with, at most, fifty empty barrels when, off the Banks of Newfoundland, he happened to run across a ship that was just coming back from a cod-fishing expedition. Captain Pamphile, although quite able to indulge in vast speculations, was far from averse, as we have seen, to more modest speculations too. So he did not neglect this opportunity of complementing his cargo. The fifty empty barrels were loaded on to the fishing vessel, which, in exchange, was only too pleased to send fifty full barrels back to Captain Pamphile. Policar observed that the lids on the full barrels were three inches lower than they had been on the empty barrels, but Captain Pamphile was prepared to overlook this irregularity, since the cod had been salted only the day before; all the same, he examined the barrels one after another to assure himself that the fish was of good quality; then, ordering them to be all nailed shut in turn, he commanded them to be carried down into the hold, apart from a single one that he kept for his own personal use.

That evening, the doctor came down to his cabin just as he was about to sit down to table. He had come to ask, in the name of the crew, for three or four barrels of fresh cod to be handed over to them. Provisions had been running out for nearly a month, and the sailors had been reduced to eating slices of whale and seal cutlets. Captain Pamphile asked the doctor whether the provisions had run out; the doctor replied that there was a certain quantity of those we have just mentioned, but that this sort of food, quite revolting even when it was fresh, was not in the slightest improved by salting. Captain Pamphile replied that he was sorry, but that Bedda & Co., of Marseilles, had just laid an order for precisely forty-nine barrels of salted cod, and that he could not miss out on such a good piece of business; in any case, if his crew wanted fresh cod, they had only to fish for it, which they were at perfect liberty to do, since he, Captain Pamphile, had absolutely no objection.

The doctor went out.

Ten minutes later, Captain Pamphile heard a great commotion on board the *Roxelane*.

Several voices were shouting:

'Get your pikes! Pikes ho!'

And a sailor cried:

'Long live Policar! Down with Captain Pamphile!'

Captain Pamphile thought it was time to make an appearance. He rose from table, slipped a pair of pistols into his belt, lit his short-stemmed pipe – something that he only did when the weather was very stormy – picked up a kind of whip of honour that had been fashioned with the greatest care and which he used only on the most memorable occasions, and climbed up on deck. There was a riot going on.

Captain Pamphile strode into the middle of the crew, divided as it was into groups, and glared left and right to see if there would be a single one of all these men who would dare to address him. Any stranger would have thought that Captain Pamphile was performing his ordinary inspection, but for the crew of the *Roxelane*, who had known him for a long time, this was something altogether different. They knew that Captain Pamphile was never so close to exploding as when he didn't say a word, and right now he had assumed a terrifying silence.

Finally, after going round two or three times, he came to a halt in front of a lieutenant who seemed, like the others, to be not altogether uninvolved in the rebellion.

'Policar, stout chap,' he asked, 'could you tell me how the wind is blowing?'

'Er… Captain,' replied Policar, 'the wind is… Did you say… the wind?'

'Yes, the wind… how's it blowing?'

'Heavens above, I don't know,' said Policar.

'Well let *me* tell you, then!'

And Captain Pamphile, with an imperturbable solemnity, examined the sky, which was overcast; then, holding his hand out in the direction of the breeze, he whistled, as sailors habitually do; finally, turning back to his lieutenant, he said, 'Well, Policar, stout chap, let *me* tell you how the wind is blowing; I think it's going to come lashing down.'

'I thought as much,' said Policar.

'And now, Policar, stout chap, would you be so obliging as to tell me *what's* going to come lashing down?'

'What's going to come lashing down?'

'Yes, like hail.'

'Heavens above, I don't know,' said Policar.

'Well, the cat-o'-nine-tails is going to come lashing down, stout chap, that's what. And so, Policar, stout chap, if you don't want to be caught out in the downpour, hurry back to your cabin and don't come out again until I tell you to – do you understand, Policar?'

'I understand, Captain,' said Policar, scuttling down the stairs.

'He's a bright lad,' commented Captain Pamphile.

Then he again walked round the deck three times and came to a halt in front of the master carpenter, who was holding a pike.

'Good day to you, Georges,' said the Captain. 'Now what's this little plaything, my friend?'

'Er… Captain…' stammered the carpenter.

'Well God bless me if it isn't my duster.'

The carpenter dropped the pike; the Captain picked it up and snapped it in two as if it had been a willow rod.

'Ah, I see,' continued Captain Pamphile, 'you wanted to give your clothes a beating. Well done, my friend, well done! Cleanliness is nearly next to godliness, as they say in Italy.'

He motioned two aides to come over.

'You two, over here, please; take this switch, and give poor old Georges's jacket a good beating with it, and you, Georges, my son, just leave your body on underneath the jacket, if you don't mind.'

'How many strokes, Captain?' asked the aides.

'Oh: twenty-five each.'

The order was executed, the two aides operating in turn with the regularity of Virgil's shepherds;[64] the Captain kept count of the strokes. At the thirteenth, Georges fainted.

'That'll do,' said the Captain, 'carry him to his hammock. He can get the rest tomorrow: to each his own.'

The Captain's order was obeyed; he walked around the deck another three times, then he came to a halt for one last time near the sailor who had shouted: 'Long live Policar! Down with Captain Pamphile!'

'Well now,' he said, 'how's that pretty little voice of yours, Gaetano, my boy?'

Gaetano tried to reply, but for all his efforts, the only sounds to emerge from his throat were indistinct and inarticulate mumblings.

'Blow me!' said the Captain, 'he's lost his voice! Gaetano, my boy, this will be dangerous if you don't seek a remedy. Doctor, send me four medical students.'

The doctor pointed to four men who came over to Gaetano.

'Come over here, me hearties,' said the Captain, 'and follow my prescription to the letter: you will take a piece of rope; you'll fix it to a pulley, and you'll wind one end of it like a cravat round this honest lad's neck, then you'll pull on the other end until you've hoisted our man up to a height of thirty feet; you'll leave him there for ten minutes, and when you let him down, he'll chatter like a blackbird and whistle like a starling. Jump to it, me hearties!'

The order was executed in silence and performed in every detail without a single murmur making itself audible. Captain Pamphile paid such close attention that he allowed his pipe to go out. Ten minutes later, the body of the rebel sailor fell to the deck without movement. The doctor went over to him and checked that he was well and truly dead; then they tied one millstone round his neck, and two to his feet, and threw him into the sea.

'Now,' said Captain Pamphile, pulling his extinguished pipe out of his mouth, 'off you all go to relight my pipe together, and only one of you is to bring it back to me.'

With every sign of the deepest respect, the sailor closest to the Captain received the venerable relic that his superior had presented to him and climbed down the ladder of the tween deck, followed by the whole crew, leaving the Captain alone with the doctor. A moment later, Two-Mouths appeared, holding the relit pipe.

'Ah, it's you, you young hooligan!' said the Captain. 'And what were you doing while those honest men were walking up and down the deck discussing their affairs? Answer, you young scamp!'

'Heavens above,' said Two-Mouths, seeing from the Captain's expression that he had nothing to fear from him, 'I was dipping my bread in the beef stew to see if it was going to taste all right, and my fingers into the saucepan to check that the sauce was nicely salted.'

'Very well, you useless boy, take the best stock from the stew and the best morsel from the saucepan, and use the rest to make soup for my dog; as for the sailors, they can eat bread and drink water for three days: it'll protect them from scurvy. Let's go and have supper, doctor.'

On leaving table, the Captain went back up on deck to carry out his evening inspection. Everything was in perfect order: the sailor on watch was at his post, the pilot at his helm, and the lookout on his mast. The brig was moving forward full sail ahead, and merrily skimming along at eight knots an hour, with the banks of Newfoundland on the left and the gulf of St Lawrence on the right; the wind was blowing west-north-west, and promised to hold good; so Captain Pamphile, after a tempestuous day, counting on a peaceful night, went down into his cabin, took off his jacket, lit his pipe and leaned out at his window, allowing his eyes to dwell now on the curls of tobacco smoke and now on the wake of his vessel.

Captain Pamphile, as the reader will have been able to judge, was more original of spirit than poetic and picturesque of imagination. However, being an authentic sailor, he couldn't help but observe the moon shining in the middle of a fine night sky and shedding its silver light on the waves of the ocean without drifting off into that gentle reverie that every man of the sea feels for the element on which he lives; so he had been leaning there for two hours or so, his body half out of the window, hearing nothing but the lapping of the waves, and seeing nothing but Saint John's Point disappearing behind the horizon like a sea mist, when he felt himself being grabbed by the collar of his shirt and the hem of his pants. At the same moment, the two hands that had permitted themselves this familiarity performed a tipping movement, one pushing down and the other pulling up, so that Captain Pamphile's feet, leaving the air, immediately found themselves higher than his head. The Captain tried to call for help, but he didn't have time; just as he was opening his mouth, the person who was carrying out this strange experiment on him, seeing that the body was now sloping at the desired angle, let go of both his pants and his collar, with the result that Captain Pamphile, obeying in spite of himself the laws of equilibrium and of gravity, plummeted down almost vertically and disappeared into the wake of the *Roxelane*, which went on her way, gracious and swift, without suspecting that she had been widowed of her Captain.

The next day at ten o'clock in the morning, since Captain Pamphile, quite contrary to his habits, had not yet carried out his inspection on the deck, the doctor went into his cabin and found it empty; at that moment, the rumour spread through the crew that their master had vanished; the ship's command fell by right to the lieutenant, and so they went to let Policar out of the cabin where he was strictly obeying the order to remain, and they proclaimed him Captain.

The first act of the new commander was to have each man issued with a portion of cod and two rations of brandy, and to let Georges off the twenty remaining strokes he was due to receive.

Three days after the event we have just related, there was no more mention of Captain Pamphile on board the brig the *Roxelane* than if this worthy sailor had never existed.

10

How Captain Pamphile, thinking he was landing on an island, landed on a whale, and became the servant of Black-Serpent.

When Captain Pamphile resurfaced, the brig the *Roxelane* was already out of range of his voice, so he didn't think it worth his while to exhaust himself uttering useless cries: he started by finding his bearings so as to see which was the nearest land, and having worked out that it must be Cape Breton, he struck out in that direction, steering by the Pole Star, which he took care to keep on his right.

Captain Pamphile swam like a seal; however, after four or five hours of this exercise, he was starting to get rather tired; in addition, the sky was starting to grow overcast, and the lantern that had been directing his progress had disappeared, so he reflected that it wouldn't be a bad idea to rest for a while. So he stopped swimming on one side, and started to float on his back.

He remained in this position for about an hour, making only such movement as was absolutely necessary to keep himself on the surface, and watching all the stars in the sky disappearing one by one.

Whatever philosophy Captain Pamphile was endowed with, it is easy to see that his situation was not exactly enjoyable; he knew the bearing of the coasts extremely well, and he knew that he must be still some three or four leagues from any land. So, sensing that his strength had returned after his brief rest, he had just started to swim with renewed ardour when he spotted, a few yards ahead of him, a black surface that he hadn't been able to see any earlier, since the night was so dark. Captain Pamphile thought that it must be an islet or rock forgotten by navigators and geographers, and struck out towards it. He soon reached it; but he found it difficult to clamber up onto it, as the surface, washed unceasingly by the waves, had become slippery; still, he managed it in the end, after several attempts, and found himself on a small rounded island, twenty yards or so long and some six feet above water level; it was completely uninhabited.

Captain Pamphile had soon explored his new domain; it was bare and sterile, apart from a kind of tree as thick as a broomstick, ten feet long, but quite without any branches or leaves. There were also a few wet strands of seaweed indicating that, at high tide, the waves must completely cover the island. Captain Pamphile attributed this to the incredible negligence of the geographers, and made a firm resolution that once he was back in France he would write a scientific paper in which he point out the error of his predecessors, and send it to the Society of Voyages.

This was as far as he had got with his various plans and projects when he thought he heard someone speak some distance away from him. He looked round on all sides, but, as we have said, the night was so dark that he couldn't see anything. He listened again and, this time, he could distinctly make out the sound of several voices; although the words were still unintelligible, Captain Pamphile was about to call out, but as he didn't know whether those approaching through the darkness were friends or enemies, he decided to wait and see. In any case, the island on which he had landed wasn't so far from land that, being as he was in the ever-busy Gulf of Saint Lawrence, there was any risk of his dying of starvation. So he resolved to keep quiet until daylight, unless he was discovered himself; he consequently moved to the tip of his island that was furthest away from the point where had thought he had heard human words – those words that, in certain circumstances, man fears more than he does the roar of ferocious beasts.

Silence had fallen again, and Captain Pamphile was starting to think that everything would go without a hitch, when he felt the ground move beneath his feet. His first thought was that it was an earthquake, but, throughout the extent of his island, he hadn't noticed the least mountain with the appearance of a volcano; he then remembered what he had often heard about those underwater formations that suddenly appeared above the surface of the water, sometimes staying there for days, months or years, giving whole colonies time to settle on them, to sow their crops and build their huts, until, in an instant, at a given time, they were destroyed just as they had been formed, without any apparent cause, disappearing all of a sudden, taking with them the over-confident populace that had settled on them. In any case, as Captain Pamphile hadn't had time either to sow or to build, and thus had no reason to regret the loss of either wheat or houses, he prepared to continue his journey swimming, feeling thankful as it was that his miraculous island had appeared at the surface of the sea long enough for him to rest awhile. So he was perfectly resigned to the will of God when, to his great astonishment, he noticed that the ground he was on, instead of sinking, seemed to be moving forward, leaving behind it a wake like that left by the stern of a ship. Captain Pamphile was on a floating island; the marvel of Latona was being repeated, just for him, and he was sailing along, on some unknown Delos, towards the shores of the new world.[65]

Captain Pamphile had seen so many things in the course of his nomadic and adventurous life that he wasn't the kind of man to be astonished by so little; he merely noted that his island, with an intelligence that he would never have dared expect of it, was heading directly towards the northern tip of Cape Breton. Since he had no particular preference for one direction rather than another, he decided not to hinder its progress and to let it continue peacefully on its course, and to take advantage of the situation to ride along with it. However, as the slippery nature of the terrain had been made even more dangerous by the movement, Captain Pamphile, although he had long since gained his sea legs, still made his way to the elevated region of his island, and, holding onto the isolated and leafless tree that seemed to mark its centre, he awaited events with patience and resignation.

However, Captain Pamphile (who had, as the reader will easily understand, become all ears and all eyes), in the slightly brighter intervals when the wind drove away a cloud and disclosed some star twinkling like a diamond on heaven's necklace, thought he could make out, like a black spot, a little island that was guiding the big one along, moving at a distance of some forty yards from it, and when the wave that came beating against the flanks of his domain was somewhat hushed, those same voices that he had heard again came to his ears, borne hither on a light breeze, uncertain and unintelligible as the murmur of the spirits of the sea.

It was only when dawn started to appear in the east that Captain Pamphile managed to find his bearings completely, and was then astonished, given the intelligence that he attributed to himself, that he hadn't realised his situation earlier. The little island that was moving along ahead was a small boat with six Canadian savages on board; the big island on which he found himself was a whale that the former allies of France were towing along; and the tree without branches or leaves against which he was leaning was the harpoon that had slain the giant of the seas and which, having gone some four or five feet deep into the wound, still stuck out a good eight or nine.

The Hurons, for their part, on seeing the double catch they had made, uttered an exclamation of astonishment. But, judging immediately that it was beneath a man's dignity to show surprise at anything, they continued to row silently towards land without paying Captain Pamphile any further attention. When he observed that the savages, for all their apparent insouciance, never took their eyes off him, he affected the greatest calm of mind, in spite of the real anxiety that his strange situation inspired in him.

When the whale had arrived a quarter of a league or so from the northern extremity of Cape Breton, the boat halted, but the huge cetacean, continuing to follow the momentum it had been given, glided towards the little boat and finally caught up with it. Then the man who seemed to be the crew's master, a big, strapping fellow five foot eight inches tall, painted blue and red, with a black serpent tattooed on his breast and wearing on his shaven head the tail feathers of a bird of paradise stuck into the sole lock of hair that he had preserved, slipped a big knife into his loincloth, picked up his tomahawk in his right hand, and advanced slowly and solemnly towards Captain Pamphile.

Captain Pamphile, who, for his part, had seen all the savages in the known world, from those who come down from the pleasure gardens on the morning of Ash Wednesday[66] to those of the Sandwich Islands who treacherously slew Captain Cook, calmly allowed him to approach without appearing to pay him the least attention.

Once he was six paces away from the European, the Huron stopped and stared at Captain Pamphile; Captain Pamphile, resolved not to yield an inch, then stared at the Huron with the same calm and tranquillity as the latter was affecting; finally, after ten minutes of mutual inspection, the Huron remarked, 'Black-Serpent is a great chief.'

'Pamphile, of Marseilles, is a great captain,' said the Provençal.

'And why,' continued the Huron, 'has my brother left his vessel to embark on Black-Serpent's whale?'

'Because,' replied Captain Pamphile, 'his crew threw him into the sea and, tired of swimming, he rested on the first object to come along without worrying who it belonged to.'

'Very well,' said the Huron; 'Black-Serpent is a great chief, and Captain Pamphile will be his servant.'

'Just say that again, would you?' retorted the Captain in bantering tones.

'I said,' replied the Huron, 'that Captain Pamphile will row in Black-Serpent's boat when he is on the water, will carry his tent of birch-tree bark when he travels by land, will light his fire when it is cold, will drive away the flies when it is hot, and will mend his moccasins when they wear out; in exchange for which, Black-Serpent will give Captain Pamphile the leftovers from his supper and the old beaver skins that are no longer of any use to him.'

'Aha!' retorted the Captain; 'and what if these arrangements do not please Pamphile and Pamphile turns them down?'

'Then Black-Serpent will remove Pamphile's head of hair and hang it at his door, with those of the seven Englishmen, nine Spaniards and eleven Frenchmen who are there already.'

'Very well,' said the Captain, who could see that he was not the stronger party; 'Black-Serpent is a great chief and Pamphile will be his servant.'

At these words, Black-Serpent motioned to his crew, who disembarked on the whale in turn and surrounded Captain Pamphile. The chief spoke a few words to his men, who immediately transported onto the animal several small crates, a beaver, two or three birds they had shot down with arrows, and everything necessary to light a fire. Then Black-Serpent went down into the dugout canoe, took a paddle in each hand, and started to row towards land.

The Captain was busy attentively watching the big chief move away, admiring the swiftness with which the little boat skimmed over the water, when three Hurons came up to him; one took off his cravat, the other removed his shirt and the third relieved him of his trousers, in which was his watch; then, immediately, two others followed, one of them holding a razor and the other a kind of palette composed of little shells filled with yellow, red and blue pigment; they motioned Captain

Pamphile to lie down and, as the rest of the crew were lighting the fire just as they might have done on a real island, plucking the birds and skinning the beaver, they proceeded to array their new comrade: while one was shaving his head, just leaving the lock of hair that savages habitually keep, the other was drawing his brush dipped in different colours over his whole body and painting him in the latest fashion adopted by the dandies of the River Outava and Lake Huron.

Once these initial preparations were complete, one of Captain Pamphile's two valets went to pick up a bunch of feathers torn from the tail of the whippoorwill that they were singeing, while the other took the skin of the beaver that was starting to roast, and returned to their victim; they fixed the bunch of feathers on the sole lock of hair that had been left on his head, and tied the beaver skin round his waist. Thereupon, one of the Hurons held up a mirror for Captain Pamphile to see himself in. He looked hideous!

Meanwhile, Black-Serpent had reached land and made his way to quite a substantial building that could be seen from afar, gleaming white as it rose above the sea's edge; he soon re-emerged accompanied by a man dressed in European style, and they deduced from his gestures that the son of the desert was showing the man of civilisation the catch he had made at sea and brought overnight within sight of shore.

After a while, the inhabitant of Cape Breton climbed in turn into a boat with two slaves, rowed towards the whale, and sailed all the way round it to get a good idea of it, but without landing on it; then, no doubt recognising that the Huron had been telling the truth, he returned to the Cape, where the chief had been awaiting him, sitting there motionless.

A moment later, the white man's slaves brought various different objects that Captain Pamphile could not at this distance make out, and put them into the Redskin's canoe; the Huron chief picked up his paddles again and started to sail back towards the provisional island where his crew and Captain Pamphile were waiting for him.

He landed just as the beaver and the whippoorwills were done to a turn, ate the beaver's tail and the wings of the whippoorwills, and, in accordance with the arrangements they had agreed on, gave the leftovers of his meal to his servants. Captain Pamphile's presence among them seemed to fill him with delight.

Then the Hurons brought the booty they had seized from their prisoner, so that, as chief, he could select the spoils of war that pleased him the best.

Black-Serpent examined with considerable disdain Captain Pamphile's cravat, shirt and trousers; on the other hand, he paid particular attention to the watch, of whose use he was obviously ignorant. Nonetheless, having turned it round and round, as it hung from a little chain and swayed this way and that from its big chain, he was convinced that it was a living creature he was dealing with, and lifted it to his ears; he listened attentively to its movement, turned it round yet again to try and discover how it worked, placed one hand on his heart while, with the other hand, he again brought the chronometer up to his ear; and, convinced that it was an animal, since it had a pulse that beat just as did his own, he laid it with the greatest care next to a little turtle as broad as a five-franc coin and as thick as half a nut, which he kept like some precious object in a box that, from the richness of its incrustations of shells, it was easy to guess had constituted part of his own individual treasure; then, as if satisfied by the portion he had appropriated for himself, he pushed away with his foot the cravat, the shirt and the trousers, generously placing them at the disposal of his crew.

Once breakfast was over, Black-Serpent, the Hurons and the prisoner moved from the whale to the canoe. Captain Pamphile then saw that the objects brought by the Hurons were two English rifles, four bottles of brandy and a barrel of powder: Black-Serpent, judging it beneath his dignity to cut up the whale he had himself killed, had bartered with a colonist and exchanged it for alcohol, ammunition and weapons.

Just at that moment, the inhabitant of Cape Breton reappeared on the shore, accompanied by five or six slaves, went down into a boat bigger than the one he had chosen for his first errand, and again put out to sea. As he was leaving the shore, Black-Serpent, for his part, gave orders to leave the whale, so as not to give its new owner any cause for anxiety. Then Captain Pamphile's apprenticeship began. A Huron, thinking he would embarrass him, placed a paddle in his hands, but since he had passed through every rank, from cabin boy to ship's captain, he used the instrument with such strength, precision and skill, that Black-Serpent, to show him how very satisfied he was, gave him his elbow to kiss.

That same evening, the Huron chief and his crew stopped on a big rock that rises some distance from a smaller one in the middle of the Gulf of Saint Lawrence. Some of them immediately busied themselves putting up the tent of birch-tree bark that the savages of north America take almost everywhere with them whenever they set off hunting or on their travels; others scattered around the rock and started to look in the crevices for oysters, mussels, sea urchins and other sea foods, and brought back so many that, even when Great-Serpent had eaten his fill, enough was left over for everyone else.

Once supper was over, Great-Serpent asked for the box in which he had shut away the watch, to see if anything had happened to it. He picked it up, as he had that morning, with the greatest delicacy, but no sooner did he hold it in his hands that he realised its heart had ceased to beat; he lifted it to his ear and could not hear a single movement; then he tried to warm it up with his breath, but, on seeing that all his attempts were in vain, he handed it back to its owner with an expression of deep disdain, saying, 'Here, take your creature – it's dead.'

Captain Pamphile, who was very attached to his watch, as it was a present from his wife, didn't need to be asked twice, and slipped the chain round his neck, delighted that his Bréguet was back in his possession. He deliberately refrained from winding it up.

As day broke, they set off again, continuing to head westwards; in the evening, they disembarked in a small isolated cove on Anticost Island, and the next day, at around four in the afternoon, having rounded Cape Gaspé, they rowed into the mouth of the Saint Lawrence river, up which they were to sail as far as Lake Ontario, whence the great chief was planning to reach Lake Huron, on the banks of which his wigwam was situated.

11

Tom's obituary. How Captain Pamphile sailed up the Saint Lawrence river for five days, and escaped from Black-Serpent towards the end of the sixth.

Captain Pamphile had, as we have seen, accepted his lot with more readiness and resignation than might have been expected from such a violent and absolute man. The fact is that, thanks to the different situations in which he had found himself during the course of a particularly stormy life, of which we have shown our readers only the most brilliant side, he had acquired the habit of making quick and decisive resolutions, and, as we have said, seeing that he was not the stronger party, he had that instant drawn on an old stock of philosophical stoicism that he always kept in reserve for such occasions and fallen back on an apparent resignation that had quite hoodwinked Black-Serpent, for all his cunning.

We should admittedly add that Captain Pamphile, being a lover of the great art of navigation, felt no small pleasure at being able to study the degree to which this art had developed among the savage nations of upper Canada.

The parts of the boat in which Captain Pamphile was embarked as the sixth member of the crew were composed of a very strong but pliant wood, yoked by pieces of birch-tree bark sewn together and covered at the joins by a thick layer of tar. As for the inside, it was lined with very slender planks of pine, placed on top of one another like the tiles of a roof.

Our observer was too impartial not to pay homage to the workers who had constructed the vehicle thanks to which he was being transported, despite his wishes, from north to south, so he had, with a single sign – but the sign of an appreciative connoisseur – indicated that he was well pleased with the lightness of the boat. This lightness, indeed, gave it two immense advantages: the first was that of being able to overtake, supposing an equal number of rowers, in under five minutes and from a considerable distance, the finest and best-constructed English boat; the second, which was entirely local, was of being easily hauled ashore and comfortably transported by two men, when the rapids with which the river is dotted force navigators to follow the shore, sometimes for the space of two or three leagues. Admittedly, these two advantages come with one drawback: a single clumsy movement will make it capsize immediately. But this drawback ceases to be one for men who, like Canadians, live as much in water as they do on land; as for Captain Pamphile, we have seen that he was a member of the family of seals, manatees and other amphibians.

On the evening of the first day's sailing upstream, the boat came to a halt in a little cove on the right bank; the crew immediately pulled it ashore, and prepared to pass the night on the soil of New Brunswick.

Black-Serpent had been so pleased with the intelligence and docility of his new servant during the forty-eight hours that they had spent together, that after leaving him, as he had the evening before, a rather generous portion of his supper, he gave him a buffalo skin on which a few hairs were still left to serve as his mattress. As for a blanket, Captain Pamphile was obliged to go without. Now, as our readers will recall, if they have a good memory, that his only clothes were a beaver skin that clung round his midriff and fell halfway down his legs, they will not be surprised that this worthy trader, used as he was to the temperature of Senegambia and the Congo, spent almost the entire night changing the position of his beaver skin so as to warm the different parts of his person one after the other; however, as every cloud has a silver lining, his insomnia helped to prove to him that he was the object of his companions' most assiduous mistrust; at every movement he made, however slight, he immediately saw a head raised and two eyes, gleaming in the darkness like those of a wolf, staring at him. Captain Pamphile realised he was being observed, and his caution redoubled.

The next morning, before daybreak, the navigators set off; they were still in that part of the river mouth that is so wide it seems a lake flowing out into the sea. So nothing obstructed their progress, and the current was almost unnoticeable; the wind, whether favourable or contrary, had little effect on the little vessel, and on each side there unfolded before their eyes an immeasurable landscape fading into the haze of the blue horizon, in the midst of which the houses appeared like white spots; from time to time, in the far distances where their swimming gaze could no longer make anything out clearly, they caught sight of the snowy peak of a few mountains belonging to the chain that extends from Cape Gaspé to the sources of the Ohio, but the distance was so great that it was impossible to know whether this fleeting apparition belonged to heaven or earth.

The day went by surrounded by these scenes, to which Captain Pamphile seemed to pay an unstinting attention and which seemed to meet with his unqualified admiration; however, this twofold feeling, however powerful it appeared, did not distract him for a single instant from his duties as a sailor. As a result, Black-Serpent, doubly flattered by his good taste and his good service, passed to him, one minute when they were resting, a pipe all ready and filled, a favour that Captain Pamphile appreciated all the more as he had been deprived of this pleasure ever since Two-Mouths had gone to relight his pipe during the rebellion on board the *Roxelane*. So he straight away bowed, saying, 'Black-Serpent is a great chief!'

To this courtesy Black-Serpent replied in turn, 'Captain Pamphile is a faithful servant.'

Here the conversation broke off, and they all started to smoke their pipes.

That evening, they landed on an island; the ceremony of supper passed, as usual, to general satisfaction. But the previous night had not failed to leave Captain Pamphile with some anxieties as to how he could best combat the cold, which, as everyone knows, is even more intense on islands level with the water surface than on a wooded landmass. However, on unrolling his buffalo skin, he found a woollen blanket in it; Black-Serpent was definitely a rather nice devil of a master and, if Captain Pamphile had had no other plans for the future, he would probably have stayed in his service, but however comfortable he felt on an island in the middle of the Saint Lawrence river, between his buffalo-skin mattress and his woollen blanket, he was only human, and inclined to prefer his bed on board the *Roxelane*; still, however inferior in quality his present sleeping arrangements, the Captain still slept uninterruptedly until daybreak.

At around eleven o'clock on the third day, Quebec started to come into sight. The Captain had some hopes that Black-Serpent would put in at this town, so, as soon as he spotted it, he started to row with an ardour that notably increased the consideration in which he was held by the great chief, and did not allow him to pay the waterfall of Montmorency all the attention that it deserves.[67] But his conjectures were mistaken; the boat sailed past the harbour, rounded Cape Diamond, and landed opposite the Chaudière Falls.

As it was still broad daylight, Captain Pamphile could then admire that magnificent cascade that falls from a height of 150 feet across a breadth of 260, spreading out like a cloth of white snow over a carpet of verdure and, between wonderfully wooded banks (in the midst of which, here and there, great masses of rocks rose up), showing their bald, white heads as prominent as the brows of old men. Supper and night went by as usual.

The next day, the boat was floated at daybreak; for all his stoicism, Captain Pamphile was starting to feel some disquiet. He could not help but reflect that the more he penetrated inland, the further he was moving from Marseilles, and that it would become ever more difficult to escape: so he was rowing with a nonchalance that the great chief had not seen in him before, but that he forgave him in view of his previous experience. Then, all of a sudden, his eyes focused fixedly on the horizon, and his paddle remained immobile; as the sailor sitting opposite him was still rowing, the boat went round on itself twice.

'What is the matter?' said Black-Serpent, rising from the depths of the boat in which he was reclining, and removing his calumet from his mouth.

'The matter,' replied Captain Pamphile, pointing southwards, 'is that either I've lost all my navigational skills, or that we're in for a heck of a storm.'

'And where does my brother see any sign that God has said to the tempest: "Blow and destroy"?'

'In that cloud, dammit!' said Captain Pamphile, 'coming up towards us as black as ink.'

'My brother has the eyes of a mole,' replied the chief. 'What he can see is not a cloud.'

'Don't make me laugh!' said Captain Pamphile.

'Black-Serpent has the eyes of an eagle,' replied the chief. 'Let the white man see, and then let him judge.'

And indeed, the so-called cloud was advancing with a swiftness and intensity that the Captain had never seen in any real cloud, whatever wind was driving it; after a few seconds, our worthy sailor, so confident in his own experience, had started to doubt his own judgment. Finally, before even a minute had gone by, all his doubts had been answered and he realised that Black-Serpent had been right; the apparent cloud was nothing other than a flock of countless pigeons emigrating northwards.

At first, Captain Pamphile could not believe his eyes: the birds were flying at such a speed and in such a mass that it was impossible to believe that all the pigeons in the world could form such a cloud. The sky, which to the north was still a bright blue, was entirely covered to the south, as far as the eye could see, by a kind of grey cloth that extended to the far horizon; soon this grey cloth had stretched out in front of the sun and immediately blotted out its rays – it looked like nightfall, advancing to meet the navigators. Then a kind of vanguard, composed of several thousands of these animals, flew over the boat, swept along with a magical swiftness; then, almost immediately, the main body of the army followed it, and the daylight disappeared as if the wing of the tempest had unfurled itself between the sky and the earth.

Captain Pamphile watched this phenomenon with an astonishment bordering on stupor. The Indians, however, being used to this sight, which they witness every five or six years, shouted for joy and made their arrows ready so as to profit from the winged manna that the Lord was sending them. For his part, Black-Serpent loaded his rifle with a tranquillity and slowness that proved he was well aware of the vast extent of the living cloud passing over his head; eventually, he lifted it to his shoulder and, not even bothering to take aim, fired; that very same moment, a kind of opening similar to that of a well allowed a transient ray of daylight to pass through; some fifty or so pigeons, caught within the circumference of the lead shot, fell like rain into and around the boat; the Indians gathered them up, every last one, to the great astonishment of Captain Pamphile, who could not see any reason for taking such pains when, with just another rifle shot or two, and without bothering to move right or left, the boat would be able to pick up a sufficient quantity to supply the whole crew, but when he turned round, he saw that the chief had lain down again, placed his weapon by his side and picked up his calumet.

'Has Black-Serpent already finished hunting?' asked Captain Pamphile.

'With one shot, Black-Serpent has killed all the pigeons he needs for his own supper and that of his followers; a Huron is not a white man, pointlessly destroying the creatures of the Great Spirit.'

'Aha!' said Captain Pamphile to himself, 'that's not such a bad argument for a savage, but I wouldn't have been at all put out to see another three or four holes being made in that feathered shroud being held out over our heads, if only to be sure that the sun is still in the right place.'

'Look, and do not worry so,' replied the chief, pointing southwards.

And indeed, on the southern horizon, a golden haze was starting to spread, while, if you turned to look north, you saw the whole landscape deep in darkness, so the head of the column must have reached the mouth of the River Saint Lawrence, at least. In a quarter of an hour it had got as far as the boat had managed in four days. Furthermore, the grey cloth was still moving as if the genies of the pole had been pulling it towards them, while the daylight, just as swift as the night had been, was rushing up, pouring down in floods on the mountains, streaming through the valleys and spreading across the surface of the meadows. Finally, the rearguard of flying creatures passed like a mist over the face of the sun that, once this last veil had vanished, continued to smile down on the earth.

However courageous Captain Pamphile, and however little danger there had been in the phenomena that had just occurred, he had, all the same, been rather ill at ease all the time this artificial night had lasted. So it was with real joy that he greeted the light, picked up his paddle once more and started to row, while Black-Serpent's other followers plucked the pigeons that he had shot down with his rifle and they with their arrows.

The next day, the boat sailed past Montreal as it had already sailed past Quebec, without Black-Serpent showing the least intention of stopping off in that city; on the contrary, he motioned to the rowers, and they moved towards the right bank of the river; this was inhabited by a tribe of Cochenonegas Indians, whose chief, squatting and smoking on the shore, exchanged with Black-Serpent a few words in a language that the Captain could not understand. A quarter of an hour later they encountered the first rapids, but instead of trying to cross them with the help of the hooks placed for that purpose in the hold of the boat, Black-Serpent gave orders to land, and himself jumped out onto the shore; Captain Pamphile followed him. The boatmen hoisted the boat onto their shoulders, the crew formed a caravan and, instead of laboriously rowing upstream, calmly followed the bank. After two hours, once the rapids were past, the bark was floated again and sailed off on the surface of the river.

It had been sailing along for three hours or so when Captain Pamphile was drawn out of his musings by a shout of joy that all of his travelling companions, with the exception of the chief, uttered at the same time. This exclamation was produced by a new sight almost as curious as that of the previous day, but this time, the miracle, instead of occurring in the air, was happening on the water. A band of black squirrels was in its turn emigrating from east to west, just as the pigeons had emigrated from south to north two days previously; the squirrels were crossing the full width of the Saint Lawrence river. Doubtless they had been assembled on the bank for some days, waiting for a favourable wind, for the current at this spot is over four miles wide, and however well these animals can swim, they would not have been able to cross it without the help that God had just sent them: indeed, a delightful breeze had been blowing for an hour from the mountains of Boston and Portland, and the whole flotilla had consequently taken to the water, spreading their tails as sails, and tranquilly crossing the river with a following wind, using their paws only as much as was absolutely necessary to maintain themselves in the right direction.

Since the savages are even fonder of the flesh of squirrels than of the flesh of pigeons, the boat's crew immediately got ready to hunt the emigrants; the big chief himself did not seem to look down on this kind of pastime. So he took a blowpipe, opened a little box of birch-tree bark marvellously embroidered with elk hairs, and took from it twenty or so small arrows, barely two inches long and as slender as iron wires; one of their extremities was armed with a point, and the other decorated with sufficient thistledown to fill the tube from which it was to be launched. Two other Indians did likewise, and two others were designated as rowers. As for Captain Pamphile, he, together with the last Indian, was put in charge of gathering the dead and extracting from their bodies the little instruments with the help of which the Indians were planning to slay them. Ten minutes later, the boat came within range of the animals, and the hunt began.

Captain Pamphile was stupefied; he had never seen such skill. At thirty and forty paces, the Indians could hit the animal they were aiming at, and almost always in the breast; as a result, within ten minutes, the river, within a fairly wide circumference, found itself covered with the dead and wounded. When there were about sixty or so, lying on the battlefield, Black-Serpent, faithful to his principles, signalled that the carnage could now cease. He was obeyed by his men with a submission that would have done honour to the discipline of a Prussian squad, and the fugitives who, this time, were quite happy to put both paws and tail combined to the best use they could, hastily reached land. The Indians did not even dream of pursuing them.

However, although this hunt had not lasted all that long, it had lasted long enough for a storm, which the Indians had not noticed, to gather in the sky. So Captain Pamphile had only half completed his task when he had to interrupt it to play his part in the manoeuvres - which were as simple as could be, consisting of rowing, with him as fourth rower, towards the shore where Black-Serpent hoped to land before the hurricane could break out; unfortunately, as we have said, the wind was blowing from the very bank they were heading for, and the waves were rising so swiftly that after a moment it was as rough as if they had been out at sea.

To make matters worse, night fell and the only light on the river was the flashes of lightning; the little boat was swept away like a nutshell, sometimes at the crest of a wave, and sometimes being dashed down into the depths of the river. Every instant it was on the point of capsizing. Meanwhile, they were approaching the shore and already, in spite of the darkness of the night, just starting to make out its hazy dim shape, when suddenly the boat, launched with the swiftness of an arrow, plunged from the crest of a wave onto a rock, and smashed as if it had been made of glass.

Then it was every man for himself. They all struck out for shore; Black-Serpent was the first to reach it. He immediately rubbed together two dry sticks and lit a great fire so that his companions would be able to make their way to him; this precaution worked, and ten minutes later, guided by this welcoming lighthouse, the whole crew – apart from Captain Pamphile – was gathered round the great chief.

12

How Captain Pamphile spent two extremely disturbed nights, one on a tree, the other in a cabin.

First night

Thanks to the care we have taken to present Captain Pamphile to our readers as a first-class swimmer, we hope that they will not have been unduly worried on seeing him falling into the water with his travelling companions; in any case, we will quickly reassure them if we tell them that, after ten minutes of relentless overarm swimming, he reached the shore safe and sound.

He had no sooner shaken himself down, an operation that didn't take long, in view of the scantiness of the clothes to which he had been reduced, than he spotted the flame that Black-Serpent had lit to rally his comrades. He immediately and deliberately turned his back on this signal and moved away from it as fast as he possibly could.

Despite the tender care the great chief had taken of him during the six days they had been together, Captain Pamphile had constantly nursed the hope that one day or another an opportunity to take his leave of him would arise; so, for fear that he might not be given a second chance, he resolved to make the most of the first, and in spite of the darkness and the storm, he plunged into the forests that extend from the river to the base of the mountains.

After walking for some two hours, Captain Pamphile, judging that he had put sufficient distance between himself and his enemies, decided to pause for a while and think how he could spend the night as well as possible.

The position was far from comfortable: the fugitive had only his beaver skin for clothing, and for the time being it would have to serve him as both mattress and blanket; he was already shivering at the idea of the night he was facing, when he heard, from three or four different directions, distant howls that diverted his thoughts from this first anxiety and brought them to bear on another, equally worrying, problem; in these howls, Captain Pamphile had recognised the nocturnal cry of hungry wolves, who are so common in the forests of Canada that, when they run out of food, they sometimes even come down into the streets of Portland and Boston.

He had still not had time to decide what to do, when new howls rang out, this time closer; he didn't have a moment to lose. Captain Pamphile, whose gymnastic education had been taken the greatest care of, included among his most distinguished talents that of being able to climb up a tree like a squirrel, so he looked round until he had found an oak tree of perfectly adequate girth, flung his arms around it as if to uproot it, and reached its lowest branches just as the cries that had alerted him were echoing out for the third time, barely forty yards from him. Captain Pamphile had not been mistaken: a band of wolves, scattered around to a circumference of about a league, had got wind of him and were galloping up to the centre where they hoped they would find their supper. They arrived too late: Captain Pamphile was perched on a branch.

However, the wolves refused to consider themselves beaten; there is nothing as obstinate as an empty stomach. They gathered round the foot of the tree and started to utter such lamentable plaints that Captain Pamphile, brave though he was, could not altogether avoid succumbing to terror when he heard this mournful, prolonged cry, even though he was actually in no danger of succumbing to the wolves.

The night was dark, but not so dark as to prevent him from seeing in the gloom, like the waves of a foaming sea, the tawny backs of his enemies; furthermore, every time one of them looked up, Captain Pamphile could see two burning coals gleaming in the shadows, and, as the disappointment was general, there were moments when those heads all rose at once, making it seem as if the ground were scattered with moving carbuncles that, as they wove among each other, traced strange and diabolical coded messages…

But soon, as he gazed fixedly at the same point, his eyes grew cloudy; the real shapes were succeeded by fantastic shapes; his intelligence itself, somewhat perturbed by the effects of a disquiet that he had hitherto hardly ever experienced, ceased to register the real danger and started to dream of superhuman dangers. A host of creatures that were neither men nor animals appeared to him in the place of the familiar quadrupeds that were roaming around beneath him; he fancied he could see demons with flaming eyes rising up, hand in hand, dancing a satanic dance around him; sitting astride his branch like a witch on her broomstick, he imagined he was the centre of an infernal sabbath in which he was being summoned to play his part.

The Captain sensed instinctively that vertigo was luring him downwards, and that if he yielded to this attraction, he was doomed; he gathered all his strength of body and mind into one last act of intelligence, lashed himself tightly to the tree trunk with the rope tying the beaver skin around his waist, and, clinging to the upper branch with both hands, flung his head back and closed his eyes.

Then madness and delirium triumphed completely. Captain Pamphile first felt his tree moving, bending and rising back like the masts of a vessel in a storm; then he imagined that, in an attempt to tear its roots out of the soil, it was making the same efforts as a man whose feet are bogged down in a marsh; after a few moments of struggle, the oak succeeded and, from the wound it had inflicted on the earth sprang streams of blood that the wolves started to drink; the tree took advantage of their avidity to flee away from them, but in a jerky fashion, like an invalid hopping along on a wooden leg. Soon, as they had devoured their food, the wolves, demons and vampires that the brave Captain had thought himself rid of set off in pursuit; they were led by an old woman whose face he could not see, holding a knife in her hand, and the whole horde rushed along at breakneck speed.

Finally the tree, exhausted, panting, breathless, seemed to run out of stamina, and lay down like a man at the end of his tether; then the wolves and demons, still being led by the old woman, bounded up, their eyes burning and their tongues flecked with blood. The Captain uttered a cry and tried to stretch out his arms, but a loud hissing noise immediately rang out behind his head, and a glacial shudder ran down his whole body; he seemed to sense ice-cold coils being tightened round him to suffocate him; then this impression gradually waned, the phantoms vanished, the howls faded, the tree was shaken just a few more times, and everything fell back into darkness and silence.

Little by little, thanks to the silence, Captain Pamphile's nerves calmed down; his blood, which had been boiling in the fever of delirium, cooled, and his spirits, now more tranquil, returned from the domains of fantasy into which they had strayed back to real, concrete nature; he looked all around him, and found himself in the middle of his dark, solitary and silent forest. He felt himself all over to check he was still all there, and eventually recognised the situation he was actually in; tied to his tree, astride a branch, he was not as comfortable as in his hammock in the *Roxelane* or on the great chief's buffalo skin, but at least safe from the attacks of the wolves, which, indeed, had disappeared. And as he looked down at the foot of his oak, the Captain thought he could also make out a shapeless, moving mass that seemed to be rolling round the tree trunk, but as the plaints he had thought he could hear soon fell silent, and as the object on which his gaze was fixed became immobile, Captain Pamphile decided it must still be part of the infernal dream he had just had and, panting, drenched in sweat, broken by exhaustion, he eventually went off to sleep as calmly and deeply as the precarious situation in which he was thus yielding to repose allowed.

Captain Pamphile was awoken at daybreak by the chatter of countless birds of different species fluttering joyously under the thick leafy canopy of the forest. He opened his eyes, and the first thing he spotted was the immense vault of greenery stretching out over his head, through the gaps in which the first rays of the sun were filtering down. Captain Pamphile was not by nature devout; still, like all sailors, he had the sense for the greatness and might of God that the everlasting sight of the ocean brings out in the souls of those who incessantly labour on its immense solitudes, so the first thing he did was to offer up thanks to him who holds the world in his hands, whether that world is asleep or awake; then, after a moment of instinctive contemplation, he lowered his eyes from heaven to earth and, in a single glance, all the things he had experienced during the night found their explanation.

Twenty paces around the oak, the earth had been dug up by the wolves' impatient claws, as if a plough had passed over it, while at the foot of the tree, one of those animals, broken and shapeless, emerged two thirds of the way out of the jaws of a huge boa constrictor, whose tail was wrapped round the tree trunk, at a height of seven or eight feet. So Captain Pamphile had found himself between two dangers that had destroyed one another mutually: under his feet the wolves, over his head a snake; that hissing he had heard, that cold he had felt, those coils that had tightened round him, were the hissing, the cold and the coils of the reptile, at the sight of which the ferocious predatory beasts besieging him had fled; just one, halted in his tracks by the fatal embrace of the monster, had been crushed within its folds. The movement of the tree that the Captain had felt had been the shakings of its death agony; then the victorious snake had started to swallow its adversary and, as is the habit of constrictors, it was digesting the one half, while the other, still exposed to the air, was awaiting its turn to be devoured.

For a moment, Captain Pamphile stood immobile, staring at the sight at his feet; several times, in Africa and India, he had seen similar snakes, but never in circumstances so likely to intimidate him, and so, although he knew perfectly well that, in his position, the reptile was incapable of hurting him, he reflected on how he could get down the tree other than by sliding down the trunk. He started by undoing the rope tied around him, then, moving backwards along the branch until he felt it start to bend, he entrusted himself to its flexibility, and then, bending it beneath his weight, hung from his two hands and found himself so near the ground that he thought he could without harm manage without the support of his branch. His hopes were well-founded, and the Captain let go of the branch, falling to the ground unhurt.

He hurried away, not without a backward glance or two; he walked towards the sun. There was no path through the forest, but with a hunter's instincts and a sailor's skill, he needed merely to glance at the ground and the sky to find his bearings immediately, so he moved forward unhesitatingly, as if he had been quite familiar with these huge solitudes; the further he plunged into the forest, the more grandiose and savage it seemed to become. Little by little the leafy canopy thickened until the sun could no longer penetrate it; the trees grew ever closer to one another, rising upwards like straight, slender pillars, and, just like pillars, holding up a roof that light could not pierce. The wind itself passed over the vault of greenery, and did not stir within this sojourn of shadows: it was as if, ever since the Creation, this part of the forest had slumbered in an eternal twilight.

In the wan light of this half-gloom, Captain Pamphile could see several large birds without being able to make out to which species they belonged, winged squirrels leaping agilely and flying from branch to branch in silence; in this kind of limbo, everything seemed to have lost its natural, primordial colour to take on the ashen hue of moths. A deer, a hare and a fox stirring at the footsteps of the man who was disturbing their repose, while still preserving their different shapes, seemed to have put on the monotonous and uniform livery of the moss across which they noiselessly ran.

Every now and again, Captain Pamphile halted and stared; gigantic tawny mushrooms, leaning against one another like shields, formed groups that were so similar in size and colour to couching lions that, although he knew perfectly well that this king of creation did not inhabit this part of his empire, he shuddered at what he saw.

Great parasitical creepers, which seemed to be short of air, coiled round trees, climbing up along them, clinging to the branches, and draped like festoons between one and the next, until they reached the canopy; here, they sought for some opening between the branches, and slipped into it like snakes so that they could unfold their scarlet, perfumed corollas in the sunlight, while those who were forced to open up en route put out flowers that were pale, odourless, sickly, and as it were jealous of the good fortune of their friends who were able to warm themselves in the light of day and under the smile of God.

At around two o'clock, Captain Pamphile felt in the general region of his stomach pangs of hunger that told him that he had not had any supper the night before, and that the hour for lunch had gone by long ago. He looked around him: birds were continuing to flitter from tree to tree, winged squirrels were leaping ceaselessly from branch to branch, as if they had been following the same route as he, but he had neither rifle nor blowpipe to bring them down with. He tried throwing a few stones at them, but he soon realised that this exercise would simply add to his appetite without obtaining any result that might appease it. And so he decided to look for other resources and to fall back on vegetables.

This time, his quest met with better fortune: after a few moments of attentive seeking, made more difficult by this semi-obscurity, he found two or three roots of the *cyperus* family, and some of those plants commonly called *carex*.[68]

This was more or less all he needed to keep his stomach happy, but Captain Pamphile was a cautious man; he reflected that no sooner had he calmed his hunger than he would start to feel thirsty, so he looked for a stream, just as he had looked for roots. Unfortunately, the former were less common.

He listened attentively: not a murmur reached him. He sniffed the air to try and catch a whiff of something, but there was no air under this canopy, for all its gigantic size: in it there reigned a heavy, sultry atmosphere, which the animals and plants condemned to creep along the ground could breathe only with an effort, and which seemed inadequate to support life.

Then Captain Pamphile made up his mind; he picked up a sharp pebble, then, instead of continuing with his pointless quest, he went from tree to tree, examining every stem closely. Eventually he seemed to have found what he had been looking for: it was a magnificent maple, young, smooth and strong. He took it in his left arm, while, with his right hand, he pushed the sharp pebble deep into its bark; a few drops of that precious vegetable blood that the Canadians use to make a sugar more delicious than cane sugar immediately sprang from it as if from a wound. Captain Pamphile, pleased with the experiment, sat tranquilly down at the foot of his victim and started his lunch; then, when he had finished, he placed his thirsty mouth to the wound from which the sap was now flowing as if from a fountain, and set off once more, haler and heartier than ever before.

At around five in the evening, Captain Pamphile thought he could see a few rays of daylight filtering through the darkness: he stepped out with a springier step than before, and reached the edge of that forest that resembled the one described by Dante, belonging neither to life nor to death, it seemed, but to some nameless intermediary power. Then he seemed to enter into an ocean of light; as he plunged into its waves, gleaming in the haze of sunset, he seemed like a diver who, having been trapped on the seabed, caught on some coral branch or entangled in some polyp, manages to break free from the deadly obstacle, swims to the water surface and draws breath.

He had reached one of those vast steppes flung like lakes of greenery and light in the midst of the vast forests of the New World; on the other side of this clearing, a new line of trees stretched out like a dark, opaque wall, while above it one could see the mountains whose tortuous range separates off the whole peninsula, their snowy summits zigzagging in the last of the daylight.

The Captain cast a satisfied look around him, glad to see that he had not gone astray from his route.

Finally, his eyes fell on a whitish, twisting pillar that stood out against the background and floated slowly skywards; it did not need a long inspection to recognise the smoke from a cabin, and almost immediately, whether it be friend or enemy, he resolved to walk towards it, the memory of the night he had just passed playing a swift and decisive part in his decision.

Second night

Captain Pamphile found a narrow path that seemed to lead from the forest to the cabin. He followed it, although it was not without some anxieties about the boiquiras[69] and copper-coloured snakes, so common in these cantons, that he walked amidst the tall, thick grass.

As he approached the smoke that guided his steps, he saw the cabin looming ahead, situated on the edge of the plain and the forest; night fell before he had reached it, but his route merely became easier and clearer to follow.

The door opened on the traveller's side and, opposite the door, at the back of the cabin, there gleamed a fire that seemed a lighthouse lit up expressly to guide him in his solitude. From time to time, there passed back and forth in front of the flame a figure that stood out in black against the hearth.

Once he was a short distance away, he realised it was a woman, and was filled with fresh confidence; finally, having reached the threshold, he stopped and asked whether there was any room for him by the side of the fire that he could see gleaming from so far away, and for which he had been yearning for so long.

A type of low grunt, which the Captain interpreted in his own way, was the reply. So he went in without hesitating, and went to sit on an old stool that seemed to be awaiting him at just the right distance from the flames.

On the other side of the hearth, his elbows on his knees and his head in his hands, immobile and unbreathing like a statue, a young Red Indian of the Sioux tribe was squatting; his great bow of maple wood was nearby, and at his feet there lay several birds of the dove species and a few small quadrupeds pierced with arrows. Neither the arrival nor the actions of Pamphile seemed to draw him out of this apparent apathy behind which savages conceal the eternal mistrust they feel at the approach of civilised man, for, at the mere sound of his footsteps, the young Sioux had recognised the traveller as a European. Captain Pamphile, for his part, gazed at him with the close attention of a man who knows that, for every chance of coming across a friend, you have ten of finding an enemy. Then, as this inspection did not reveal anything other than what he could see, and as what he saw left him unsure, he decided to speak to him.

'Is my brother sleeping,' he asked, 'for him not even to look up when a friend arrives?'

The Indian started, and, without any words to accompany his deed, he lifted his brow and pointed out to the Captain one of his eyes protruding from its socket and dangling from a nerve, while from the cavity it had occupied a trickle of blood was flowing down his face and onto his chest; then, without uttering a single word, his head fell back into his hands.

An arrow had snapped while the string of his bow was tensed, and one of the fragments of the broken reed had gouged out the Indian's eye; Captain Pamphile realised what had happened from a single glance, and did not pursue his questions any further, out of respect for the strength of soul of this savage hero of the desert.

Then he turned to the woman.

'The traveller is weary and hungry; can his mother give him a meal and a bed?'

‘There is a cake under the ashes and in that corner a bearskin,’ said the old woman; ‘my son can eat the one and sleep on the other.’

‘Don’t you have anything else?’ continued Captain Pamphile who, after the frugal dinner of which he had partaken in the forest, would not have been displeased to find a more substantial supper.

‘Yes, I do,’ replied the old woman, coming over with swift steps and staring avidly at the gold chain hanging round Captain Pamphile’s neck, and bearing the watch that the big chief had given him back. ‘I have… My son has a very fine chain there!… I have salted buffalo meat and some fine venison. I would be really happy to have a chain like that.’

‘Well, bring me your salted buffalo and your venison pie,’ replied Captain Pamphile evasively, saying neither yes nor no to the woman’s request; ‘then, if you chanced to have, in some corner, a bottle of maple brandy, it wouldn’t be out of place, I feel, in such good company.’

The old woman moved away, looking around every now and then to gaze once more at the jewel that she so obviously hankered after; then, finally, lifting a curtain of reeds, she went into another part of the cabin. No sooner had she disappeared than thc young Sioux quickly looked up.

‘Does my brother know where he is?’ he murmured in a low voice to the Captain.

‘By heaven, I don’t,’ the latter replied nonchalantly.

‘Does my brother have any weapon to defend himself with?’ he continued, lowering his voice even more.

‘None,’ replied the Captain.

‘In that case, let my brother take this knife, and not go to sleep.’

‘What about you?’ said Captain Pamphile, hesitating to accept the weapon he was being offered.

‘Me? I have my tomahawk. Quiet!’

With these words, the young savage dropped his head in his hands again and resumed his motionless posture, as the old woman lifted the reed curtain and came in with the supper. Captain Pamphile slipped the knife under his belt, and the old woman cast her eyes on the watch once more.

‘My son,’ she said, ‘met with a white man on the warpath; he slew the white man and took this chain from him, then he rubbed it to clean the blood off it. That is why it shines so brightly.’

'My mother is mistaken,' said Captain Pamphile, starting to guess at the unknown danger the Indian had warned him of. 'I made my way up the River Ottawa as far as Lake Superior, to hunt the buffalo and the beaver, but when I had obtained many skins, I went into the town, and exchanged half of my catch for firewater, and the other half for this watch.'

'I have two sons,' continued the old woman, placing the meat and the brandy on the table, 'who for ten years have hunted the buffalo and the beaver, and never have they taken so many skins into town that they have been able to come home with a chain like that. My son said he was hungry and thirsty,' she continued, 'my son can eat and drink.'

'Is my brother of the prairies not having supper too?' asked Captain Pamphile, addressing the young Sioux and bringing his stool up to the table.

'Pain gives one nourishment,' replied the young hunter without making a single movement; 'I am neither hungry nor thirsty; I am sleepy and I am going to sleep. May the Great Spirit protect my brother!'

'How many beaver skins did my son give for that watch?' interrupted the old woman, harping again on her favourite subject.

'Fifty,' replied Captain Pamphile at random as he bravely attacked a fillet of buffalo.

'I have here ten bear skins and twenty beaver skins; I will give them to my son just for the chain.'

'The chain comes with the watch,' said the Captain, 'they cannot be separated; in any case, I do not wish to part with either of them.'

'Very well,' said the old woman, smiling like a witch, 'let my son keep them!… Every living man is master of his own possessions. Only the dead own nothing.'

Captain Pamphile glanced quickly at the young Indian, but he appeared to be in a deep sleep, so he returned to his supper, to which, just in case, he did the same honour as if he had found himself in a less precarious position; then, once he had finished his meal, he flung an armful of twigs on the fire and went off to lie down on the buffalo skin that was stretched out in a corner of the cabin, not with any intention of going to sleep, but so as not to awaken any suspicions on the part of the old woman, who had gone back into the second room and disappeared.

A moment after Captain Pamphile had lain down, the curtain rose quietly and the horrible head of the old shrew reappeared, fixing her burning little eyes on each of the sleepers in turn; when she saw they were making no movement, she came into the room, went to the door of the cabin that led outside, and listened as if she were waiting for someone, but when no sound reached her ear, she turned round and, as if loath to waste any time, went and took down from the walls of the cabin a long kitchen knife. Then, straddling a grindstone, she started to turn it with her foot and began to sharpen her weapon carefully. Captain Pamphile saw the water fall drop by drop on the stone, and did not fail to notice every move that the flickering light of the hearth illuminated. These preparations spoke volumes; Captain Pamphile drew his knife from his belt, opened it, tried its point with his finger, drew his thumb along its edge, and, satisfied by his inspection, awaited the event, motionless and pretending to be in the deepest and most tranquil sleep.

The old woman continued with her infernal operation, but then she suddenly stopped and pricked up her ears. The noise she had heard sounded again, closer; she rose swiftly, as if her thirst for murder had restored to her limbs all their old suppleness, hung the knife back on the wall and again went to the door; this time, the men she was awaiting had doubtless arrived, since she silently motioned them to make haste, and came back into the cabin to take another quick look at her guests. Neither of them had made a movement, and they still seemed wrapped in the deepest sleep.

Almost immediately, two young men, tall of stature and strong of build, appeared on the threshold of the cabin; they were carrying on their shoulders a deer they had just killed. They halted and gazed in sinister silence at the guests they found in their cottage, then one of them asked his mother in English why she had taken those savage dogs into her home. The old woman signalled him to be silent: the hunters then came over to throw the dead deer at the feet of Captain Pamphile. They disappeared behind the reed curtain; the old woman followed them, bearing the bottle of maple brandy that her guest had hardly touched; the cabin was now occupied by just the two sleepers.

Captain Pamphile remained immobile for another moment or so; the only noise that could be heard was the calm, regular breathing of the Indian; this sleep was feigned so perfectly well that Captain Pamphile started to think that, while pretending to sleep, he really had gone off to sleep. Then, trying to imitate the model he had in front of him, he turned over, as if agitated by one of those capricious movements communicated to the body by the watchful brain, and by this means, instead of having his face turned towards the wall, he found himself facing the Indian.

He remained for another few moments in this new position, motionless, then he half-opened his eyes. He saw the young Sioux in the same position in which he had left him; however, his head was now propped up by his left hand alone; the other had started to dangle next to him, and was now resting near his tomahawk.

Just then, a slight noise was heard; the Indian's fingers immediately clenched the handle of his club, and the Captain saw that, just like himself, the Indian was awake and ready to face the danger that threatened them both.

Just then, the reed curtain rose and two young men slipped under it, one after the other, creeping along noiselessly like snakes; behind them, a moment later, appeared the head of the old woman, whose body remained hidden in the darkness of the other room; although she thought there was no point in participating in the scene that was about to happen, she wanted at least, if need be, to urge on the murderers with voice and gesture.

The young men rose slowly and silently, and without taking their eyes off the Indian and Captain Pamphile; one of them was holding a kind of curved billhook, with its sharp edge facing inwards: he made to advance straight away on the Indian, but his brother motioned him to wait until he in turn had armed himself. Whereupon, he went over to the wall on tiptoe and took down the knife; then they exchanged one final glance of complicity, before turning to look at their mother as if to ask her advice.

'They're asleep,' said the old woman in a low voice. 'Go ahead.'

The two young men obeyed, each of them moving over to the victim he had chosen; the one raised his arm to strike the Indian, the other leaned over to stab Captain Pamphile.

At that very same moment, the two murderers staggered back, each of them uttering a loud cry: the Captain had plunged his knife right up to its handle into the breast of the one, and the young Indian had split open the head of the other with his tomahawk. Both of them continued to stand there for a moment, swaying on their legs as if they were drunk, while the travellers had, instinctively and spontaneously, drawn closer to one another; then the two young men fell, like trees uprooted by a tempest. At the same time, the old woman uttered an oath and the young Sioux a cry of triumph: then, taking the string of his bow, he dashed into the other room, and soon re-emerged dragging the old woman by the hair, and, pulling her out of the cabin, tied her to a young birch tree some ten paces from the hut, and gagged her. Then he returned, bounding along like a tiger, picked up the knife that one of the murderers had dropped, and prodded them with its point to see if they were still alive; seeing that neither of them was making any movement, he motioned to Captain Pamphile to leave; then, when the latter had mechanically obeyed, he took from the hearth a flaming branch of pine wood, set fire to the four corners of the hut, came out bearing his torch, and began to execute around the cabin a strange dance accompanied by a song of victory.

However much Captain Pamphile was accustomed to scenes of violence, he could not help giving this one his fullest attention. And indeed, the place, the isolation, the danger he had just been in – all gave the act of justice that had been performed a character of savage vengeance; he had of course sometimes heard it said that, from the Niagara Falls to the shores of the Atlantic, it was an old and well-established juridical custom to burn down the dwelling of murderers, but he had never actually witnessed such justice being carried out.

Leaning against a tree and as motionless as if he had just been tied up and gagged himself, he at first saw a thick black smoke emerging through all the openings, then tongues of fire rose through the roof like red-hot lances; soon, on all sides, columns of fire arose, following the undulating breeze, sometimes twisting like snakes, sometimes floating like banners.

Meanwhile, looking like the demon of the blaze, the young Indian carried on turning, dancing and singing. A moment later, all the flames coalesced into one, forming one vast blaze that shed its light for half a league around, extending on the one side across the vast green steppe, and on the other plunging under the dark dome of the forest; finally, the heat became so violent that the old woman, although she was ten steps away from the fire, uttered shrieks of pain. All of a sudden the roof fell in, and a column of flames arose as if hurled forth by the crater of a volcano, flinging thousands of sparks into the sky; then each wall in turn collapsed and, at every crash, the blaze lost a little of its heat and light. Darkness gradually reoccupied the ground it had lost; finally there was nothing left of the accursed cabin other than a pile of burning coals heaped over the corpses of the murderers.

Then the savage stopped dancing and singing, lit a second branch of pine from his torch, and presented it to the Captain.

'Now,' he said, 'in which direction is my brother going?'

'To Philadelphia,' replied the Captain.

'Well, let my brother follow me, and I will act as his guide until he has reached the other side of the forest.'

With these words, the young Sioux plunged into the depths of the forest, leaving the old woman half burned by the smoking debris of her cabin.

Captain Pamphile cast one last look back at this scene of desolation, and followed his young and courageous travelling companion. At daybreak, they reached the outskirts of the forest and the foothills of the mountains; here the Sioux halted.

'My brother has arrived,' he said; 'from the top of these mountains, he will see Philadelphia. Now, may the Great Spirit protect my brother!'

Captain Pamphile looked for something he could give to the savage in reward for the devotion he had shown him, and as his only possession was his watch, he started to take it off, but his companion stopped him.

'My brother owes me nothing,' he said. 'After a fight with the Hurons, Young-Elk was taken prisoner and led to the shores of Lake Superior. He was already tied to the stake: the men were getting their knives ready to scalp him, and the women and children were dancing around him, singing the song of death, when some soldiers who had been born, like my brother, on the other side of the salty river, dispersed the Hurons and freed Young-Elk. I owed my life to them, and I have saved yours. When you meet one of those soldiers, tell them that we are quits.'

At these words, the young savage plunged into the forest. Captain Pamphile followed him with his eyes as far as he could see him; then, once he had disappeared, our worthy sailor broke off a young ebony tree that he could use both as a walking stick and as a weapon, and started to climb the mountain.

Young-Elk had not been lying: once the Captain was at the summit, he saw Philadelphia rising like a queen between the green waters of the Delaware and the blue waves of the Ocean.

13

How Captain Pamphile made the acquaintance of Tom's mother on the banks of the River Delaware, and what followed.

Although Captain Pamphile could tell by looking that he would need two good days to get from where he was to Philadelphia, he nonetheless continued on his route with remarkable zest, stopping only to look for birds' eggs or roots; as for water, he had soon met with the sources of the Delaware, and the river, which was in full spate, had relieved him of any anxiety in this regard.

So he travelled cheerfully on, seeing rest and quiet awaiting him after so many hardships, admiring the wonderful landscape unfolding in front of his eyes, in that happy frame of mind in which the solitary traveller regrets only one thing, the fact that he does not have any companion with whom to share his overflowing thoughts, when, reaching the summit of a small mountain, he thought he could make out, half a league ahead, a black speck that was moving towards him. For a moment he tried to work out what it might be, but as the distance was too great, he set off again, continuing on his way without worrying any further about the object, which he soon lost sight of, as the terrain across which he was walking was very undulating. So he carried on, whistling a tune that was very popular on the Cannebière[70] and twirling his stick, when the same object presented itself to his sight once more, several hundred yards closer; this time, the Captain was the object of the same scrutiny on the part of the character we have just introduced as he himself had been. Captain Pamphile made a kind of telescope out of his hand, gazed for a while through the improvised tube, and realised that it was a Negro.

This encounter seemed all the more fortunate in that Captain Pamphile, not particularly keen to spend a third night like the two previous ones, hoped to ask him for information about bed and board; so he stepped out, regretting that the undulating terrain forced him to lose sight of the man who might be able to give him such useful information, but whom he hoped to see again on the summit of a small hillock that constituted the halfway mark, more or less, of the path between them. Captain Pamphile had not been out in his strategic calculations: at the summit of the mountain, he found himself face to face with what he was looking for, but its colour had deceived the Captain; it wasn't a Negro, but a bear.

Captain Pamphile took in at a single glance the extent of the danger threatening him, but we will tell our readers nothing new if we inform them that, in circumstances like this, the worthy sailor was a resourceful man: he looked all round, inspecting the topography of the terrain, and saw there was no way of avoiding the animal. To the left, the river, encased within its deep banks, and too rapid to be swum across without one's being exposed to a peril perhaps even greater than that which one was fleeing; on the right, sheer rocks, scalable by lizards but inaccessible to any other animal; behind and before, a road or rather a track as broad as the one on which Oedipus encountered Laius.

On its side, the animal had come to a halt some ten paces or so from Captain Pamphile, seeming to examine everything for itself with the closest attention.

Captain Pamphile, who in the course of his life had met a host of poltroons disguised as brave men, deduced that the bear might well be as afraid of him as he was of the bear. So he walked towards it, and the bear did likewise; Captain Pamphile started to think that he had been mistaken in his conjectures, and stopped; the bear continued to walk. The situation was becoming as clear as daylight: it was not the bear that was afraid. Captain Pamphile turned on his left heel, so as to allow his adversary to pass freely, and started to beat a retreat. He had not gone back three steps before he came up against the sheer rocks; he backed right up against them so as not to be taken by surprise from his rear, and awaited the event.

He did not have long to wait: the bear, who was of the biggest species, advanced along the road as far as the place where Captain Pamphile had left it; once there, he described the same angle that the cunning strategist against whom he was matched had traced, and came straight up towards him. The situation was critical: Captain Pamphile could expect no help from anyone; the only weapon he possessed was his stick, a rather paltry means of defence; the bear was only two steps away, he lifted his stick... At this gesture, the bear rose up on its hindquarters and started to dance.

It was a tame bear, which had broken its chain and escaped from New York, where it had had the honour to give a performance in front of Mr Jackson, the President of the United States.[71]

Only at this point did Captain Pamphile, reassured by his enemy's choreographic manoeuvres, notice that the latter was muzzled, and that a length of broken chain was dangling from its neck; he immediately calculated the advantages to be drawn from such an encounter by a man reduced to the penury in which he found himself, and, as neither his birth nor his education had given him any of those false aristocratic notions by which anyone else in his place might have been preoccupied, he reflected that the profession of bear-trainer was perfectly honourable, relative to a host of other professions he had seen being exercised by several of his compatriots, both in France and abroad. And so he picked up the end of the dancer's rope, gave the bear a tap on the muzzle with his stick to explain that it was time to stop its minuet, and carried on his way to Philadelphia, leading it on a leash as if it had been a hunting dog.

That evening, as he was crossing the meadow, he noticed that his bear kept stopping in front of certain plants that were unknown to him. The nomadic life he had led had given him the ability to carry out far-reaching profound studies on the instincts of animals. He presumed that these repeated halts, although without any effect, must have some reason behind them; indeed, at the first demonstration of this kind that the animal made, Captain Pamphile stopped and gave him all the time he needed to indulge his scrutiny. He did not have to wait long for the results: the bear dug in the ground, then, a few seconds later, he uncovered a mass of tubers that looked mouth-watering. Captain Pamphile sampled them; they tasted like a cross between truffle and potato.

This was a very useful discovery, so he gave his bear every freedom to look for new ones; an hour later, there was a sufficient harvest of them to provide for the supper of both man and beast. After their meal, Captain Pamphile spotted a solitary tree, and once he had checked that its leaves did not conceal the smallest reptile, he tied his bear to the trunk, and used it as a short ladder to reach the lowest branches. Once on them, he settled down as he had done already in the forest, but his night was perfectly quiet, and the wolves kept their distance, as they could smell the bear.

The next morning, Captain Pamphile woke up altogether calm and well-rested. The first thing he checked was his bear: it was quietly sleeping at the foot of the tree. Captain Pamphile climbed down and woke it up, then they both amicably set off on the road to Philadelphia, which they reached at eleven o'clock in the evening.

Captain Pamphile had stridden along like Tom Thumb's ogre.

He started to look for an inn, but he couldn't find a single hotel keeper willing to put up a bear and a savage at such a late hour; so he was starting to feel more lost in the middle of the capital of Pennsylvania than he had been in the centre of the forests of the Saint Lawrence river, when he spotted a tavern all warm and well-lit, from which there came such a medley of sounds of glasses clinking, roars of laughter and oaths that it was obvious there was a crew here busy spending the pay it had just been given. Hope immediately returned to the Captain: either he had forgotten what kind of man a sailor is, or there would be wine, money and a bed for him here – three absolutely essential things, given his situation; so he was confidently walking towards it, when all of a sudden, he stopped as if rooted to the spot.

Amid all this hubbub, the shouts and the swearing, he thought he had recognised a Provençal song being sung by one of the drinkers: so he stood there, his head held forward, pricking up his ears, still filled with doubt as it all seemed so unlikely to him; but soon, on hearing one particular refrain being taken up in chorus, he could no longer be in any uncertainty: there were compatriots of his there. Thereupon, he took a few more steps forward and again halted, but this time, his face took on an expression of astonishment bordering on stupidity: not only were these men compatriots of his, not only was this song a Provençal song, but the man singing it was Policar! The crew of the *Roxelane* was feasting on the proceeds of its loading in Philadelphia.

Captain Pamphile did not hesitate for a moment as to the decision he needed to take; thanks to Black-Serpent's barber and painter, he was disguised in such a way that not even his best friend would have recognised him, so he boldly opened the tavern door and entered with his bear. A general shout of 'Hurrah!' greeted the newcomers.

One doubt remained in the mind of Captain Pamphile: he had forgotten to rehearse his bear, so he had absolutely no idea of what it was capable, but the intelligent animal took responsibility itself for its own programme. No sooner had it entered the cabaret than it started to trot round so that everyone would form a circle; the sailors climbed onto chairs and benches; Policar sat on the stove, and the show began.

Captain Pamphile's bear already knew everything that a bear can be taught; he could dance a minuet like Vestris,[72] and straddle a broom-handle just as well as any sorcerer, and point out the drunkest man in the company well enough to make the clever ass jealous; and so, once the session was over, there was but one shout, uttered so unanimously that Policar declared that, however much the bear's master was asking for his bear, he would buy it off him and present it to the crew; this decision was greeted by general acclaim. So the offer was repeated on a more formal footing; Captain Pamphile asked ten *écus* for his animal. Policar, who was feeling generous, offered fifteen, and having handed over the money, came into immediate possession of the animal. As for Captain Pamphile, he came away at the first trick in the second performance, without anyone paying him the least attention, or any of the sailors conceiving the slightest suspicion.

Our readers are too intelligent not to have guessed the reason for Captain Pamphile's disappearance; however, since some of them might not be altogether certain of the facts, we will give a short and precise explanation for the usage of lazy minds or those who dislike mere conjectures.

Captain Pamphile had not been wasting his time, once he had entered the tavern, he had closely observed his bear's tricks with one eye and, with the other, he had counted the sailors; every single one of them was there, from the highest to the lowest, so it was obvious that there was nobody on board. Only Two-Mouths was not present in the gathering; Captain Pamphile deduced that he had been left on the *Roxelane*, in case the vessel took it into its head to return to Marseilles all by itself. Following this altogether mathematical argument, Captain Pamphile headed down to the harbour, following Water Street, which extends parallel to the quays.

Once he had reached the port, he glanced quickly round all the vessels at anchor, and, in spite of the darkness, he recognised, some 400 yards away, the *Roxelane*, swaying graciously, rocked by the rising tide. Apart from this, not a light on board, nothing to indicate that the boat was inhabited: Captain Pamphile had guessed correctly. Without losing a moment, he dived head first into the river and started to swim in silence towards the ship.

Captain Pamphile swam round the *Roxelane* twice to assure himself that there was no one keeping watch on board; then, satisfied by his inspection, he slipped under the bowsprit, reached the rope ladder, and started to climb up, stopping at every rung to listen for any noise. Everything remained silent; finally, the Captain clambered over the edge and found himself on the deck of his boat; here, he could breathe again: he was finally at home.

Captain Pamphile's first need was to change his clothes: those he was wearing were too close to a state of nature, and might belie his identity. So he went down into his old cabin and found everything in the same place, as if nothing had happened. The only change that had been made was that Policar had had his own things brought in, and, being a meticulous kind of man, had tidied those of Captain Pamphile away in a trunk. This respect for his movable property had been taken so far that Captain Pamphile had only to hold out his hand to the place where he usually kept his phosphor lighter to find it in the same place. As a result, with the ninth match he struck, Captain Pamphile had light.

He immediately proceeded to wash himself; it was a great deal that he had retaken possession of his boat, but it wasn't enough: he still needed to get his own face back, and this was more difficult. The great chief's painter had done his job conscientiously; Captain Pamphile almost left the skin of his face on his towel. Finally, the exotic adornments disappeared, and as he continued to rub, our worthy sailor found himself reduced to his personal adornments; then he looked at his reflection in a little mirror and, although he was not particularly enamoured of his person, he felt a certain pleasure in seeing himself looking his old self again.

Once this first transformation had been accomplished, the rest became the easiest thing in the world: Captain Pamphile opened his trunk, slipped on his trousers with the stripe going down the length, put on his waistcoat with the stripe going across, put on his frock coat of coarse wool with a cross on the back, unhooked his straw hat from the peg where it was hanging, tied his red belt round his waist, slipped his pistols with their silver fittings into his belt, extinguished the light, and went back on deck; he found it just as empty and silent as before. Two-Mouths was still nowhere to be seen, as if he had possessed Gyges' ring and turned the stone inwards.[73]

It was lucky that Captain Pamphile was acquainted with the habits of his subordinate, and knew where to find him when he wasn't in the place he should have been. And indeed, when he unhesitatingly went over to the steps down to the galley, and carefully walked down the creaky steps, on looking through the half-open door he spotted Two-Mouths busy preparing his supper, cooking up for himself a piece of fresh cod, maître d'hôtel style .

Apparently, just at the moment the Captain arrived, the fish had been cooked for sufficiently long, for Two-Mouths stopped laying his place at the table, took his cod out of the saucepan and put it on a plate, set the plate on the table, shook his flask, realised it was half-empty, and, in case he ran out halfway through his meal, went out via the door that opened onto the storeroom, so as to fetch an extra supply of liquid; the supper was all ready and waiting, Captain Pamphile was hungry, he went in and sat down.

Either because the Captain had not tasted any European food for a fortnight, or because Two-Mouths did actually possess a distinguished talent in an art that he exercised, after all, as a mere amateur, the man enjoying his supper – although it hadn't been made for him – found it excellent and proceeded accordingly. He was just at the most brilliant moment of his performance when he heard a cry; he immediately looked round and saw Two-Mouths on the threshold, stupefied, pale and motionless: he took Captain Pamphile to be a ghost, although the latter was indulging in an activity that belongs exclusively to the inhabitants of this world.

'Well then, you young rascal,' said the Captain, continuing with his meal, 'what do you think you're doing there? Can't you see I'm choking with thirst? Come on, let's have a drink, quick!'

Two-Mouths' knees started to tremble and his teeth chattered.

'Didn't you hear me?' continued Captain Pamphile, holding out his glass. 'Come on, just a drop! You can manage that, can't you?'

Two-Mouths came over with as much reluctance as if he had been walking to a gibbet, and tried to obey, but in his terror, he poured half of the wine into the glass and half onto the table. The Captain pretended not to have noticed this clumsiness, and lifted his glass to his lips. Then, after taking a sip of the contents, he clacked his tongue.

'Blow me!' he said, 'it looks like you know the right place to go. Where did you get this wine from, Monsieur le sommelier? Do tell me!'

'Er… er…' replied Two-Mouths, now at the uttermost degree of terror, 'from the third cask on the left.'

'Aha! Bordeaux Lafite. Do you like Bordeaux Lafite?… I asked you if you like Bordeaux Lafite! You could give me an answer, you know!'

'Certainly,' replied Two-Mouths, 'certainly, Captain… But…'

'But it doesn't taste so good when diluted, is that right? Very well, drink it straight, my boy.'

He took the flask out of Two-Mouths' hands, poured him a second glass of wine and handed it to him. Two-Mouths took it, hesitated for another moment, and then, adopting a desperate resolve, the cabin boy said, 'To your health, Captain!'

And he tossed back the whole glassful without taking his eyes off the man who had poured it. The effect of this tonic was swift; Two-Mouths started to regain his confidence.

'Well now,' said the Captain, on whom this improvement in the physical and moral faculties of Two-Mouths had not been lost, 'now that I know you have a taste for cod done in maître d'hôtel style and a liking for Bordeaux Lafite, let's talk business for a while. What's been happening since I left the ship?'

'Well, Captain, they appointed Policar in your place.'

'Fancy that!'

'Then they decided to set sail for Philadelphia and sell half the cargo there, instead of returning straight away to Marseilles.'

'Just as I thought.'

'So they sold it off, and for three days they've been eating everything they can't drink, and drinking everything they can't eat on the proceeds.'

'Yes, yes,' replied the Captain, 'I saw them hard at it.'

'That's all, Captain.'

'Blow me! But it strikes me that's quite enough. And when are they supposed to be leaving?'

'Tomorrow.'

'Tomorrow? Oho! It was high time for me to return! Listen, Two-Mouths, my friend, do you like nice soup?'

'Yes, Captain.'

'Nice beef?'

'Sure.'

'Nice poultry?'

'Very much.'

'And a nice drop of Bordeaux Lafite?'

'Can't say no to that.'

'Very well, Two-Mouths, my friend, I'm appointing you master chef of the *Roxelane*, with a basic salary of one hundred *écus* per year and a twentieth part of all captures.'

'Really?' said Two-Mouths, 'swear to God?'

'Word of honour.'

'Done! I accept! What do I need to do for all that?'

'You need to keep your mouth shut.'

'Easy.'

'Never tell a soul that I'm not dead.'

'Fine!'

'And, if by any chance they don't leave tomorrow, bring to my hiding place a bit of nice cod and some of that excellent Lafite.'

'Enough and to spare! And where will you be hiding, Captain?'

'In the powder magazine, so that I can blow you all up if things don't go the way I want.'

'That's fine, Captain; every effort will be made to ensure you aren't too dissatisfied.'

'So, it's agreed?'

'Yes, Captain.'

'And you'll bring me Bordeaux and cod twice a day?'

'Yes, Captain.'

'Very well, good evening to you.'

'Good evening, Captain! Good night, Captain! Sleep well, Captain!'

These three wishes were pretty pointless: our worthy sailor, robust though he was, was dropping with sleep, and so, once he had gone into the powder magazine, and the door had been closed from inside, he hardly took the time to make up a kind of bed for himself between two kegs and to roll a barrel under his head as a sort of bolster, after which he fell into a sleep as deep as if he had not been obliged to leave his boat at any moment for the circumstances we have mentioned: the Captain slept for a solid twelve hours, his fists clenched.

When he woke up, he could feel, from the movement of the *Roxelane*, that it had started moving again; during his sleep, the ship had indeed weighed anchor and was moving out to sea, not suspecting the extra crew member it was carrying on board. Amid all the noise and confusion that always accompany a departure, the Captain heard someone scratching at the door of his den: it was Two-Mouths, bringing his rations.

'Well, my boy,' said the Captain, 'have we set sail, then?'

'As you can see, we're moving.'

'And where are we going?'

'To Nantes.'

'And where are we?'

'Off Reedy Island.'

'Good. Are they all aboard?'

'Yes, all of them.'

'No new recruits?'

'Oh yes: a bear.'

'Good! And when will we be at sea?'

'Oh, this evening; we've got the wind and the current on our side, and at Bombay Hook we'll find the tide.'

'Good! And what time is it?'

'Ten o'clock.'

'I am extremely satisfied with your intelligence and your accuracy, and I'm adding a hundred pounds to your salary.'

'Thank you, Captain.'

'And now, scarper, and bring me my dinner at six.'

Two-Mouths signalled that he would be on the dot and went out, delighted at the way the Captain was treating him.

Ten minutes later, when the Captain had just finished his dinner, he heard cries coming from Two-Mouths; he immediately realised from their regularity that they were occasioned by lashes from a cat-o'-nine-tails. He counted twenty-five, not without a certain disquiet, for he had a feeling that he might be partly involved in the punishment being meted out to his supplier. However, as the cries ceased, nothing indicated anything untoward on board, and the *Roxelane* continued to sail just as swiftly, his disquiet was soon calmed. An hour later, he felt from the rolling of the ship that it must be level with Bombay Hook, the movement of the tide having succeeded that of the current. In this way the day went by. At seven in the evening there was another scratching at the door of the powder magazine, Captain Pamphile opened, and Two-Mouths came in for a second time.

'Aha, my boy,' said the Captain, 'what's the news on board?'

'Nothing, Captain.'

'I thought I could hear you singing a tune I recognise.'

'Ah! This morning?'

'Yes!'

'They gave me twenty-five lashes with the cat-o'-nine-tails.'

'Now why did they do that? Tell me!'

'Why? Because they saw me coming into the powder magazine, and asked me what I was coming here to do.'

'They are so inquisitive! And what did you tell those nosy fellows?'

'Oh, that I was going to steal some powder to make rockets.'

'And they gave you twenty-five lashes for that?'

'Oh, it's nothing! It's windy, and it's already dried up.'

'Another hundred pounds for the lashes.'

'Thank you, Captain.'

'And now, give yourself a bit of a rub-down inside and out with some rum, and go to bed. I don't need to tell you where the rum is?'

'No, Captain.'

'Good evening to you, my brave lad.'

'Good night, Captain.'

'By the way, where are we?'

'We're passing between Cape May and Cape Henlopen.'

'Good, good!' murmured the Captain, 'in three hours we'll be at sea.'

And Two-Mouths closed the door, leaving the Captain in this state of expectation.

Four hours went by without bringing any change to the respective situations of the different individuals who comprised the crew of the *Roxelane*, but the last couple of hours went by more slowly and more anxiously for Captain Pamphile. He listened with increasing attentiveness to the different noises that told him of what was happening all around and above him; he heard the sailors bedding down in their hammocks, and through the chinks in his door he saw the lights being extinguished; gradually, silence fell; then the sound of snoring could be heard, and Captain Pamphile, now sure that he could venture forth from his hiding place, half-opened the door of the powder magazine and poked his head out into the tween deck: it was as quiet as a nuns' dormitory.

Captain Pamphile climbed the six steps leading to his cabin, and made his way on tiptoe to the door; he found it ajar, stopped for a moment to draw breath, then peeped inside. It was illuminated only by a few rays of moonlight, slanting in from the aft window; they fell on a man who was curled up at this window and gazing at an object that seemed to absorb all his attention. He was so intent on this object that he did not hear Captain Pamphile opening the door and bolting it shut behind him. When he saw how preoccupied was this man, whom he had immediately recognised as Policar (although he had his back to him), the Captain's intentions seemed to change. He had half-drawn his pistol from his belt, but he pushed it back in, and approached Policar slowly and silently, stopping at every step and holding his breath so as not to attract his attention; then, when he finally came within reach, bearing in mind the manoeuvre to which he had fallen prey in similar circumstances, he seized Policar in one hand by his jacket collar, and in the other by the hem of his pants, performed the same see-saw movement that he had felt being executed on himself, and sent him, before he could have any time to put up the least resistance or to utter the briefest cry, to examine more closely the object he had been gazing at so attentively.

Then, seeing that the event that had just occurred had in no way disturbed the sleep of the crew, and that the *Roxelane* was continuing to sail along at ten knots per hour, the Captain calmly went to sleep in his hammock, whose value he now appreciated all the more, having been dispossessed of it for a while, and soon he was sleeping the sleep of the just.

Now what Policar had been gazing at so attentively was a hungry shark following in the wake of the vessel, in the hope that something might fall from it.

The next morning, at daybreak, Captain Pamphile got up, lit his pipe, and went up on deck. The sailor on watch, who was walking up and down to ward off the cold, saw the Captain's head emerge from the stairwell first, and then, in succession, his shoulders, his chest and his legs. He halted, thinking he must be dreaming; it was indeed Georges, whose clothes Captain Pamphile had given a dusting down with the handle of a pike a fortnight ago.

The Captain strode past him without appearing to notice his amazement, and went to sit down, as was his wont, on the poop hatchway. He had been there for about half an hour when another sailor came up to relieve the one on watch, but no sooner had he come up through the hatch than he in turn saw the Captain and stopped: it was as if our brave sailor possessed, like Perseus, the head of Medusa.

'Well,' said Captain Pamphile after a moment of silence, 'what are you up to then, Baptiste? Aren't you going to relieve old Georges there?

He's freezing, he's been keeping watch for three long hours. What's the meaning of all this? Come on, get a move on!'

The sailor obeyed mechanically, and took over from his comrade.

'Well done!' continued Captain Pamphile; 'everyone does their stint, that's only fair. Now, Georges, my friend, you come over here; take my pipe, it's gone out; go and relight it for me, and make sure everyone brings it back to me!'

Georges, trembling, took the pipe, staggered like a drunkard down the steps to the tween deck, and reappeared a moment later, the lit pipe in his hand. He was followed by all the rest of the crew, silent and stupefied; the sailors lined up on the deck without uttering a single word.

Then Captain Pamphile got up and strolled from one end of the vessel to the other, sometimes lengthways, sometimes breadthways, as if nothing at all had happened; each time he came and went, the sailors moved aside to let him pass, as if merely to touch him would have been fatal, and yet he had no weapon; he was alone, while there were seventy of these men and they had at their disposal the full arsenal of the *Roxelane*.

After a quarter of an hour of this silent inspection, the Captain stopped at the commander's handrail, gazed all around, went down the steps and back into his cabin, and ordered his breakfast.

Two-Mouths brought him a slice of cod done in maître d'hôtel style and a bottle of Bordeaux Lafite. He had taken up his post as master chef.

This was the only change that was made on board the *Roxelane* during the crossing from Philadelphia to Le Havre, where it docked after thirty-seven days of a peaceful journey, bringing back one man less and one bear more.

Now as this bear happened, by chance, to be a female and, by some miracle, this female happened to be pregnant when Captain Pamphile encountered her on the banks of the Delaware, she gave birth on arrival in Paris, where her master had taken her to present his respects to M. Cuvier.

Captain Pamphile immediately started to think how he could turn this situation to his advantage and, in spite of the fact that his merchandise was unlikely to be very saleable, he finally managed to sell off one of his bear cubs to the owner of the Hotel Montmorency, where our readers may have seen it walking round on the balcony, until an Englishman bought it and took it off to London, and he sold the other to Alexandre Decamps, who baptised it with the name 'Tom' and entrusted it to Fau, who, as we have said, gave it an education that would have made of it a quite superior bear, superior even to the great she-bear of the Icy Sea, had it not been for the unfortunate event that we have recounted, and to which Tom succumbed in the flower of his age.

And this is how Tom had come from the shores of the Saint Lawrence river to the banks of the Seine.

14

How James I, unable to digest the butterfly's pin, suffered from a perforation of the peritoneum.

'Misfortunes arrive in a whole troop,' says a Russian proverb that deserves to become French, as it is so accurate: hardly had a few days gone by since the death of Tom than James I gave unmistakeable signs of ill health that filled the whole colony with alarm, apart from Gazelle who, retiring into her shell for three quarters of the day, seemed quite unmoved by anything that did not affect her personally and who was, moreover, as we know, not one of James's closest friends.

The first symptoms of the illness were a continual somnolence, accompanied by heaviness of head; in two days, his appetite vanished entirely and gave way to a thirst that became more and more raging; around the third day, the slight attacks of colic he had been experiencing up until then assumed such intensity and caused such a permanent pain that Alexandre Decamps climbed into a cabriolet and went to fetch Doctor Thierry. The latter straight away recognised the seriousness of the illness, although he was unable to diagnose it definitely, hesitating between an invagination of the entrails, a paralysis of the intestines, or an inflammation of the peritoneum. In any case, he bled two basins' worth of the patient's blood, promised to return that same evening to perform another bleeding, and ordered, in the mean time, that thirty leeches be applied to the abdominal region; furthermore, James was to be put on thin liquids, and all the most effective anti-phlogistic treatments.[74] James permitted all of this with a docility indicating that he himself realised the gravity of his illness.

In the evening, when the doctor returned, he found that the illness, far from yielding to the treatment, had made new inroads; there was increased thirst, complete lack of appetite, swelling of the stomach and inflammation of the tongue; the pulse was weak, rapid, concentrated and frequent, and the sunken eyes indicated the suffering that poor James was enduring.

Thierry carried out a second bleeding, again of two basins' worth, to which James yielded with resignation, for in the morning, after a similar operation, he had for a time felt better. The doctor ordered that the thin liquids be continued all night long; they sent for a carer to administer them to him every hour on the hour; soon a little old woman appeared, looking just as if she were a female version of James, and when she saw the patient, she asked for a rise in the fee she was usually given, on the vain pretext that she was used to looking after men and not monkeys, and that, as she was breaking with her principles, she would need to receive compensation for her indulgence; things were sorted out as they usually are when people have to go against their principles, and she was paid double.

They had a bad night: James stopped the old woman from sleeping, and the old woman beat James; the noise of the fight came to the ears of Alexandre, who got up and went into the patient's room. James, exasperated at the old woman's underhand treatment of him, had summoned up all his remaining strength and, just as she was stooping over him to strike, he had torn off her bonnet and was tearing it to pieces.

Alexandre arrived just in time to break up the fight; the old woman gave her reasons, James mimed his; Alexandre realised that it was the old woman who was in the wrong; she tried to justify herself, but the fact that the bottle of drink for James was still almost full, even though the night was two thirds past, condemned her.

The old woman was paid and dismissed, despite the ungodly hour, and Alexandre, to James's great joy, sat by the bed and continued the vigil begun by the horrid old witch he had just sent away. Then the energy that the patient had for a moment deployed gave way to total prostration. James fell back as if he was at death's door. Alexandre thought that the fatal moment had come, but on leaning over James he saw that it was just exhaustion, not the death agony.

At around nine in the morning, James shuddered and rose on his bed, showing signs of joy; that instant, footsteps were heard, and the bell was rung. James immediately tried to get up, but he fell limply back; straight away, the door opened and Fau appeared. Doctor Thierry had warned him that minute of James's illness, and he was coming to pay his pupil a visit.

James was overjoyed, and seemed for a moment to forget all about his sufferings, but soon his stoicism yielded to physical weakness; he started to suffer from dreadful attacks of nausea, followed, half an hour later, by vomiting.

At this juncture the doctor arrived: he found the patient lying on his back, his tongue whitish, dry and covered with a mucous coating. His breathing was frequent and uneven; the quarrel between James and the old woman had meant the illness had made alarming progress. Thierry immediately wrote to one of his colleagues, Doctor Blazy, and got one of Decamps's young art students to take it over. A consultation had become necessary, as Thierry could no longer vouch for the patient's recovery.

Around midday, Doctor Blazy arrived; Thierry brought him into James, gave him the details of the illness, and told him what prescription he had given. Doctor Blazy acknowledged the wisdom and competence of the treatment; then, having in turn examined the unhappy James, his conclusion, like Thierry's, was that he was suffering from a paralysis of the intestines caused by the quantity of lead white and Prussian blue that James had devoured.

The patient was so weak that they did not dare to carry out another bleeding, and the men of science fell back on the resources of nature. The day went by in this way, interrupted every moment by a new crisis; in the evening, Thierry came back and had only to take a single glance at James to see that the illness had made even more inroads. He shook his head sadly, did not make any more prescriptions, and said that, if the patient were to show a sudden craving for anything, they could give him anything he asked for: this is what happens to condemned men the day before they are led to the guillotine. This declaration of Thierry's threw everyone into consternation.

In the evening, Fau arrived, declaring that nobody other than he would watch over James. As a result of the doctor's decision, he had stuffed his pockets with chocolates and almonds both fresh and sugared; as he could not save James, he at least wanted to make his last moments as sweet as possible.

James received him with an expression of utmost joy; when he saw him settling down in the chair where the old woman had sat, he realised how devoted his master was, and thanked him with a friendly little grunt. Fau started to give him a glass of the potion ordered by Thierry; James, obviously so as not to vex Fau, made the most incredible efforts to swallow it, but he almost immediately brought it back up, so violently that Fau thought he was going to pass away in his arms; however, a few minutes later, the stomach contractions stopped, and James, although still trembling all over, so terrible had been the attack, was granted a moment, if not of rest, at least of exhaustion.

At around two in the morning, the first brain haemorrhages started to show themselves; not knowing what to give James to calm him down, they offered him chocolates and almonds: the patient immediately recognised these objects, which held a highly distinguished place in his gastronomic memories. A week before, he would have been happily whipped and hanged if it meant he could have chocolates and almonds. But illness is a harsh punishment. It had left James with the desire and taken away the possibility: James sadly chose the pralines which contained almonds and sugar as well and, being unable to swallow, he stuffed them into the pouches which nature had granted him on either side of his jaw. So, after a moment, his cheeks were sagging down onto his chest, as was the case with Charlet's sideburns before he had them cut off.[75]

However, although James could not, to his great regret, swallow the pralines, he felt a certain pleasure in the intermediate operation he had just performed: moistened by the saliva, the sugar that coated the almonds melted gently, which was a far from unpleasant sensation for the dying creature, and, as the sugar melted, the volume of provisions shrunk, soon leaving room in the pouches for new pralines to be inserted into. James held out his hand; Fau understood, and offered James a whole handful of sweeties among which the patient chose the ones he found most suitable, and his pouches assumed an altogether respectable rotundity once more; as for Fau, he drew new hope from this desire since, having seen the pouches shrinking, he had attributed the phenomenon of melting to the act of chewing, and had deduced from this a distinct improvement in the state of the patient, who was now eating, having been unable even to drink not so long ago.

Unfortunately, Fau was mistaken: at around seven in the morning, the cerebral haemorrhages became alarming; this had been foreseen by Thierry, for, when he came in, he did not ask how James was, but simply whether he was dead yet. At the answer in the negative, he appeared most astonished, and went into the room where Fau, Jadin, Alexandre and Eugène Decamps were all gathered: the patient was in his death agony. Then, since he could do nothing to save him, and seeing that in two hours he would have ceased to exist, he sent the servant to Tony Johannot with the strict request to bring James II over, so that James I could die in the arms of an individual of his own species, and at least communicate to him his last wishes and his final desires.

The sight was heartrending: everyone loved James, who, apart from the defects inherent in his species, was what young chaps like to call a bon viveur; there was only Gazelle who, as if to insult the dying creature, had come into the room from the studio, dragging along a carrot that she started to eat under the table with an impassiveness that pointed to an excellent stomach but a very hard heart. James looked at her askance several times with an expression that might have done little honour to a Christian, but was altogether excusable on the part of a monkey. At this juncture, the servant came in; he was carrying James II.

James II had been given absolutely no warning of the sight that was awaiting him, and his first reaction was one of fear. The deathbed on which was laid one of his kin, all those animals of another species surrounding the dying creature (he recognised them as being men, in other words a race used to persecuting his own) – all this filled him with such fear that he started to shake in every limb.

But Fau immediately went over to him, holding a praline; James II took the sweetie, turned it round this way and that to see if it wasn't some kind of a trick, tasted it with the tip of his teeth and then, convinced by the evidence of his senses that they didn't wish him any harm, gradually recovered from his panic.

Then the servant set him down near the bed of his compatriot, who, making one last effort, turned round to see him, the marks of death already evident on his face. Then James II understood or at least seemed to understand the mission he was being called upon to fulfil; he went up to the dying monkey, who was unrecognisable with his cheek pouches stuffed full of almonds; then, taking his paw and uttering sympathetic murmurs, he seemed to invite James I to confide his last thoughts in him. The patient made a visible effort to summon up all his energy, and managed to sit up; then, mumbling a few words in his mother tongue into his friend's ear, he pointed out the still impassive Gazelle with a gesture similar to the one made by the Maréchale d'Ancre in Alfred de Vigny's fine play, when she points out to her son, at the point of death, Albert de Luynes, the murderer of his father.[76] James II nodded to show that he had understood, and James I fell back motionless.

Ten minutes later, he brought both his hands up to his head, gazed one more time at all those surrounding him, as if to wish them a final farewell, pulled himself up with one last effort, uttered a cry and fell back in the arms of James II.

James I was dead.

Among all present there was a moment of deep stupor, which James II initially seemed to share. With staring eyes, he gazed at the friend who had just passed away, as immobile as the corpse itself; then, when after five minutes' examination, he had assured himself that there wasn't the shadow of life left in the body before him, he brought his two hands up to the dead monkey's mouth, opened it by pulling the two jaws apart, inserted his hand into the cheek pouches, pulled out the almonds from the pralines and immediately stuffed them into his own mouth; what they had taken to be the devotion of a friend had merely been nothing more than the cupidity of an heir!…

Fau tore the corpse of James I from the arms of the unworthy executor of his will, and handed it over to Thierry and Jadin, who were both demanding to have it, the first in the name of science, and the second in the name of art: Thierry wanted to open the body to see what illness he had died from; Jadin wanted to make a cast of the head so as to preserve his death mask and thus enrich his collection of famous death masks. Priority was granted to Jadin, so that he could carry out his procedure before death could make the features of the face unrecognisable, then it was agreed that he would hand the corpse over to Thierry, who would proceed with the autopsy.

As making the mould would leave Thierry with a good hour to kill, he took advantage of this to go and fetch Blazy, whom he was to accompany to Fontaine's,* where the body was going to be taken, to be placed at the disposal of the two doctors.

Once these arrangements had been made, Jadin, Fau, Alexandre and Eugène Decamps immediately took a fiacre to Fontaine's, taking James I with them and leaving James II and Gazelle in total control of the house.

The procedure, performed with the greatest care, was a great success, and the imprint of the face was taken with an exactitude that at least consoled James's friends with the idea that they would still have a semblance of the departed.† They had just fulfilled this sad final function when the two doctors came in: art had performed its task, and science was now asking to perform its task in turn. Jadin was the only one brave enough to stay behind for this second operation; Fau, Alexandre and Eugène Decamps withdrew, unable to take it upon themselves to witness this sad sight.

The result of the autopsy was that the peritoneum was severely inflamed, with white patches visible here and there, then an oozing of serous bloody liquid; all this was an effect and not a cause. So the doctors pursued their investigation; eventually, roughly halfway along the small intestine, they discovered a slight ulceration which led to the point of a pin, whose head had got stuck in the intestine; then they remembered the fateful business with the butterfly, and everything became clear. So death had been inevitable, and the two doctors had

* Famous moulder in the Faubourg Saint-Germain.

† If you get a voucher from M. Jadin, you can purchase the death mask of James I for the price of the moulding. M. Jadin lives at 5b, rue de la Rochefoucauld.

the consolation of seeing that, although they had been somewhat mistaken about the cause of the illness, James's ailment had been fatal, and that all the resources of art would not have been able to save him from the accident caused by greed.

As for Fau, Alexandre and Eugène Decamps, they were sadly climbing back up the staircase in no. 109 when, on the second floor, they started to smell a strange smell of frying; the higher they went, the stronger the smell became, and once they reached their landing, they realised that this exhalation was coming from their apartment. They quickly pushed open the door – when they had left, the cook had not been at home, and so they could not understand these culinary preparations. The smell was emerging from the studio.

They rushed in; they could hear something being cooked in the frying pan, and a thick cloud of smoke was emerging from it. Alexandre flung open the door and on the red-hot baking sheet found Gazelle on her back, and being braised in her shell.

The vengeance of James I had been carried out by James II.

He was pardoned, since he had been acting with the best intentions, and he was sent back to his master.

15

How Tony Johannot, finding he did not have enough wood to get through the winter, purchased a she-cat, and how, when this cat had died, James II got a frozen tail.

Some time after the events we have just been relating, winter had arrived, and everyone had made arrangements to spend it in as comfortable a way as possible; however, as Matthieu Laensberg was forecasting quite a mild winter to end the year, many people had bought in relatively little firewood.[77] One of these people was Tony Johannot, either because he had every confidence in the predictions of Matthieu Laensberg, or for some completely different reason that we have been discreet enough not to pry into. The result of this negligence was that, around 15th January, the witty illustrator of *The King of Bohemia and His Seven Castles*,[78] going off to find a woodpile for his stove, noticed that, if he continued to light a fire both in his studio and his bedroom, he would only just have enough fuel for about two weeks, if that.

Now for the last week it had been possible to skate on the canal, the river was carrying ice floes as in the days of Julian the Apostate,[79] and M. Arago,[80] disagreeing with the canon of Saint Bartholomew, was announcing, from the pinnacle of the Observatory, that the cold (already 15 degrees below) would continue to sink until it reached 23; this was only six degrees less cold than it had been during the retreat from Moscow. And, as the past served as an example for the future, everyone was starting to think that it was M. Arago who was right, and that Matthieu Laensberg might possibly have been mistaken just this once.

Tony came out of the woodshed, anxiously brooding over the painful discovery he had just made: he needed to decide whether to freeze during the day or to freeze during the night. However, on mature reflection, while fiddling with some details in a painting of *Admiral Coligny Being Hanged At Montfaucon*,[81] he thought he might have found a way of arranging matters: he could take his bed out of his bedroom and out it in the studio. As for James II, a bearskin folded in four would do the trick. And indeed, that very evening, both of them had moved, and Tony went off to sleep lulled by the gentle warmth and congratulating himself on having received from heaven such a resourceful and fertile imagination.

The next day, when he awoke, he was at first unsure of where he was; then, on recognising his studio, his eyes, directed by the paternal preoccupation that the artist feels for his work, turned towards his easel; James II was sitting on the back of a chair, at just the height of the easel, and within reach of it. At a first glance, Tony thought that the clever animal, by dint of gazing at the painting, must have become a connoisseur, and that, as he seemed to be examining the canvas from very close up, he was admiring its perfection of detail. But soon Tony realised that he had made a big mistake: James II adored white lead and, as the painting of *Coligny* was more or less finished, and Tony had done all his highlights with that ingredient, James was licking up every last trace of it.

Tony leapt out of bed, and James off his chair, but it was too late: all the expanses of flesh done with that colour had been licked away down to the canvas, with the result that the admiral's corpse had already been swallowed; you could still see the gibbet and the rope, but the hanged man himself had gone. The whole execution needed to be done again.

At first, Tony flew into a terrible temper with James; then, reflecting that on balance it was his fault, since he could easily have tied the animal up, he went to get a chain and a cramp, stuck the cramp into the wall, fixed one end of the chain to it, and having thus prepared everything for the following night, set to work with a will on his *Coligny*. The admiral had been more or less hanged all over again by five o'clock in the evening. Then, deciding that he'd done enough work for one day, he went out for a stroll along the boulevard, came back to dine in the English Tavern, and then went off to the theatre, where he stayed until half past eleven.

When he returned to his studio, which he found to be still nice and warm from the heat of the day, Tony observed with satisfaction that nothing had been disturbed in his absence and that James was asleep on his cushion, so he in turn went to bed in perfect quiet of mind and soon went off to sleep the sleep of the just.

Around midnight, he was awoken by a rattling of old iron: you'd have thought all the ghosts in Ann Radcliffe[82] were dragging their chains around the studio. Tony didn't really believe in ghosts, and, thinking that someone had come to steal the rest of his wood, he stretched out his hand to pick up an old damascened halberd, decorated with a tassel that was part of a trophy hanging from the wall.

He soon realised his error.

In a moment, he recognised the cause of all this din, and ordered James to go back to bed. James obeyed, and Tony relapsed into his momentarily interrupted sleep, with all the ardour of a man who has worked well all day. Half an hour later, he was awoken by stifled plaints.

As Tony's street was rather off the beaten track, he at first thought that a murder was being committed under his windows. He jumped out of bed, picked up a pair of pistols and ran across to open the window. The night was calm and the street quiet; not a sound disturbed the solitude of the this part of town, apart from the dull rumble that never stops, hovering over Paris like the breathing of a sleeping giant. Then he shut his window again and realised that the plaints were coming from the bedroom.

Since James and he were alone in the room, and since his only reason for complaint was that he had been woken up, he went over to James. James had got bored and had whiled away the time by walking round and round the leg of the table under which he had been lying, but after five or six turns, his chain had shortened; James hadn't noticed and had continued his manoeuvre. The result was that he had eventually been brought to a halt by the collar and, as he insisted on keeping going forward without even dreaming of turning around, he throttled himself a bit more with every effort he made to pull himself free. Hence the plaints that Tony had heard.

To punish James for his stupidity, James would have been only too glad to leave him in the situation he had got himself into, but if he condemned James to slow strangulation, he would never get any sleep himself. So he untied the rope as many times as James had tied it up, and James, happy to find that his respiratory paths were now free, humbly and silently went back to bed. Tony, for his part, did the same, hoping that nothing would now disturb his sleep until the next morning. But Tony was mistaken: James's sleeping habits had been disturbed and eaten away into his night, with the result that, now he had slept his eight hours, for that was James's figure, he could no longer get a wink of sleep. And so, twenty minutes later, Tony jumped out of bed for a third time; this time, it was neither a halberd nor a pistol that he picked up, but a whip.

James saw him coming, recognised his intentions, and huddled under his cushion, but it was too late. Tony was pitiless and James was given a thrashing that was conscientiously made to fit the crime. This kept him quiet for the rest of the night, but this time it was Tony who couldn't get back to sleep, whereupon he bravely got up, lit his lamp and, having no daylight to paint by, started one of those delightful woodcuts that have made him the king of illustrations.

It is easy to understand how, in spite of the pecuniary advantages Tony drew from his insomnia, things could not go on in the same conditions; so, when day dawned, he seriously thought of finding a means of reconciling the demands of his sleep with the interests of his wallet. He was plunged into these abstract meditations when he saw a pretty alley cat by the name of Michette coming into his studio. James was fond of her since she did everything he wanted, and she in turn was fond of James because he would keep the fleas off her.

No sooner had Tony reminded himself of this sweet intimacy than he decided to take advantage of it. The cat, with her winter fur, could perfectly easily replace the stove. So he picked up the cat, who, unaware of the plans that had just been laid for her, made no attempt to flee, and he placed her in James's cage, pushed in James behind her, and went back into the studio so as to peep through the keyhole and observe how it all turned out.

At first the two captives tried every way to escape from their prison, using whatever means were suggested to them by their different personalities. James jumped against the three walls of his den in turn, and then came back to shake the bars, then did the same thing twenty times over without realising it was completely pointless. As for Michette, she stayed where she had been put, looked all around without moving anything other than her head, and then, returning to the bars, rubbed up against them gently with one side of her body, and then with the other, arching her back and curling her tail; then, at the third attempt, she tried, still purring away, to poke her head between each pair of bars; finally, when she had ascertained that this was impossible, she uttered two or three short and plaintive miaows, but on seeing that these produced no result, she went off to make a nest for herself in a corner of the den, rolled around in the hay, and soon gave every appearance of an ermine muff as seen from one of its extremities.

As for James, he continued to jump, somersault and grumble for about a quarter of an hour; then, seeing that all his gambolling about was in vain, he went to huddle down in the corner opposite the cat. Still heated by the exercise he had just taken, he squatted down for a moment, making repeated gestures of indignation; then, as the cold started to spread through his body, he started to shiver in all his limbs.

It was at this point that he spotted his friend warmly wrapped up in her fur, and that his egotistic instincts showed him the secret of the advantage he could draw from his enforced cohabitation with his new companion, and so he went quietly over to Michette, lay down next to her, slipped one of his arms under her body, and inserted the other into the upper opening of the natural muff that she formed. He then rolled his tail into a spiral around his neighbour's tail, and she obligingly pulled the whole lot between her legs; he immediately seemed to be perfectly reassured as to his future.

This conviction was soon shared by Tony who, satisfied by what he had seen, withdrew his eye from the keyhole, rang for his housekeeper and ordered from her, in addition to James's carrots, nuts and potatoes, a bowl of mash for Michette.

The housekeeper followed this request to the letter, and everything would have gone perfectly well as regards the everyday fare of Michette and James if the latter had not upset all these arrangements thanks to his greed. From the very first day, he had noted, in the two meals he was regularly served, the first at nine in the morning and the second at five in the evening – meals that, thanks to the indulgent slowness of his digestive system, lasted all day long – the introduction of a new course. As for Michette, she had recognised perfectly well her bowl of mash and milk in the evening, and, although being perfectly well satisfied with the service, had started to eat both of them with that disdainful delicacy that all observers have noted in cats from good households.

To begin with, preoccupied by the appearance of the food, James had watched her get on with it; then, as Michette, being a well-brought-up cat, had left a little of the mash in milk on her plate, James had come up behind her, tasted it and, finding it excellent, had finished it off. At dinner he had tried the same experiment and, finding the mash with meat equally to his liking, he had – still snuggled up warmly to Michette – spent the night wondering why they were giving *him*, a fully fledged resident, carrots, nuts, potatoes and other raw vegetables, which irritated his teeth, while they offered to a lady who was a stranger to the house the creamiest and most delicate of mashes.

The result of this sleepless night was that James decided that Tony's behaviour was altogether unfair and resolved to re-establish things in their natural order by eating the mash and leaving the carrots, nuts and potatoes to Michette.

As a result, the next morning, just as the woman who helped out had finished serving the double breakfast of James and Michette, and Michette was approaching her saucer, purring, James tucked her under his arm with her head facing the other way from the saucer, and held her in this position for as long as there was anything left to eat; then, once the mash was finished, and James had eaten his fill, he let Michette go so that she could go and at her leisure enjoy a breakfast of vegetables. Michette went over and sniffed them all in turn, carrots, nuts and potatoes; then, not best pleased by what she had found, she came back, miaowing disconsolately, and lay down next to James, who, now that his stomach was comfortably full, concentrated on immediately extending the gentle warmth he felt to his abdominal region, his paws and his tail, extremities that were much more sensitive to the cold than all the rest of his body.

At dinner, the same manoeuvre was performed as before, only this time, James congratulated himself even more on his change of diet, and the mash with meat seemed to him just as superior to the milk than the mash with milk had been to the carrots, the nuts, and the potatoes. Thanks to this more comfortable food and to Michette's fur, James spent an excellent night, without paying the slightest attention to the plaints of poor Michette, who, with her empty stomach racked by pangs of hunger, miaowed piteously from evening until morning, while James was snoring like a prelate, his dreams bathed in a golden glow. This went on for three days, to the great satisfaction of James and the detriment of Michette.

Finally, on the fourth day, when dinner was brought, Michette did not even have the strength to make her usual protests, and she stayed lying down in her corner, so that James, freer in his movements now that he was no longer obliged to restrict Michette in hers, dined better than he had ever dined before; once his dinner was over, he went, as was his custom, to lie down next to his cat, and feeling that she was colder than usual, enwrapped her more tightly than usual in his

* The different moral lessons of our story can be drawn perfectly simply, so we do not feel it is necessary to spell them out to our readers, relying rather on the pure and simple narrative of events; this way we do not deprive them of an opportunity to meditate on the punishment that egotism and greed always bring down on themselves.

paws and his tail, grumbling sullenly at the way his stove was losing its heat.

The next day, Michette was dead, and James's tail was frozen.*

That day, it was Tony who, worried by the increasing chill of the night, went to visit his two prisoners as soon as he woke up. He found that James had paid the price for his egotism and was chained to a corpse; he picked up the dead female and the living male, both of them pretty much as immobile as each other, and took them into his studio. However much he tried to warm her up, no heat would ever revive Michette; as for James, as he was merely numb, and little by little the movement returned to his whole body, except around the region of his tail, which remained frozen, and which, having been frozen while it was still wound in a spiral round that of Michette, preserved the shape of a corkscrew, a shape hitherto quite uncommon, not to say unheard of, among the simian species, and which immediately gave James the most fabulously chimerical silhouette one can possibly imagine.

Three days later, it started to thaw. Now, along with the thaw came an event that we cannot pass over in silence, not because of its importance as such, but because of the disastrous consequences it had for James's tail, already somewhat endangered by the accident we have just related.

During the freeze, Tony had received two lion skins that one of his friends, who for the time being was hunting in the Atlas mountains, had sent him from Algiers. These two lion skins, freshly cut from the animals' bodies, had been badly affected by the cold on arrival in France, which had led to them losing their smell, and were waiting in Tony's room where they had been left. Tony was hoping to get them tanned one day or another, so he could decorate his room with them. Now, once the thaw arrived, everything thawed out, except for James's tail, so the skins, as they softened, regained that acrid, musky odour that announces from afar to panic-stricken animals the presence of the lion. The result of this circumstance was that James (who, in view of the accident he had suffered, had been given permission to stay in the studio), with the subtle sense of smell peculiar to his race, caught a whiff of the terrible odour that was gradually spreading through the apartment, and started to show signs of manifest disquiet, which Tony took to be a malaise caused by the curtailing of one of his most essential limbs.

This disquiet had lasted for two days; for two days, James, eternally preoccupied by one and the same idea, would breathe in all the draughts that blew up to him, leap from chairs into tables and from tables onto shelves, eating hastily and, looking fearfully around him all the while, drinking hastily, and choking on his drink – in short, was leading a most agitated kind of life, when it so happened that I went to visit Tony.

As I was one of James's good friends, and never turned up in the studio without bringing him some titbits, as soon as James set eyes on me, he ran up to check that I hadn't lost my good habits. Now the first thing that struck me, when I offered James a Havana cigar of the kind he was very fond of, not so he could smoke it in the way our elegant men about town do, but so he could chew it, imitating the sailors of the *Roxelane*; well, as I was saying, the first thing that struck me was that fantastic tail that I had never seen on him before; then, subsequently, that nervous trembling, that feverish agitation that I had never observed in him before. Tony gave me the explanation for the first phenomenon, but he was as ignorant of the reason for the second as I was; he was thinking of sending for Thierry to consult him on this subject.

I left him, encouraging him to put this good intention into effect, when, passing through the bedroom, I was struck by the odour of pelts that could be smelled in it. I asked Tony for the reason, and he showed me the two lion skins. This single gesture made everything clear to me: obviously, it was these lion skins that were tormenting James. Tony refused to believe me, and, as he continued to think that James was suffering from some serious illness, I suggested that he try an experiment that would demonstrate fully and clearly that, if James was suffering, it was from fear. This experiment was one of the simplest and easiest you could think of: it consisted purely and simply in asking each of his two young art students, who had taken advantage of our temporary absence to play billiards, to drape a lion skin across their shoulders, and send them into the studio on all fours, dressed like the Hercules who had slain the Nemean lion.

Already, ever since the bedroom door had been opened and the odour of the lions had been wafting more strongly and directly to him, James's anxiety had been visibly increasing: he had flung himself onto a double-sided ladder, and once he was on the top rung, he turned to look at us, sniffing the air and uttering little cries of alarm, indicating that he sensed the danger approaching and guessed the direction from which it must be coming.

And indeed, a moment later, one of the art students, suitably caparisoned, went down on all fours and marched towards the studio, followed immediately by his friend; James's disquiet reached a new height. Eventually he saw the head of the first lion appearing in the door, and this disquiet became real terror – a senseless, irrational, hopeless terror: the terror of the bird struggling to escape from the gaze of the snake; the terror that breaks your physical strength, and paralyses your mental faculties; the terror of vertigo, which means that to your panic-stricken eyes the sky is falling and the earth shaking, so that, as all your strength collapses at once, you fall panting to the ground as if in a dream, without uttering a single cry; this is what the mere sight of the lions had produced.

They took a step closer to James, and James fell from his ladder.

We ran over to him; he had fainted; we picked him up: he had quite lost his tail! The freeze had made it as fragile as glass, so that, as he fell, it had smashed.

We had not wished to take the joke quite so far, so we despatched the lion skins to the attic, and, five minutes later, the art students returned in their natural shape and form. As for James, a moment later, he gloomily opened his eyes, uttering little whimpers, and on recognising Tony, he flung his arms around his neck and hid his face in his breast.

Meanwhile, I prepared a glass of Bordeaux to restore to James the courage he had lost, but James didn't have the heart to eat or drink anything: at the slightest noise, he quivered all over. But little by little, as he continued to sniff the air, he started to realise that the danger had passed.

Just then, the door reopened, and in one bound James had leapt from Tony's arms onto the ladder, but instead of the monsters he had been expecting to see emerging from that door, James saw his old friend the cook arrive; this view made him feel a little safer. I took advantage of this occasion to place under his nose a saucer full of Bordeaux wine. He looked at it mistrustfully for a moment, looked back at me as if to assure himself that it was indeed a friend who was presenting the tonic brew to him, feebly dipped his tongue into it, and then brought it back into his mouth as if he wished to please me, but having realised, with the fine sense of taste characteristic of him, that the unknown liquid had a most admirable aroma, he came back voluntarily; the third or fourth time he lapped up the wine, his eyes started to sparkle, and he uttered little grunts of pleasure that indicated his return to more pleasant sensations, and finally, once the saucer was empty, he sat up on his behind, looked all around to see where the bottle was, spotted it on the table, darted over to it with a nimbleness that proved that his muscles were starting to recover their original elasticity, and, drawing himself up in front of the bottle, which he took in his hands the same way that a clarinet player picks up his instrument, he inserted his tongue into its neck. Unfortunately, his tongue was several inches too short to render him the service he had been expecting of it, at which point Tony took pity on James and poured out a second saucer of wine for him.

This time, James didn't need to be asked twice: far from it – he put his lips to it so avidly that he at first swallowed as much wine through his nose as he did through his mouth, and was obliged to stop so he could sneeze. But this interruption was as rapid as a thought. James immediately got down to business again, and in an instant the saucer was as clean as if it had been wiped with a towel; James, meanwhile, was starting to get seriously tipsy; any trace of alarm had vanished and given way to a cocksure, swaggering air; he again looked at the bottle, which Tony had moved to another piece of furniture, and tried to take a few steps towards it; but almost immediately, sensing that his safest bet was to double the number of points of support he could rest on, he dropped down onto all fours again and made his way, with the intent gait of growing drunkenness, towards the goal he had set himself; he had already crossed two thirds or so of the space that separated his point of departure from the bottle when, en route, he came across his tail.

This sight drew him for a few moments out of his preoccupation. He stopped in front of it and stared at it, waved the bit of whip still left; and, after remaining motionless for a few seconds, he went round it to examine it in greater detail; then, once his investigation was concluded, he negligently picked it up, turned it this way and that in his hands like an object that made him only moderately curious, sniffed it one last time, nibbled it gingerly, and, finding it rather insipid to the taste, dropped it with an expression of profound disdain, and continued on his way towards the bottle.

This was the best episode of drunkenness that I have ever seen in my life, and I pass it on for all connoisseurs to appreciate.

Never afterwards did James mention his tail, but not a day went by but he asked for his bottle. As a result, nowadays, this last hero of our story is not just enfeebled by age, but addled by alcohol too.

16

How Captain Pamphile offered a prize of 2,000 francs and the cross of the Legion of Honour for the answer to the question whether Joan of Arc's name was spelled with a Q or a K.

So long as our readers have not, as a result of the intense interest they will have taken in the death of James I, lost all memory of the events that preceded those we have just related, they will probably recall that on his return from his eleventh journey to India, after loading up with tea, spices and indigo at the expense of Captain Kao-Kiou-Koan, and having bought a parrot in the Rodrigues Islands, the respectable sailor whose true story we have just narrated had dropped anchor successively in the bay of Algoa and the mouth of the Orange river.

On each of these coasts, he had, as the reader will also recall, traded first with a Kaffir chief by the name of Outavaro and then with a Namaquois chief by the name of Outavari, purchasing 4,000 elephant tusks. Now it was, as we have said, to give his two esteemed trading partners time to fulfil their part of the deal that the Captain had tried his luck on that cod-fishing venture we have related during which he had been subjected to such terrible tribulations, and which had, nonetheless, come to a conclusion that redounded to his greater glory, thanks to his courage and his presence of mind, supported by the devotion of Two-Mouths, who on this occasion had been, as the reader will remember, raised to the high rank of master chef of the trading brig the *Roxelane*.

And so, Captain Pamphile's first thought, once he had profitably sold off his cod at Le Havre and his bear cubs in Paris, had been to begin preparations for a third journey, which presented him with opportunities that were no less sure of success than the twelve previous ones. And so, faithful to his previous activities, whose happy results he had appreciated only too well, he had taken the carriage to the rue de Grenelle-Saint-Honoré in Orleans, had got off at the Hôtel du Commerce, and, to the usual questions of the hotelier, had replied that he was a member of the Department of Historical Sciences of the Institute, and that he had come to the county town of the Loiret *département* to carry out research into the real spelling of Joan of Arc's name, which some people write with a Q and others with a K, not to mention those who, like me, write it with a C.

At a time when all sober and serious minds are turned towards historical studies, a pretext of this kind must have seemed perfectly plausible to the inhabitants of Orleans; the discussion was, indeed, a matter of enough importance for the Academy of Inscriptions and Letters to devote considerable attention to it, sending one of its most distinguished members to investigate in depth this important question. As a result, on the very same day as he arrived, our illustrious traveller was introduced by his host to a member of the town council, who introduced him the next day to the deputy mayor, who introduced him the day after that to the mayor, who, before the week was out, introduced him in turn to the Prefect; he, flattered by the honour which was being paid, via his person, to the whole city, invited the Captain to dinner so that an answer to this great problem could be reached more quickly and surely; the other guest was the last descendant of Bertrand de Pelonge who, as everyone knows, led Joan the Maiden from Domrémy to Chinon, and from Chinon to Orleans, where, having taken a wife, his race had perpetuated itself down to our own time, and shone in all its splendour in the person of M. Ignace-Nicolas Pelonge, a wine and spirit wholesaler in the Place du Martroy, a sergeant-major in the National Guard and a corresponding member of the Academies of Carcassonne and Quimper-Corentin. As for the suppression of the *de,* which – like Cassius and Brutus[83] – was conspicuous by its absence, this was a sacrifice that M. de Pelonge senior had made to the cause of the People during the famous night in which M. de Montmorency burned his letters of nobility, and M. de La Fayette renounced his title of marquis.[84]

The worthy Captain met with even better fortune than he had hoped: what he esteemed – as one may well imagine – in Citizen Ignace-Nicolas Pelonge, sergeant-major in the National Guard and wine and spirit wholesaler, was not the lustre shed on him by his ancestors, but that which he had acquired for himself; Citizen Ignace-Nicolas Pelonge was known for despatching, not just to different parts of France but also abroad, considerable quantities of vinegar and brandy. Now, as the reader knows, Captain Pamphile needed quite a considerable quantity of alcohol, as he had committed himself to delivering to Outavari and Outavaro fifteen hundred and 2,500 bottles respectively, in exchange for an equal number of elephant tusks, so he was grateful to accept the invitation that M. le Préfet had issued to him.

The dinner was a veritable symposium. The guests, who knew the kind of man they were dealing with, had all arrived well-stocked with all the treasures of local erudition, and each of them possessed such a great deal of irrefutable evidence for his opinion that, when the dessert came, some had sided with Guillaume Gruel, and others with Pierre de Fenin,[85] so that they were just about to start hurling the dinner plates provided by the government at each other when Captain Pamphile managed to reconcile all opinions, inviting their representatives to send a learned article on the subject to the Institute, promising to take 2,000 francs from the Montyon Prize, and a cross of the Legion of Honour from the honours lists of 27th, 28th and 29th July, so as to award them to the man whose opinion prevailed.[86]

This offer was greeted with enthusiasm, and the Prefect, rising to his feet, proposed a toast in honour of the respectable body that had done the city of Orleans such a great honour by sending one of its most distinguished members to draw from local sources one of the rays of that light with which the sun of Paris illumines the whole world.

Captain Pamphile rose with tears in his eyes, and, in a voice quivering with emotion, replied, in the name of the body of which he was a member, that if Paris were indeed the sun of science, Orleans, thanks to the information that he had just received and that he would hasten to transmit to his illustrious colleagues, could not fail to be declared, before too long, its moon. The guests all swore in chorus that this was their whole ambition, and that the day this ambition was fulfilled, the *département* of Loiret would be the proudest *département* of all the eighty-six *départements* of France, whereupon the Prefect placed his hand on his heart, told his guests that he held them all in his heart, and invited them to take coffee with him in his salon.

This was the moment that they had all been waiting for to seduce Captain Pamphile; they were fully aware of the influence that such a distinguished member, who had demonstrated such vast erudition during dinner, must have on the decisions of his colleagues; furthermore, he had cleverly insinuated that he would probably be appointed as rapporteur of the commission, and that, in this capacity, his opinion carried great weight. As a result, his neighbour on the right, instead of allowing him to continue on his way to the salon door, drew him into the first corner of the dining room and here asked him what he had thought of the raisins. The Captain, who had nothing against that estimable fruit, praised it to the skies, whereupon his neighbour on the right took his hand, squeezed it with a knowing smile, and asked him for his address. The worthy scientist replied that his scientific address was at the Institute, but that his real residence was in Le Havre, whither he had betaken himself so that he would be in a better position to observe the rise and fall of the tides, and any despatch of goods whatsoever could be sent to him at this port, addressed to his brother Captain Pamphile, commander of the trading brig the *Roxelane*.

The same thing happened for the neighbour on his left, who had been eagerly waiting for the moment when the rapporteur of the commission would be free; this man was an entirely estimable man, who enquired, with the same interest as his neighbour the grocer had done, how much Captain Pamphile was partial to sweets and preserves. The Captain replied that it was generally recognised what a very sweet tooth the Academy had, and in proof of his statement he was quite happy to admit to him that this honourable assembly, which met every Thursday with the ostensible pretext of discussing literary or scientific questions, had no other aim, during these sessions behind closed doors, than to assure itself – while eating preserve of roses and drinking gooseberry syrup – of the progress being made by the art of people such as Millelot and Tanrade.[87] For some time, what was more, it had been aware of the abuses of centralisation, as regards confectioneries, and that *pâtes d'Auvergne* and Marseilles nougat had been recognised as worthy of academic encouragement; he himself was happy to have learned from experience that *confitures d'Orléans*, which he had never heard of before now, were not a whit inferior to those of Bar and Châlons: this was a discovery that he would not fail to communicate to the Academy at one of its very next sessions. The neighbour on the left shook Pamphile by the hand and asked for his address, and Captain Pamphile, having given him the same reply as he had to his neighbour on the right, finally found himself free to enter the salon, where the Prefect was awaiting him to take coffee.

Although the Captain was a worthy aficionado of Arabica, and the variety whose liquid flame he was savouring seemed to him to have come directly from Moka, he reserved all his praise for the little glass of brandy that accompanied it, comparing it to the best cognac he had ever tasted. The descendant of Bertrand de Pelonge accepted this praise with a bow: he was the usual supplier to the Prefecture, and the arrow of flattery that Captain Pamphile had just sent winging on its way towards him had struck a bull's-eye.

There followed a long discussion between Citizen Ignace-Nicolas Pelonge and Captain Amable-Désiré Pamphile, in which the wines and spirits wholesaler showed considerable practical experience, and the academician a profound understanding of theory. The result of this conversation, in which the question of liquids had been debated in depth, was that Captain Pamphile learned what he wanted to know, namely that Citizen Ignace-Nicolas Pelonge was just about to send fifty large casks of that very same brandy, containing 500 bottles, to the firm of Jackson and Williams, of New York, with whom he entertained a business relationship, and that this despatch, currently being loaded on the Quai de l'Horloge, was to be transported down the Loire as far as Nantes, where it would be placed on board the three-master the *Zéphir*, under its captain Malvilain, about to sail for North America: the whole journey should take fifteen to twenty days.

There was not a minute to lose, if Captain Pamphile wished to arrive at the right time. And so, that very same evening, he bade farewell to the authorities in Orleans, claiming that the clarity of the information he had received rendered any longer sojourn in the capital of the *département* of the Loiret superfluous; so he shook the grocer and the confectioner by the hand once more, embraced the wines and spirits wholesaler, and left Orleans that same night. Even those who had been least favourable to the Academy had completely revised their opinion of that estimable body.

17

How Captain Pamphile, having landed on the coast of Africa, was forced to pick up a cargo of ebony wood instead of the cargo of ivory that he had come for.

The day after his arrival at Le Havre, Captain Pamphile received a half-quintal of raisins and six dozen jars of jam, which he ordered Two-Mouths to stow away in his private office; then he busied himself with the preparations for the sailing. These did not take long, given that the worthy sailor almost always sailed on his ballast and, as we have already seen, usually loaded his cargo only when out at sea. Thus, a week later, he was doubling the point of Cherbourg, and a fortnight later he was cruising between the 47th and 48th degrees of latitude, cutting neatly across the route that the three-master the *Zéphir* was due to take on its journey from Nantes to New York. The result of this clever manoeuvre was that one fine morning, as Captain Pamphile, half drowsy and half alert, was daydreaming lazily in his hammock, he was suddenly drawn out of his somnolence by the cry of the sailor on watch who had sighted a sail.

Captain Pamphile rolled out of his hammock, grabbed a telescope, and, without even bothering to put on his pants, went up onto the deck of his vessel. This somewhat mythological appearance of his might have seemed somewhat unbefitting, perhaps, on board a more conventional ship than the *Roxelane*, but we have to confess, to the shame of the crew, that not one of its members played the slightest attention to this conspicuous infraction of the rules of modesty, so used were they to the

Captain's eccentricities. The Captain himself, meanwhile, calmly walked across the deck, climbed onto the ship's rail, straddled several of the ratlines of the shrouds, and, with the same impassivity as if he had been more fittingly dressed, he started to examine the ship that had come into sight.

A moment later, he was in no doubt: it was indeed the ship he had been expecting, so orders were immediately given to place the carronades on their pivots and the eight-pounder on its carriage; then, seeing that his orders were about to be executed with the usual promptness, Captain Pamphile ordered the helmsmen to hold to the same course, and went down into his cabin, so as to present himself to his colleague Captain Malvilain in a more decent guise.

When the Captain came back on deck, the two ships were about one league away from each other, and you could recognise in the new arrival the honest and grave demeanour of a merchant ship that, being laden, with all its sails and with a good breeze, can make quite a decent five or six knots per hour. As a result, even if had attempted to make a getaway, the *Zéphir* would have been caught up by the lively, skittish *Roxelane* within two hours; but it did not even make the attempt, confident as it was of the peace sworn by the Holy Alliance and the extinction of piracy, whose obituary it had read a week before its departure in the *Constitutionnel*. So it continued to advance, putting its trust in treaties, and it had come within half a cannon shot of Captain Pamphile, when these words echoed on board the *Roxelane* and were carried by the wind to the astonished ears of the captain of the *Zéphir*.

'Ahoy there! Three-master! Put out a boat, and send us your captain!'

There was a momentary pause; then these words, wafted from the three-master, in turn reached the *Roxelane*, 'We are the trading vessel the *Zéphir*, under Captain Malvilain, laden with brandy, and sailing from Nantes to New York.'

'Fire!' said Captain Pamphile.

A flash of light accompanied by a cloud of smoke, and followed by a violent bang, immediately left the prow of the *Roxelane* and, at the same moment, the blue of the sky could be seen through a hole in the mizzen sail of the innocent and inoffensive three-master, which, under the impression that the ship firing on it had misheard or misunderstood, repeated once more, more distinctly even than the first time:

'We are the trading vessel the *Zéphir*, under Captain Malvilain, laden with brandy, and sailing from Nantes to New York.'

'Ahoy there! Three-master!' replied the *Roxelane*, 'put out a boat, and send us your captain!'

Then, seeing that the three-master was still hesitating to obey, and that the eight-pounder had been reloaded, 'Fire!' the Captain said a second time.

And the cannonball was seen skimming over the crests of the waves and crashing into the woodwork, eighteen inches above the waterline.

'In heaven's name, who are you and what do you want?' cried a voice made even more plaintive by the effect of a loudhailer.

'Ahoy there! Three-master!' replied the *Roxelane* impassively, 'put out a boat, and send us your captain!'

This time, whether the brig had understood or not, whether or not it was really deaf or just pretending, there was no means of evading the summons: a third cannonball under the waterline, and the *Zéphir* would have sunk, so the unfortunate captain did not waste time replying, but any eye with a little training could see that his crew were making preparations to lower the rowing boat into the sea.

A moment later, six sailors were sliding down a rope one after the other; the captain followed them, sat in the stern, and the rowing boat, moving away from the sides of the three-master, like a child leaving its mother, pulled with all its oars to cross the distance separating the *Zéphir* from the *Roxelane*, and advanced to starboard, but a sailor on the side of the ship signalled to the rowers to head hard to port, in other words on the side of honour. Captain Malvilain could not complain; he was being received with the courtesies due to his rank.

At the top of the ladder, Captain Pamphile was awaiting his colleague; now, as our worthy sailor was a man of *savoir-vivre*, he began by apologising to Captain Malvilain for the way he had requested him to come over and pay a visit; then he asked after his wife and children, and once he had been reassured as to their health, he invited the commander of the *Zéphir* to enter his cabin, where, he said, he had important business to discuss with him.

Captain Pamphile always issued his invitations in such an irresistible way that there was no means of refusing them. So Captain Malvilain yielded with good grace to the wishes of his colleague who, having told him to go first, despite the polite demurrals he expressed with regard to this honour, closed the door behind him, ordering Two-Mouths to show off his talents, so that Captain Malvilain would take away a decent idea of the good fare enjoyed on board the *Roxelane*.

Half an hour later, Captain Pamphile half-opened the door, and handed to Georges, who was on orderly duty in the dining room, a letter addressed by Captain Malvilain to his lieutenant; this letter contained orders to bring on board the *Roxelane* twelve of the fifty large casks of brandy on board the *Zéphir*, belonging to Ignace-Nicolas Pelonge and company. This was just 2,000 bottles more than Captain Pamphile strictly needed, but, being a cautious man, the worthy sailor had thought of the inroads that a sailing of two months might make on his cargo; in any case, he was in a position to take the lot, and when he reflected in private on that omnipotence that his host was using so sparingly, Captain Malvilain gave thanks to Our Lady of Guérande that he had got off so lightly.[88]

Two hours later, the transport of the goods had been completed, and Captain Pamphile, faithful to his system of civility, had been so polite as to have the procedure executed during dinner, so that his colleague would see nothing of what was happening. They had just got to the after-dinner conserves and raisins, when Two-Mouths, who had surpassed himself in the execution of the meal, came over to say a word in the Captain's ear; the latter gave a nod of satisfaction and asked for coffee to be served. It was brought in immediately, accompanied by two bottles of brandy, which the Captain recognised, at the first little glassful, as being the same that he had tasted at the home of the Prefect of Orleans; this gave him a very positive impression of the probity of Citizen Ignace-Nicolas Pelonge, whose despatches were so faithful to his samples.

Once coffee had been taken and the twelve large casks of brandy had been stowed away, Captain Pamphile no longer had any reason to detain his colleague on board the *Roxelane*, and conducted him, with the same politeness he had shown in receiving him, to the stairs on the port side, where his rowing boat was awaiting him, and where he took his leave of him, though not without keeping an eye on him until he reached the *Zéphir*, with all the interest of a growing friendship; then, once he had seen him back on deck, and from the manoeuvrings of the vessel deduced that his vessel was about to set sail, he raised his loudhailer to his lips once more – but this time it was to wish him bon voyage.

As if the *Zéphir* had merely been waiting for him to give it permission, it then spread all its sails, and the ship, yielding to the action of the wind, immediately set off westwards, while the *Roxelane* set course for the south. Captain Pamphile, however, continued to signal his friendship, and Captain Malvilain to respond in kind, and it was only when night followed the day that this exchange of friendly feelings was interrupted. The next day, at sunrise, the two ships had lost sight of one another.

Two months after the event we have just related, Captain Pamphile dropped anchor at the mouth of the Orange river and started to sail upstream, accompanied by twenty well-armed sailors, on his way to visit Outavari.

Captain Pamphile, who was an observant fellow, noticed with great surprise how much the country had changed since his last visit. Instead of those fine plains of rice and maize whose roots bathed in the very waters of the river, instead of the many herds that had previously come, mooing and bleating, to drink from its banks, there was nothing but fallow land and a profound solitude. For a moment, he thought he had made a mistake and taken the Fish river for the Orange river, but, having taken soundings, he saw that his calculations had been correct: and indeed, after twenty hours of sailing, he hailed within sight of the capital of the Little-Namaquois.

The capital of the Little-Namaquois was populated only by women, children and old men, who were in a state of the most profound distress. This is what had happened.

Immediately after the departure of Captain Pamphile, Outavaro and Outavari, the one lured by the 2,500 and the other by the 1,500 bottles of brandy that they were to obtain in exchange for their supply of ivory, had separately set off to hunt down the elephants – which, unfortunately, were in a great forest that separated the States of the Little-Namaquois from those of the Kaffirs, a kind of no man's land that belonged neither to the former nor to the latter. No sooner had the two chiefs encountered each other in this territory than, seeing that they had come for the same reason and that the speculation of each would necessarily harm that of the other, the leaven of the ancient hatred that had never entirely died out between the Son of the East and the Son of the West sprang back to life. Each of them had set off on a hunting expedition, and so all of them were armed for combat, with the result that instead of working together to gather the 4,000 tusks, and to share out their prize amicably, as a few hoary-headed elders proposed, they came to blows, and on the very first day, fifteen Kaffirs and seventeen Little-Namaquois were left dead on the battlefield.

From this time forward there had been all-out war, war to the death, between these hordes: in this war, Outavaro had been slain and Outavari wounded, but the Kaffirs had named a new chief, and Outavari had recovered. As a result, as they found themselves in the same respective situation as before, the rivalry between them had merely resumed all the more fiercely, with each country exhausting its supply of warriors in an attempt to reinforce its strength; finally one last effort had been made by the two peoples to maintain the supremacy of their different chiefs: all young men aged twelve or more, and all the men under sixty, had joined their respective armies, and the two combined forces of the two nations had decided to confront one another in just a few days, so that a general battle could decide the outcome of the war.

This was why there were only women, children and old men left in the capital of the Little-Namaquois, and they were, as we have said, in the most profound distress; as for the elephants, they were cheerfully beating their flanks with their trunks, and making the most of the fact that nobody was keeping an eye on them to come right up to the gates of the village and eat the rice and maize.

Captain Pamphile straight away saw how he could turn this situation to his advantage: he had made his bargain with Outavaro and not with his successor; he was thus freed of any commitments towards the latter, and his natural ally was Outavari. He recommended to his troops to carry out a very close inspection of the rifles and pistols to ensure that everything was in good shape; then, having ordered every man to provide himself with four dozen cartridges, he asked for a young Namaquois who would be bright enough to act as his guide and pace their progress so that they would arrive at the camp in the middle of the night.

All was carried out with the greatest skill, and, two days later, at eleven in the evening, Captain Pamphile was brought into Outavari's tent just as the latter, having decided to give battle the next day, was holding council with the foremost and wisest men in the nation.

Outavari recognised Captain Pamphile with that certainty and that swiftness of recall that distinguish savage nations, so no sooner had he seen him than he rose to his feet, came over to greet him, and placed one hand on his heart and the other on his mouth, as a sign that his thoughts and the words he was about to utter were in agreement. Now, what he was about to say, and what he did say to the Captain, in bad Dutch, were that since he had not observed the agreement made with Captain Pamphile, since he had been unable to keep his side of the bargain, his lying tongue and his deceitful heart were at the latter's disposal, and that he simply had to cut out the former and tear out the latter and give them to his dogs to eat – as befits the tongue and the heart of a man who does not keep his word.

The Captain, who spoke Dutch just as well as did William of Orange, replied that he wasn't interested in the heart and tongue of Outavari, that his dogs had had plenty to eat, since they had found their route strewn with the corpses of Kaffirs, and that he had come to strike a bargain that would be much more advantageous to both of them than that which his faithful friend and ally Outavari had just, with such loyalty and disinterest, proposed. Pamphile offered to help him in his war against the Kaffirs, on condition that all the prisoners taken after the battle would belong to him in all propriety, for him and his heirs to do with as they pleased: Captain Pamphile, as will be seen from his style, had been a lawyer's clerk before becoming a pirate.

It was too good a proposition to be turned out, so it was received with the acclamation not only of Outavari, but indeed by the entire council; the oldest and wisest of the elders even pulled his plug of tobacco out of his mouth and lowered his cup from his lips to offer both of them to the white chief, but the white chief majestically declared that it was for him to offer gifts to the council, and he ordered Georges to go and fetch two ells of Virginia carrot and four bottles of Orleans brandy, which were received and enjoyed with deep gratitude.

After this collation, since it was one o'clock in the morning, Outavari sent everyone to bed at their respective posts, and remained alone with Captain Pamphile, so as to lay plans for the next day's battle.

Captain Pamphile, convinced that a general's first duty is to gain a thorough knowledge of the localities on which he is to operate, and having no hope of procuring a map of the area, asked Outavari to lead him to the highest point in the vicinity, as the moon was shedding sufficient light for objects to be made out just as clearly as in a western twilight. As it happened, a low hill rose on the outskirts of the forest, on which the right wing of the Little-Namaquois was encamped. Outavari motioned Captain Pamphile to follow him in silence, and, walking ahead, he led him by paths along which they were sometimes forced to leap like tigers, and sometimes forced to creep like snakes. Fortunately Captain Pamphile had, in the course of his life, passed through many worse difficulties, both in the swamplands and the virgin forests of America, so he leaped and crept so well that after a march of half an hour he had arrived with his guide at the summit of the hill.

Here, however used Captain Pamphile might have been to the great spectacles of nature, he could not but halt for a while and gaze in admiration on the sight that stretched out before his eyes. The forest formed a huge semicircle in which the remnants of two whole peoples was enclosed; it was a dark mass that cast its shadows over both camps, and which one's eye would have tried to penetrate in vain, while beyond that shadow, joining one end of the semicircle to the other, and forming the string of the bow, the Orange river gleamed like a stream of liquid silver, while in the distance the landscape melted away out of sight in that endless horizon beyond which stretches the land of the Great-Namaquois.

This vast expanse, which even at night preserved its warm and clearly demarcated hues, was lit up by the brilliant moon of the tropics, which alone knows what happens amid the great solitudes of the African continent; from time to time, the silence was broken by the roar of the hyenas and jackals that were following the two armies, and over which there rose, like a rumble of thunder, the distant snarl of some lion. Then everything fell silent, as if the whole world had recognised its master's voice, from the song of the Bengali telling of his love as he swayed in the calyx of a flower to the hiss of the snake that, erect on its tail, called to its female as it raised its blue-spangled head above the heather; then the lion in turn fell silent, and all the various sounds that had fallen mute at his roar again filled the solitude and the night.

Captain Pamphile remained for a few moments, as we have said, in thrall to the impression that such a sight was bound to produce, but, as the reader knows, the worthy sailor was not the kind of man who would allow himself to be diverted for long by bucolic influences from a business as serious as that which had brought him here. So his second thoughts brought him back down with a bump to his material interests; then he saw, on the other side of the small stream that flowed from the forest and debouched into the River Orange, the entire army of the Kaffirs asleep in their camp, guarded by a few men who, from their immobility, could have passed for statues: like the Little-Namaquois, they seemed to be determined to give battle the following day, and were resolutely awaiting their enemies.

Captain Pamphile had taken in their position in a single glance and calculated the chances of a surprise attack, and, as his plan was sufficiently well-laid, he signalled to his companion that it was time to get back to their camp, which they did, taking the same precautions as when they had left it.

No sooner were they back than the Captain awoke his men, took twelve with him, and left eight with Outavari; then, accompanied by a hundred or so Little-Namaquois, whom their chief ordered to follow the white captain, he plunged into the forest, taking a broad circular detour, and finally took up an ambush position with his troop on the outskirts of the forest that rang along the edge of the Kaffirs' camp.

From here he placed several of his sailors at regular distances so that between every two mariners there were ten or twelve Namaquois; then he sent everyone to bed and awaited the opportune moment.

The opportune moment was not long in coming: at daybreak, great cries announced to Captain Pamphile and his troop that the two armies had attacked one another. Soon an impressively loud volley of gunfire could be heard amid the clamour; just then, the whole enemy army turned tail in the greatest disorder, and tried to get back into the forest. This was just what Captain Pamphile had been waiting for: he and his men had only to show themselves for the rout to be complete.

The unhappy Kaffirs, surrounded ahead and behind, and trapped on the one side by the river and on the other by the forest, made no attempt to escape: they fell to their knees, convinced that their last hour had come – and indeed, it is probable that not one would have escaped, given the way the Little-Namaquois were laying into them, had Captain Pamphile not reminded Outavari that this was not the way they had agreed to proceed. The chief interposed his authority, and, instead of striking out with mace and knife, the victors contented themselves with tying up the hands and feet of the vanquished; then, having completed this operation, they picked up not dead men, but living prisoners. The rope binding their feet was loosened sufficiently for them to be able to walk, one way or another, towards the capital of the Little-Namaquois. As for those who had escaped, they were of no further concern, as there were too few of them to cause any more anxiety.

Since this great and definitive victory was due to the intervention of Captain Pamphile, he was granted all the triumphal honours. Women came up to him bearing garlands. Young women strewed rose petals in his path. The elders awarded him the title of *White Lion*, and all of them laid on a great banquet for him; then, after all the celebrations, the Captain thanked the Little-Namaquois for their hospitality, declared that he could spend no more time on his pleasures, and that he now needed to get down to business; and so asked that Outavari hand over his prisoners to him. Outavari recognised the fairness of this request, and led him to a great wooden hall into which they had been crammed on the very same day they arrived. Now, three days had elapsed; some had died of their wounds, others of hunger, yet others of heat – so it was high time, as the reader will clearly see, for Captain Pamphile to think of his merchandise, since it was starting to go rotten.

Captain Pamphile moved through the ranks of the prisoners, accompanied by the doctor, touching the sick men himself, examining wounds, observing as they were dressed, separating the good from the bad as the angel will on the Day of Judgment; then, his inspection concluded, he drew up a list: there were still 230 Negroes in excellent condition.

And there was no gainsaying that these were men who had been tried and tested: they had resisted battle, a long march, and hunger. They could be bought and sold with confidence; there was no wastage to be feared; so the Captain was so pleased with his bargain that he presented Outavari with a large cask of brandy and twelve ells of tobacco in carrots. In exchange for this very civil gift, the chief of the Little-Namaquois lent him eight big boats to take away all his prisoners in, and, himself climbing into the Captain's rowing boat with his family and the greatest men of his kingdom, he asked to accompany the Captain as far as his ship.

The Captain was greeted by the sailors who had remained on board with a joy that gave the chief of the Little-Namaquois a very high idea of the love that the Captain inspired in his subordinates; then, as the Captain was, first and foremost, a man of order, who would not allow any emotion to distract him from his duties, he left the doctor and Two-Mouths to do the honours of the *Roxelane* to his guests, and went down into the hold with his carpenters.

In point of fact, a grave difficulty had arisen here that required nothing less than Captain Pamphile's intelligence to be resolved. On leaving Le Havre, the Captain had been anticipating an exchange of goods; now the objects exchanged naturally replaced one another. But, through an expected combination of circumstances, not only was Captain Pamphile exporting, he was also importing. So he needed to find some means of lodging, in a ship that was already pretty heavily laden, 230 Negroes.

Luckily, they were men: if they had been merchandise too, it would have been physically impossible, but the human machine is such an admirable machine, endowed with such flexible joints; it can stand so easily on its feet or its head, on the right side or the left, on the belly or the back, that you would need to be really rather inept not to take advantage, so Captain Pamphile had soon found a way of getting the best of both worlds. He had his eleven large casks of brandy taken into the lions' den and the sail locker, since he did not want to mix his merchandise up, claiming quite justly that either the Negroes would spoil the brandy or that the brandy would spoil the Negroes; then he measured the length of the hold. It was eighty feet long: more than was necessary. Every man should count himself satisfied when he occupies one square foot on the earth's surface, and, according to Captain Pamphile's calculations, everyone would have an extra line and a half to play with. As you can see, this was real luxury, and the Captain could have packed in another ten men.

Now the master carpenter, following the Captain's orders, proceeded in the following way.

He set up to port and starboard a plank, ten inches high, at an angle with the boat's hull, which could be used as a footrest; this way, and thanks to this means of support, seventy-seven Negroes could very easily be put against each side of the ship, especially since, so as to prevent them from rolling all over each other if the weather turned stormy, which would otherwise inevitably have happened, an iron ring was placed between each of them, to shackle them to their places. Admittedly, the ring occupied some of the room that Captain Pamphile had been counting on, so that instead of having a line and a half too much, each man turned out to have three lines fewer; but what is three lines for a man? Three lines! You'd need to have a perverse mind to quarrel over three lines, especially when you still have 142.

The same operation had been performed for the bottom of the boat: the Negroes, thus arranged in two rows, left a space of twelve feet free. In the middle of this space, Captain Pamphile had a kind of camp bed made up, as wide as the back supports, but, as it would need only seventy-six Negroes to fill it, every man gained a half line and three twelfths. So the master carpenter very judiciously called the bench in the middle the *pashas' bench.*

Since this bench was six feet long, it left on either side an interval of three feet for service and walk-through. This was, as the reader will see, more than was necessary; moreover, the Captain made no bones about the fact that, as the boat would be crossing the tropics twice over, the ebony wood could not fail to swell or shrink a little, which, unfortunately, would make room for the most difficult; but every speculative enterprise has its risks, and a trader who is endowed with some measure of foresight must always anticipate a certain amount of wastage.

Once these measures had been decided on, it was for the master carpenter to realise them; so, when Captain Pamphile had done his philanthropic duty, he went back up on deck to see if his guests were being treated properly.

He found Outavari, his family and the great men of his kingdom tucking into a magnificent feast presided over by the doctor. The Captain took his place at the upper end of the table, certain of being able to rely entirely on the skill of his authorised representative. And indeed, no sooner had the meal been finished and the chief of the Little-Namaquois, his august family and the great men of his kingdom been settled back in their canoe, than the master carpenter came to tell Captain Pamphile that everything in the hold was now ready, and that he could go down to inspect the stowage, whereupon the worthy Captain did precisely that.

He had not been misled: everything had been arranged with the most wonderful exactitude, and every Negro, fixed to the ribs of the ship so tightly that he seemed part of the vessel, looked like a mummy merely awaiting the moment to be placed in his coffin; indeed, a few inches had been saved over those further down, making it possible to circulate round the kind of gigantic grill on which they were stretched, so that the idea passed through Captain Pamphile's mind that he might add to his collection the chief of the Petits-Namaquois, his august family and the great men of his kingdom. Luckily for Outavari, hardly had he been settled in the royal canoe than his subjects, who did not place the same trust in the White Lion as did their king, took advantage of the liberty they had been given to row for all they were worth. So when Captain Pamphile went back on deck with the wicked idea that had come to him down in the hold, the canoe was already disappearing round a corner of the Orange river.

On seeing this, Captain Pamphile sighed: there went fifteen to twenty thousand francs, and it was his own fault he had lost them.

18

How Captain Pamphile, having sold off his cargo of ebony wood at a profit in Martinique, and his alcohol in the Greater Antilles, met up with his old friend Black-Serpent, Cacique of the Mosquitos, and bought himself the title of cacique for half a large cask of brandy.

After two and a half months of an uneventful crossing during which, thanks to the paternal care that the Captain took of his cargo, he lost only thirty-two Negroes, the *Roxelane* entered the port of Martinique.

This was an excellent moment to unload his cargo; thanks to the philanthropic measures agreed on by all civilised governments acting in concert, slave trading, which these days is exposed to the most ridiculous dangers, leaves the colonies short of manpower.

So Captain Pamphile's merchandise was at a real premium when he docked at Saint-Pierre Martinique; only the richest could afford it.

It also has to be admitted that the Captain's cargo comprised nothing but prize specimens. All these men captured on the battlefield were the bravest and sturdiest of their nation; in addition they did not have the stupid faces and the beastly apathy of Negroes from the Congo: their relations with the Cape had almost civilised them; they were now only half savage.

So the Captain sold them for 1,000 piastres a piece, which gave him a total of 990,000 francs; now, in his capacity as Captain, as he had half shares, he alone raked in – once all expenses had been paid – 422,000 francs, which, as the reader will see, was quite a handy sum.

Then an unexpected turn of events gave Captain Pamphile a further way of making a profit from another portion of his load. Instead of fifty large casks of brandy that the firm of Jackson and Company of New York had been expecting from the firm of Ignace-Nicolas Pelonge of Orleans, they had received only thirty-eight. So they had been forced, in spite of the usually reliable way they met their engagements, to break their word as regards certain of their practices. Now Captain Pamphile learned in Saint-Pierre that the Greater Antilles had run completely dry of alcohol and since he still had, if you remember, eleven and three quarter large casks of that liquor for which he had not found any use, he resolved to set sail for Jamaica.

Captain Pamphile had not been misled: the Jamaicans' tongues were hanging out in a most dreadful way for lack of brandy, which they had run out of three months ago, so the worthy Captain's arrival was greeted as a veritable gift of providence. Now since you don't haggle with providence, the Captain sold his large casks off at a rate of twenty francs a bottle, which added to his first dividend of 422,000 francs a new profit of 50,000 pounds, which, when added to the first, gave a total of 472,000 francs; so Captain Pamphile, who, up until then, had never desired anything more than the *aurea mediocritas* of Horace,[89] decided to set sail straight away for Marseilles, where, if he assembled all the funds he had set aside across all the different parts of the globe, he could realise a small fortune of seventy-five to eighty thousand pounds income.

Man proposes, God disposes. No sooner had Captain Pamphile left Kingston Bay than a gust of wind blew him towards the Mosquito Coast, situated at the head of the Gulf of Mexico, between the Bay of Honduras and the Saint John river.

Now as the *Roxelane* had suffered some damage and needed a topgallant mast for the flying jib, the Captain decided to land, although a crowd of natives had come running up onto the shore, and some of them, armed with rifles, appeared ready to put up a fight, so, having cast off the rowing boat, and ordered that a small twelve-pounder carronade be set up on its prow just in case, he went down into it with twenty men and, unalarmed by the hostile demonstrations of the natives, rowed vigorously towards the coast, resolved to procure a topgallant mast and a strut for the flying jib, at whatever price.

The Captain had calculated correctly on counting on this frank and precise demonstration of his will, for as he advanced towards the shore, the natives, who could make out perfectly well with the naked eye the warlike dispositions of the Captain, retreated into the interior of the land, where in the distance it was possible to make out a few paltry huts, the tallest of which was surmounted by a flag that was too far away for its coat of arms to be recognised. As a result, when the Captain landed, the two troops, still separated by the same space, found themselves a thousand paces (more or less) from each other, a distance at which it was difficult to talk to one another except in sign language, and this is indeed just what Captain Pamphile immediately did. For, no sooner had he disembarked than he planted in the ground a stick at the end of which there floated a white towel, which, in every country in the world, means that you are showing a friendly disposition.

This signal was no doubt understood by the Mosquitos, for hardly had they spotted it than the man who appeared to be their chief, and who, in this capacity, was wearing an old uniform, which he was wearing without a shirt or trousers, probably because of the heat, laid his rifle, his tomahawk and his dagger down, and, raising his two hands into the air to indicate that he was weaponless, advanced towards the shore. This demonstration was immediately understood in the clearest terms by the Captain; not wishing to be left behind, he in turn laid his rifle, his sabre and his pistols down on the beach, raised his hands in the air too, and advanced towards the savage with the same confidence as was being shown by the latter.

When he was fifty paces away from the chief of the Mosquitos, Captain Pamphile halted so as to scrutinise him with greater attention; it seemed to him that his face was not unknown to him, and that this was not the first time he had had the honour to gaze on it. For his part, the savage seemed to be having rather similar thoughts, and the Captain seemed to awaken in his memory various vague, old memories; finally, as they couldn't go on staring at each other for ever, they started walking again; then, having come within ten paces of each other, they stopped again, each of them uttering an exclamation of surprise.

'Heng!' said the Mosquito gravely.

'Blimey!' cried the Captain with a laugh.

'Black-Serpent is a great chief!' continued the Huron.

'Pamphile is a great captain!' replied the sailor.

'What brings Captain Pamphile to the lands of Black-Serpent?'

'Two paltry little lengths of willow branch, one to make a topgallant mast with, the other to make a strut for a flying jib.'

'And what will Captain Pamphile give Black-Serpent in exchange?'

'A bottle of brandy.'

'Captain Pamphile is welcome here,' said the Huron after a moment's silence, holding out his hand in sign of agreement.

The Captain took the Huron's hand and shook it so hard he almost crushed it, to convey to him that it was a deal. Black-Serpent endured the torture like a true Indian, with calm eyes and a smile on his lips, and when the sailors on one side and the Mosquitos on the other saw this, they uttered three great and joyous acclamations.

'And when will Captain Pamphile hand over the brandy?' asked the Huron, disengaging his fingers.

'This very instant,' replied the sailor.

'Pamphile is a great captain,' said the Huron with a bow.

'Black-Serpent is a great chief,' replied the sailor, returning his bow.

Then both of them, turning away from each other with the same gravity returned with even tread to their respective troops, to give them an account of what had transpired.

One hour later, Black-Serpent was holding the bottle of brandy.

The same evening, Captain Pamphile spotted two palm trees that were just right for the job.

However, since the master carpenter required a week to put his mast and his jib up, the Captain, reflecting that the understanding between his crew and the naives might be interrupted, ordered a line to be drawn along the shore: the sailors were forbidden to cross this line under any pretext. Black-Serpent, for his part, also fixed certain limits that his people were instructed not to cross; then, in the middle of the space between the two camps, a tent was erected that was to serve as a conference chamber for the two chiefs when their respective affairs required them to speak face to face.

The next day, Black-Serpent walked across to the tent, calumet in his hand.

Captain Pamphile, seeing the peaceable demeanour of the chief of the Mosquitos, also came forward, his pipe in his mouth.

Black-Serpent had swallowed his bottle of brandy, and wanted another one.

Captain Pamphile, without being all that curious, was not at all averse to discovering how it was that, on the isthmus of Panama, now chief of the Mosquitos, was a man whom he had last seen on the Saint Lawrence river, when he had been chief of the Hurons.

Now as they were both prepared to make a few concessions to obtain what they desired, they came up to one another as if they had been two friends delighted to meet up again; then, as proof of their perfect brotherhood, Black-Serpent took Captain Pamphile's pipe, and Captain Pamphile took Black-Serpent's calumet, and they both gravely puffed clouds of smoke into each other's faces; then, after a moment's silence, Black-Serpent said, 'The tobacco of my Paleface brother is very strong.'

Captain Pamphile replied, 'That means that my Redskin brother wishes to refresh his mouth with firewater.'

'Firewater is the milk of the Hurons,' replied the chief with a contemptuous dignity that proved that, in this regard, he felt the full extent of his superiority over Europeans.

'So let my brother drink,' said Captain Pamphile, drawing a flask from his pocket. 'And when the baby's bottle is empty, it can be refilled.'

Black-Serpent took the flask, brought it to his lips, and, in one gulp, drank about a third of it.

The Captain then took it, shook it to measure roughly how much had gone, and, bringing it to his lips, paid it homage in a way that was no whit inferior to that of his fellow drinker. The latter wished to take it back in his turn.

'One moment,' said Captain Pamphile, placing the two-thirds-empty flask between his legs; 'let's have a bit of a chat about what's been happening since we last met.'

'What does my brother wish to know?' asked the chief.

'Your brother wishes to know,' replied Captain Pamphile, 'whether you came here by land or by sea.'

'By sea,' the Huron laconically replied.

'And who brought you here?'

'The chief of the redcoats.'

'Let Black-Serpent's tongue be loosened and let him tell his story to his Paleface brother,' replied Captain Pamphile, handing the flask back to the Huron, who emptied it in one go.

'Is my brother listening?' asked the chief, whose eyes were starting to sparkle.

'He is listening,' replied the Captain, employing in his reply the same laconic brevity that the question had dictated.

'When my brother left me in the middle of the tempest,' said the chief, 'Black-Serpent continued to make his way up the river of great waters, no longer in his boat, which had been smashed, but on foot, following the banks. He walked in this way for another five days, and found himself on the shores of Lake Ontario; then, crossing over to York, he had soon reached Lake Huron, where his wigwam was; but in his absence, great events had been occurring.

'The English, forcing the Redskins back before them, had gradually reached the shores of Lake Superior: Black-Serpent found his village inhabited by Palefaces and his place taken by strangers at the hearth of his ancestors.

'Then he withdrew to the mountains from which the Outalawa springs, and summoned his young warriors; they unburied the tomahawk and came swiftly to him, as numerous as the elks and the deer had been before the Palefaces had appeared at the sources of the Delaware and the Susquehannah. Then the Palefaces were afraid, and in the name of the governor they sent an ambassador to Black-Serpent. They presented him with six rifles, two barrels of powder and fifty barrels of firewater, if he would sell the roof of his fathers and the fields of his ancestors, and, in exchange for this roof and these fields, he would be given the land of the Mosquitos, which had just been surrendered to the Palefaces by the Republic of Guatemala. Black-Serpent resisted for a long time, although he was tempted by these offers, but he had the misfortune to taste the firewater, and from that moment on, all was lost: he agreed to the treaty and the exchange was carried out. Black-Serpent flung a stone behind his back, saying: "May the Manitou fling me far from him, as I am doing with this stone, if ever I set foot in the forests, on the prairies or the mountains that extend from Lake Erie to Hudson Bay, and from Lake Ontario to Lake Superior."

'Thereupon he was taken to Philadelphia, embarked on a vessel and taken to Mosquitos; then Black-Serpent and the young warriors who had accompanied him built the huts that my brother can see from here. When they were finished, the chief of the Palefaces raised the flag of England over the biggest of them, leaving Black-Serpent with a paper written in an unknown language.'

With these words, Black-Serpent sighed and pulled a piece of parchment from his breast and unrolled it in front of Captain Pamphile's eyes; it was the deed of transfer to him, ceding all the lands situated between the Bay of Honduras and the lake of Nicaragua, under the protection of England, and with the title of Cacique of the Mosquitos.

The British Government reserved the right to build one or more forts, in such places as it would please to choose, on the lands of the Cacique.

Of all nations, England is distinguished by its foresight: presuming that one day or another, the isthmus of Panama would be pierced either at Chiapa or at Cartago, it had dreamed in advance of establishing an American Gibraltar between the Atlantic Ocean and the Boreal Ocean.

On reading this deed, a strange idea came into Captain Pamphile's head; he had speculated on everything – tea, indigo, coffee, cod, monkeys, bears, brandy and Kaffirs, but he had never yet bought a kingdom.

But this cost him more than he had initially expected, not because of the sea that bathed the coasts and was well stocked with fish, nor because of the tall coconut trees that provided its shore with shade, nor indeed because of the vast forests that covered the mountain chain that cuts the isthmus in two and separates the Guatemalans from the Mosquitos: no, all that was a matter of indifference to Black-Serpent. What he *was* deeply interested in, however, was the red seal that decorated the lower part of his parchment. Unfortunately, there was no deed without a seal, for this seal was that of the chancellery in London.

The seal cost the Captain 150 bottles of firewater, but, into the bargain, he also obtained the parchment.

19

How the Cacique of the Mosquitos gave his people a constitution so as to facilitate a loan of twelve million.

Some seven years or so after the events that we have just been relating, a fine brig, flying a flag tierced in fess sinople, argent and azure under the royal ensign of England that fluttered proudly above it in sign of suzerainty, gave a twenty-one-gun salute to the fortress at Portsmouth, which returned the compliment with the same number of cannon shades!

It was the *Soliman*, a fine sailing vessel, detailed from the large military fleet of the Cacique of the Mosquitos, bringing to London and Edinburgh the Consuls of His Majesty, who had come, bearing the deed of transfer handed over by the British Government to their master, to seek the official recognition of His Majesty William IV.

Considerable curiosity had been aroused as soon as an unknown flag had been sighted off Portsmouth, but this curiosity increased as soon as it was discovered what important personages it was bringing. Everyone immediately rushed down to the port to see the disembarkation of the two illustrious envoys of the new sovereign whom Great Britain had just placed among its vessels. It seemed to the English, so avid for novelty, that there ought to be something strange about the two consuls, something with a whiff of the savage state from which the beneficent patronage of England was soon to draw them. But on this particular point, the predictions of the onlookers were to prove completely mistaken: the rowboat landed two men, of whom the one, already aged fifty or fifty-five, short, plump and ruddy-cheeked, was the English consul; the other, aged twenty-two to twenty-three, tall and thin, was the consul of Edinburgh; both were wearing a made-up uniform that was a mixture of military costume and civilian dress. Furthermore, their complexion, tanned by the sun, and their strong southern accents, indicated, at first glance and first hearing respectively, sons of the equator.

As soon as they had disembarked, they enquired after the home of the commander of the place, to whom they thereupon paid a visit of an hour or so. Then they returned on board the *Soliman*, still accompanied by the same crowd of people. That evening the boat set sail and a week later the happy event of their arrival in London was related in *The Times, The Standard* and *The Sun*. They had, said these newspapers, produced a great sensation in the capital. This came as no surprise to the Governor of Portsmouth, who had been most surprised – as he said to anyone willing to listen – at the wide general knowledge shown by the two envoys of the Cacique of the Mosquitos, who both spoke a really rather acceptable French, and one of whom – the English consul – had some excellent ideas about trade and even more than a smattering of medical training, while the other, the Edinburgh consul, was particularly distinguished by a very lively wit and a profound understanding of the culinary science of the different peoples of the world that, despite his youth, his parents had sent him off to explore, no doubt foreseeing the lofty responsibilities to which Providence had called him.

The two Mosquito consuls had been just as much of a success with the authorities in London as they had been with the Governor of Portsmouth. The ministers to whom they had introduced themselves had, admittedly, noted in them a complete ignorance of the world's usages, but this absence of fashion, which could hardly in all conscience be demanded of men born under the tenth degree of latitude, was fully redeemed by the varied knowledge they possessed, and which are sometimes unknown to the agents of the most civilised nations.

For example, the Lord Chancellor had come back one evening with a very hoarse voice after a sitting in the lower house where he had been obliged to argue with O'Connell over a new taxation project for Ireland. The London consul, who just happened to be there when he returned, asked Milady for the yoke of an egg, a lemon, a little glass of rum and a few cloves, and prepared with his own hands a drink that was very pleasant to the taste and in frequent use, so he said, in Comayagua for this sort of indisposition, a drink that the Lord Chancellor had swallowed in the fullest confidence, finding himself to be completely cured the following day. Indeed, this episode caused such a stir in the diplomatic world that, ever since, the London consul has always been addressed as *doctor*.

Something else, no less extraordinary, happened to the consul of Edinburgh, Sir Edward Two-Mouths*. One day when people at the Ministry of Education were discussing the different recipes of different nations, Sir Edward Two-Mouths showed such a vast knowledge of the subject, from the Indian curry that was so highly favoured in Calcutta to the bison's-hump pie that was such a favourite in Philadelphia, that he

* In the Mosquitos language, Duas-Boccas.

made the mouths of all those in the honourable assembly water. When the consul saw this, he offered with unparalleled obligingness to arrange for the Minister of Education, before too long, a dinner in which the guests would be served uniquely with dishes that were quite unknown in Europe. The Minister of Education, taken aback by such kindness, refused for a long time to accept such an offer; but Sir Edward Two-Mouths was so frank and energetic in his insistence that His Excellency finally yielded and invited all his colleagues to this culinary solemnity. Indeed, on the day appointed, the consul to Edinburgh, who had ordered the ingredients a good two days in advance, arrived early in the morning and, without any hint of snobbishness or pride, went down into the kitchen, rolled up his shirtsleeves and got down to work among the cooks and the chef's assistants, to whom he issued orders as if he had never done anything else all his life long. Then, half an hour before dinner, he took off the serviette he had tied round his waist, put on his consular uniform and, with all the simplicity of real merit, he entered the salon with the same tranquillity as if he were just got out of his carriage.

It was this dinner that proved a revolution in the English cabinet and was compared to Belshazzar's feast by *Le Constitutionnel*, in a thundering article entitled *Perfidious Albion.*

Thus, Sir Edward Two-Mouths aroused the most intense feelings of regret in the gastronomic club of Piccadilly, when, imperiously summoned by his duty, he was forced to leave London for Edinburgh.

So the doctor remained alone in London.

After a while, he notified the diplomatic corps of the imminent arrival of his august master, His Highness Don Gusman y Pamphilos, which caused a great sensation in the aristocratic world.

Indeed, one morning, a foreign vessel was sighted sailing up the Thames, bearing on its foghorn the Mosquitos flag, and on its mizzenmast the standard of Great Britain; this was the brig the *Mosquitos*, of the same bearing and strength as the *Soliman*, but gleaming with gilt decoration, and that same day it dropped anchor in the Docks. It had brought to London His Highness the Cacique in person.

If there had been a considerable crowd of onlookers to watch the consuls coming ashore, it is easy to understand how many there must have been to see their master disembarking. The whole of London came out into the streets, and the diplomatic corps could hardly make a way through the serried throng to greet the new sovereign.

He was a man of forty-five to forty-eight, in whom everyone immediately recognised the typical Mexican type, with his darting eyes, his sunburnt complexion, his black sideburns, his aquiline nose and his jackal's teeth. He was wearing the uniform of a Mosquito general, adorned simply by the badge of his order; he spoke English tolerably well, but with a very noticeable Provençal accent. This stemmed from the fact that French was the first language he had learned, and he had learned it from a teacher from Marseilles; furthermore, he replied to all compliments gracefully, spoke to each minister and each chargé d'affaires in his own language – for His Highness the Cacique was a polyglot of the highest order.

The following day, His Highness was received by His Majesty William IV.

A week later, the walls of London were plastered with lithographs showing the different uniforms of the armies of land and sea of the Cacique of the Mosquitos, then with landscape depictions of the Bay of Cartago and Cape Gracias a Dios, just where the Golden river flows out into the sea.

Finally came an exact view of the main square in the capital city, with the palace of the Cacique at the far end, the theatre on one side and the stock exchange on the other.

All the soldiers were plump and in the pink of health, and this phenomenon was explained by a note at the foot of the prints indicating the pay earned by each soldier: it was three francs a day for ordinary soldiers, five francs for corporals, eight francs for sergeants, fifteen francs for non-commissioned officers, twenty-five francs for lieutenants and fifty francs for captains. As for the cavalry, it picked up twice this rate of pay, because it was obliged to feed its horses; this magnificence, which would have been considered spendthrift in London and Paris, was perfectly simple in Mosquitos, where gold flowed down the rivers and literally sprouted underground, so that you had only to bend down and pick it up.

As for the landscapes, they were the most sumptuous panoramas one could ever see: Ancient Sicily, which nourished Rome and the whole of

Italy with the overflow of its twelve million inhabitants, was no more than a desert in comparison with the plains of Panamakas, Caribania and Tinto: there were fields of maize, rice, sugar cane and coffee, amid which the paths had hardly been cleared for the farmers to circulate; all this land was naturally productive, without man needing to tend to it in the least. However, the natives did plough it, as it often happened that with their ploughshares they would uncover gold ingots weighing two or three pounds, and diamonds of thirty to thirty-five carats.

Finally, as far as could be judged from the three magnificent palaces that rose over the main square of the Mosquitos, the city was built in a mixed style, which melded together the simplicity of Ancient Greece, the fanciful ornamentation of the Middle Ages and the noble impotence of the modern style; thus the Cacique's palace was based on the model of the Parthenon, the theatre had a façade in the same taste as the cathedral in Milan, and the stock exchange resembled the church of Notre-Dame-de-Lorette. As for the populace, they dressed in magnificent clothes, all resplendent with gold and precious stones. Negro women followed the women with parasols made from the feathers of toucans and hummingbirds, lackeys gave alms in gold coins, and in one corner of the picture there was a poor man who was feeding his dog sausages.

A fortnight after the Cacique's arrival in London, there was only one topic of conversation, from Dublin to Edinburgh: the Mosquito Eldorado. People in the streets would stop and gawp at these magnificent prospects in such numbers that the constable's truncheon proved inadequate to disperse the crowds; when the Cacique saw this, he sought out the Lord Mayor, requesting that he forbid the exhibiting of any print or poster depicting anything to do with his kingdom. The Lord Mayor, who up until now had refrained from doing so merely for fear of offending His Highness Don Gusman y Pamphilos, that very same day ordered that the designated objects be seized from all the shops where prints were sold, but if they were out of sight, they were far from out of mind, and the day after this exemplary seizure (unprecedented in such a free country as Great Britain), over fifty people presented themselves at the consul's, declaring that they were ready to emigrate if the information they had come to obtain lived up to their expectations.

The Consul told them that the impression they might have formed of that fortunate land was as different from the reality as night was from day and stormy weather from fine weather; that, as everyone knows, lithography was a very imperfect means of representing nature, since it had at its disposal nothing but dull, grey tones to render not just all the different colours, but also the innumerable nuances that comprise the charm and harmony of creation. For instance, he went on, the birds that flew across the landscapes and had the inestimable advantage over the birds of Europe that they fed on harmful insects and were unable to smell grain, all seemed, under the lithographer's pencil, house sparrows or larks, while in reality they shone with such fresh and vivid colours that they looked like living rubies and topazes. Furthermore, if his visitors would deign to pass into his study, he would show them these same birds, that they would recognise not from their plumage but from the shape of their beaks and the length of their tails, and that if they were compared to the paltry resemblance that the painter had imagined he had captured, they would be able to judge of the remainder from one single sample.

The worthy folk went into the study, and, as the doctor, a great enthusiast for natural history, had in his various travels gathered together a valuable collection of all those airborne flowers called hummingbirds and waxbills, they emerged feeling perfectly satisfied.

The next day, a bootmaker presented himself at the Consul's and asked whether, in Mosquitos, industry was free. The Consul replied that the government in that country was so paternal that you did not even need to pay for a patent – and this established a competition that benefited both manufacturers and consumers, given that all peoples from the surrounding areas came to replenish their supplies in the capital of the Cacique's territory, where they found everything so much cheaper than in their countries that this difference alone meant their journey had more than paid for itself. The only privileges that needed to be created, since they did not yet exist – and it was in England that he had given the Cacique the idea – were those associated with being made suppliers by royal appointment to the person of His Most Serene Highness and his household. The bootmaker immediately asked whether there was a royal bootmaker in Mosquitos. The Consul replied that many requests had been made, but that none had yet been especially distinguished; furthermore, the Cacique was hoping to put the job out to tender, which would always spare a great deal of commotion, given that this measure would foil every intrigue and eliminate venality, that fundamental vice of European governments. The bootmaker asked how much it would cost to purchase the post of bootmaker to the Crown. The doctor consulted his registers and replied that the post of bootmaker to the Crown could be purchased at 250 pounds sterling. The bootmaker leapt for joy: that was nothing! Then, pulling from his pocket five banknotes that he presented to the Consul, he begged him to consider him forthwith as the sole tenderer, which was only fair now that he had fulfilled the condition required, namely the payment, in cash and in full, of the tender. The Consul found the request so altogether reasonable that he replied simply by filling out a patent that he handed to the petitioner there and then, signed with his hand and bearing the seal of His Highness. The bootmaker emerged from the consulate convinced that his fortune was made, and delighted that he had made such an insignificant sacrifice to ensure it was his.

From then on, there was a queue at the office of the consulate: the bootmaker was followed by a tailor, the tailor by a pharmacist; within a week, every branch of industry, commerce or art had its patented representative. And then came the purchase of ranks and titles: the Cacique appointed colonels and created barons, sold titles of personal nobility and of hereditary nobility. One gentleman, who already had the Golden Spur and the Order of Hohenlohe, even made advances to purchase the Star of the Equator, which he had founded to reward civil merit and military courage, but the Cacique replied that, on this point alone, he would depart from the example given by European governments, and that it would be necessary to earn this cross in order to obtain it. Despite this refusal, which indeed did him the greatest honour in the minds of English radicals, the Cacique had taken in one month the sum of 60,000 pounds sterling.

Around this time, and after a dinner at Court, the Cacique just happened to mention a loan of four millions. The Crown Banker, a Jew who lent money to every sovereign, smiled with pity at this request and replied to the Cacique that there was no point in trying to borrow less than twelve million, since any business proposition under this figure was left to cheats and dodgy brokers. The Cacique replied that this wasn't going to stop him, and as far as he was concerned, he would take twelve million just as easily as four. So the banker told him to call by at his office, where he would find his clerk who was responsible for loans of less than fifty million; he would have received his orders and would be able to treat with this young man; for his part, he only ever dealt with speculations of more than a thousand million.

The next day, the Cacique called by at the banker's office; everything had been prepared as arranged. The loan was at six per cent; Mr Samuel would first issue all the funds, then he would ensure he found tenderers. However, this was on one condition sine qua non. The Cacique started and asked what this condition was. The clerk replied that this condition was that he grant his people a constitution.

The Cacique was utterly taken aback by the request – not that he was in the least reluctant to grant a constitution: he knew the value of such documents and would have granted twelve of them for a thousand *écus*, and *a fortiori* one for twelve million, but he did not know that Mr Samuel was a man to foster the liberty of peoples by double entry: he had even heard him uttering in his half-German half-French patois a political profession of faith that was so out of kilter with the request he had made of him just now that he could not but express his astonishment to the third clerk.

The latter replied to the Cacique that His Highness was not mistaken about his master's political opinions, but in absolute governments, it was the prince who was responsible for state debts, while in constitutional governments it was the state that was responsible for the prince's debts, and, however much Mr Samuel was prepared to trust the word of kings, he had even more confidence in the commitments of peoples.

The Cacique, who was a man of discernment, was forced to admit that what this third clerk had told him was not unreasonable, and that Mr Samuel, whom he had taken for a Turcaret,[90] was, on the contrary, a man of great good sense, and so he promised to bring back, the next day, a constitution just as liberal as those that were in force in Europe. Its main article would be conceived in the following terms:

ON THE LITTLE REPUBLIC

> The debts that, until the day of the summoning of the next parliament, have been contracted by His Highness the Cacique, are declared debts of State, and guaranteed by all the revenues and properties of the State.
>
> A law would be brought before Parliament at the next session to determine the portion of public revenues that would be devoted to paying the interest and the successive redemption of the capital of the current debt.

These were Mr Samuel's own terms.

The Cacique did not change a comma and, the next day, he brought back the entire constitution, as can be seen in the documentary evidence (see appendix); it was signed by his hand and sealed with his seal. The third clerk deemed it to be in order and took it to Mr Samuel. Mr Samuel added at the bottom *good for printing*, tore a leaf from his pocketbook, wrote under it 'Good for twelve million payable at the end of the present month' and signed it *Samuel*.

A week later, the constitution of the Mosquitos nation had appeared in all the English newspapers and was reproduced in all the European papers; it was on this occasion that *Le Constitutionnel* published that remarkable article that everyone still remembers, entitled: *Noble England*.

It will be easy to understand that such largesse, on the part of a prince from whom it had not been asked, doubled the trust that was placed in him and tripled the number of emigrants. The number rose to 16,639, and the Consul was just signing the 16,639th passport when, handing the aforementioned paper to the 16,639th emigrant, the Consul asked him what money he and his companions were taking with them. The emigrant replied that they were taking banknotes and guineas. To which the Consul replied that he felt it was his duty to inform the emigrant that the banknotes lost six per cent of their value in the Mosquitos bank, and gold lost two *schellings* per guinea, and this loss was something that could easily be understood, because of the distance between the two countries and the rarity of relations between them, as all trade generally was carried out with Cuba, Haiti, Jamaica, North America and South America.

The emigrant, who was a sensible man, understood this reason perfectly well, but, taken aback at the deficit that the exchange rate would necessarily make in his small fortune as soon as he reached his destination, he asked His Excellence the Consul whether, as a special favour, he might give him Mosquitos silver and gold in exchange for his guineas and his banknotes. The Consul replied that he kept his silver and gold since, being pure of any alloy, they gained in value over English silver and gold, but that he could give him, at a commission of just half a per cent, banknotes of the Cacique that, once he had reached Mosquitos, would be exchanged freely against the silver and gold of the country. The emigrant asked if he could kiss the Consul's feet, but the latter replied, with a truly republican dignity, that all men were equal, and gave him his hand to kiss.

From this day, the exchange facility was made available.

It lasted a week.

Within a week, the exchange had produced 80,000 pounds sterling, discount not included.

At around the same time, Sir Edward Two-Mouths, Consul at Edinburgh, informed his colleague in London that he had taken, by means more or less similar to those that had been used in the capital of the three kingdoms, a sum of 50,000 pounds sterling. The doctor at first thought this was not very much, but he reflected that Scotland was a poor country that could not produce as much wealth as England.

For his part, His Highness the Cacique Don Gusman y Pamphilos received, at the end of the current month, the banker Samuel's twelve million.

CONCLUSION

The emigrants departed on eight ships chartered in common and, after three months' navigation, came within sight of the coast that you know of, and dropped anchor in the Bay of Cartago.

The only city they found there were the huts we have described, and the only populace were the people of Black-Serpent; they led them to their chief, who asked them if they had brought firewater with them.

Some of these unfortunates, having left no resources behind in England, decided to stay in Mosquitos; the others resolved to return to England. On the way home, half of this half died of starvation and wretchedness.

The quarter who returned to London had no sooner set foot on land than they rushed to the palace of the Cacique and the residence of the Consul. The Cacique and the Consul had disappeared a week previously, and nobody had any idea what had happened to them.

For our part, we believe that the Cacique is living incognito in Paris, and we have reasons to believe that he is not altogether uninvolved in many of the industrial enterprises that have been set up there recently.

If we learn anything more definite, we will not hesitate to inform our readers.

As we were just going to press, we read in the *Gazette médicale*:

> Up until now, the phenomenon of spontaneous combustion has been observed only in humans; a similar case has just for the first time been reported by Dr Thierry in an animal belonging to the simian species. For five or six years, this creature, after the painful loss of one of his friends, had contracted the habit of indulging in a daily intemperance as regards wine and strong liquor; on the very day of the accident, he had drunk three little glasses of rum and had retired, as was his wont, to a corner of the apartment, when all at once, from his direction was heard a crackling noise similar to that of sparks rising from a hearth. The woman who was cleaning the room quickly turned to the source of the noise, and saw the animal enveloped in a bluish flame similar to that of spirit of wine, without making the slightest movement to escape from the fire. The stupefaction into which this spectacle plunged her deprived her of the strength to go to the animal's help, and it was only when the fire was extinguished that she dared to approach the spot where it had broken out, but by then it was too late: the animal was completely dead.

The monkey on which this strange phenomenon was seen belonged to our celebrated painter, M. Tony Johannot.

(Editor's note)

DOCUMENTARY EVIDENCE

THE CONSTITUTION OF THE NATION OF MOSQUITOS IN CENTRAL AMERICA

Don Gusman y Pamphilos, by the Grace of God Cacique of the Mosquitos, etc.

The heroic people of this land, having at all times preserved its independence by its courage and its sacrifices, enjoyed it peaceably during an era when all other parts of America were still groaning under the yoke of the Spanish Government. In the great and memorable period of the emancipation of the new hemisphere, the peoples of this vast region had not been subjugated by any European people; Spain had exercised no real authority over them, and had been forced to limit itself to chimerical claims against which the bravery and constancy of the natives had unceasingly protested. The nation of the Mosquitos had preserved intact this primitive liberty that it held from its Creator.

With the aim of consolidating its existence, to defend its freedom, the first of all the benefits of a people, and to guide its progress towards the happiness of the whole society, this land has chosen us to govern it; already, in this immortal struggle for American freedom, we had shown the peoples of this continent that we were not unworthy to contribute to the enfranchisement of this noble half of the human species.

Profoundly aware of the duties that Providence was imposing on us by calling us, through the choice of a free people, to govern this fair land, we thought it best to postpone until this day the creation of the institutions that are to bring about its happiness more quickly; we deemed it necessary to determine beforehand the needs of the nation to which these institutions were to be applied.

This time has now come. We are happy to be in a position to acquit ourselves of this duty, at a time when victory has just consecrated forever the destinies of this continent, and, after fifteen years, to bring to an end a struggle in which we were among the first to brandish the standard of independence and seal with our blood the imprescriptible rights of the American peoples. Thereto we have decreed and ordered, and do decree and order as follows:

In the name of almighty and merciful God:

ARTICLE ONE

All the parts of this country, whatever their names at present, will in future form but a single State that will forever be indivisible, to be known as the State of Poyais.

The different titles under which we have hitherto exercised our authority will in the future be merged and united as that of Cacique of Poyais.

ARTICLE TWO

All the present inhabitants of the country, and all those who in future will be granted letters of naturalisation, will comprise but one nature, under the name of Poyaisians, irrespective of origin, birth and colour.

ARTICLE THREE

All Poyaisians are free in duties and rights.

ARTICLE FOUR

The State of Poyais will be divided into twelve provinces, viz.:

The island of Boatan,
The island of Guanaja,
The province of Caribania,
The province of Romania,
The province of Tinto,
The province of Cartago,
The province of Neustria,
The province of Panamakas,
The province of Towkas,
The province of Cackeras,
The province of Wolwas,
The province of Ramas.

DIVISION

Every province is divided into districts, and every district into parishes; the limits of every province are determined by law.

In each province, there is a steward appointed by the Cacique.

The steward will be responsible for the particular administration of the province; he will be assisted by a council of notables, chosen and organised by a law.

In each district there is a deputy steward, and in each parish a mayor.

The appointment of deputy stewards and mayors, and their functions, will be determined by a law.

THE CACIQUE

The Cacique is the commander-in-chief of all the forces of land and sea.

He is responsible for raising these forces, arming them, and organising them, in accordance with what will be determined by the law.

He appoints to all civilian and military posts that the constitution has not reserved to the people to appoint.

He is the general administrator of all the revenues of State, in conformity with the laws on their nature, their tax base, their collection, and their accounting.

He is responsible in particular for the maintenance of domestic order, he makes peace treaties and declares war. However, treaties are subject to approval by the Senate.

He sends and receives ambassadors and every sort of diplomatic agents.

He alone has the right to propose laws to parliament and to approve them or reject them, after the sanction of parliament.

The laws are enforceable only after his sanction and promulgation.

He can make regulations for the enforcement of the laws.

All lands that do not belong to individuals are declared to be domains of the Cacique.

Their revenue and the product of their sale are set apart for the upkeep of His Highness the Cacique, his family and his civilian and military household.

The Cacique can, in consequence, dispose of the said domains in any way that he sees fit.

On his accession, the Cacique swears an oath to the constitution, as witnessed by parliament.

The Cacique delivers to foreigners his letters of naturalisation.

The Cacique has the right to dispense mercy.

The person of the Cacique is inviolable; his ministers hold sole responsibility.

In case of ill health, or in the case of absence, for any serious reason, the Cacique can choose one or more commissioners who will govern in his name.

Our eldest son, the issue of our marriage with Doña Josepha-Antonia-Andre de Xerès de Aristequicta y Lobera, born in Caracas, in the Republic of Colombia, is declared heir presumptive to the dignity of Cacique of the Mosquitos.

In one of the forthcoming sessions of parliament, a law will be put forward to provide for the case of the Cacique's minority.

PARLIAMENT

Parliament exercises the legislative power, concurrently with the Cacique.

No money can be borrowed in future, and no tax either direct or indirect can be raised unless it has been decreed by parliament.

At the opening of each session, the members of the two chambers of parliament swear an oath of fidelity to the Cacique and the constitution.

Parliament determines the value, the weight, the type and the title of coinage; it fixes weights and measures.

Each chamber of parliament makes regulations for the order of its work, and polices its sessions.

Each of the two chambers of parliament can request the Cacique to present a bill on a certain determinate object.

Parliament is comprised of two chambers: the Senate and the CHAMBER OF REPRESENTATIVES.

THE SENATE

The Senate is composed of fifty senators.

Four years after the promulgation of the present constitution, this number may be increased by law.

The fifty senators who are to compose the senate will be appointed by the Cacique, for the first time exclusively.

Senators are appointed for life.

In future, when a place in the Senate becomes vacant, the Senate will appoint to the vacant place one of the three candidates put forward by the Cacique.

To be a senator, it will be a requirement that one be at least thirty-one, have resided in the country for at least three years, and be a landowner possessing land 3,000 acres in extent.

The Senate is chaired by the chancellor.

The bishop or bishops of Poyais will be ex officio members of the Senate.

The sessions of the Senate are public.

CHAMBER OF REPRESENTATIVES

The Chamber of Representatives will comprise sixty deputies (five per province), until some later law has increased its number.

In order to be a representative of the people of Poyais, one must be twenty-five and be a landowner possessing land 1,000 acres in extent.

The Chamber of Representatives verifies the powers of its members.

Each province will appoint five deputies to form the first session of the chamber.

In the next session of parliament, a law shall be put forward to divide the said number of sixty deputies between the different provinces, in accordance with their population.

Further, in the same next session, the parliament will be able to grant the right of having a special representation to those of the towns of our State that it believes, by reason of their size, should be elevated to the title of cities.

For the election of the deputies of districts, all the inhabitants, born or naturalised citizens of this State, who will pay a direct contribution of whatever kind, and who, having reached the age of twenty-one, will be neither servants, nor slaves, nor subject to a prohibition on residence, nor bankrupt, nor ex-convicts, will assemble in the principal town of the district, at a date that will be indicated by our letters patent, and will appoint deputies from the persons having the qualities necessary thereto.

Deputies are appointed for four years, and the chamber is renewed entirely.

The Cacique appoints the president of the chamber of deputies from a list of three candidates presented to him by this chamber.

Electoral assemblies are chaired by one of their members, chosen from among them by the Cacique.

Laws on customs and other taxes direct or indirect cannot be brought forward except it be in the Chamber of Representatives, and only with its approval can they be sent to the Senate.

The Cacique will determine by decree the opening and closing of the session of parliament, which must be summoned at least once a year.

The Cacique can dissolve the Chamber of Representatives provided that he summon another one within three months.

The Chamber of Representatives has the right to accuse ministers before the Senate for misappropriation of public funds, malpractice, misdemeanours or usurpation of powers.

The sessions of the Chamber of Representatives are public.

RELIGION

The Catholic, Apostolic and Roman religion is the religion of State.

Its ministers are endowed, and the territory in which they are to exercise their ministry is determined by law.

All religions are protected by the State.

Differences of belief cannot serve as a reason or a pretext for admission or exclusion from any public office or post.

Persons professing a religion other than the Catholic religion who desire to erect a temple for their use will be required to make a declaration of intent to the civil authority, at the same time assigning a fund for the upkeep of the minister who is to be appointed for the service of this temple.

THE PUBLIC DEBT

The debts which, until the next summoning of parliament, have been contracted by His Highness the Cacique, are declared debts of State and guaranteed by all the revenues and all the properties of the State.

A law will be introduced at the next session of parliament to determine the portion of public revenue that will be devoted to the service of the interests and the successive redemption of the capital of the current debt.

JUDICIAL POWER

Judges are appointed by the Cacique, from three candidates who will be put forward by the Senate.

There will be six judges of State who will travel round the provinces in succession to hold assizes in which civil and criminal justice will be administered.

A later law will organise the application of the jury in criminal affairs.

In each district a justice of peace will be established responsible for settling trials and, in case they cannot be settled, to place trials under the jurisdiction of the State judge, during the assizes.

Appeals against judgments made by the assizes of each province will be judged by the Senate.

Appeals against the decrees of the supreme court will be brought before parliament.

No inhabitant can be arrested other than on the orders of a judge, carrying implicitly the mention of the reason, which can only be the accusation of a crime or misdemeanour recognised by the law.

No jailor can, on pain of being charged with arbitrary detention, receive or detain a prisoner without a warrant for his arrest, in the above form.

As soon as possible, a code of civil laws and a code of criminal laws will be drawn up, uniform for the whole country.

The present constitution will be submitted to the acceptance of parliament, which is summoned to this effect on the 1st September next.

In London, the 20th March of the year of grace 1837, and the first of our reign.

Signed: DON GUSMAN Y PAMPHILOS.

LETTER FROM M. ALPHONSE KARR[91]

My dear Alexandre,

Allow me to address an objection to you.

There are in France thirty-two million inhabitants; if each of them occupies the attention of the public for an equal time, i.e. if fame is equitably shared out among them, they will each have one and a third minutes in their whole lives (which I suppose to be eighty years long) in which to be the object of this precious attention.

This is the reason for which people grasp at everything that makes some noise in the world, and wish to be in the public eye, so that many people are somewhat envious of the criminal under the guillotine and console themselves only by saying I knew him very well or I went down the same road the day after the murder.

I know of nothing more amusing than those books so full of humour and malicious naivety that you publish sometimes when you are not writing fine dramas or witty comedies.

Here is one that will absorb everyone's attention for a fortnight, here where a revolution can be carried out in three days; so, according to the calculations I was making just now, you will be taking up the portion of fame of some 13,000 people, 13,000 people who will never be spoken of.

I have a right to be in your book, and I am using my right: James II belonged to me before he belonged to Tony Johannot. Our fine and witty Tony could tell you how, one day, he showed me a monkey and how this monkey leapt up at me, took me by the head and kissed me on both cheeks in the most moving way.

James II had lived with me for a year when I lost him; I feared at every moment that I would meet him on the boulevards dressed as a troubadour from the comic opera, now a scholar and indulging in the ignominious profession of a street clown. I was really pleased to meet him at Tony's, since he is much too witty to give any of his wit away to animals.

So, my dear Alexandre, I request and require you, as the newspapers say, to include the present objection with your documents.

Yours ever,

– ALPHONSE KARR.

NOTES

1. Chevet and Beauvais was a delicatessen that supplied the monarchy: the fine foods on display were a magnet for window-shoppers.
2. Linnaeus' classification of plants and animals is still the basis for taxonomy; the abbé Ray, a contemporary of Dumas's, was a naturalist who had modified the Linnaean system.
3. The National Guard was founded as a civil militia in 1789 to maintain order in Paris.
4. A fourth-century BC marble sculpture, rediscovered in the late fifteenth century. Marcantonio Raimondi's 1530s engraving transmitted the famous pose throughout Europe.
5. Count Georges Louis Leclerc de Buffon (1707–88) was one of the most influential naturalists of the Enlightenment, and anticipated some aspects of the theory of evolution.
6. Alexandre Gabriel Decamps (1803–60) was a painter friend of Dumas (who gives Decamps's correct 1830 address). Mlle Camargo is named after Marie Anne de Cupis de Camargo (1710–70), a celebrated opera singer.
7. Decamps's *Chiens Savants* was exhibited in the Salon of 1831.
8. The French poet La Fontaine (1621–95) produced the best-known French version of the tale of the tortoise and the hare in his *Fables*.
9. Virgilio Malaguti, an Italian printer, joined forces with a fellow Italian, Gaetano Ratta, to attack and rob the money-changer M. Joseph, leaving him for dead (he did eventually die); they were executed in 1826.
10. Louis Godefroy Jadin (1805–82), landscape painter who travelled with Dumas in France and Italy.
11. 'Mother of God, pray for us' (Latin).
12. A sabre with a curving blade, commonly used in Turkey in this period.
13. Louis Gabriel Eugène Isabey (1803–86) was a painter in the French Royal Navy, entrusted with depicting on canvas the French capture of Algiers in 1830. Joseph Vantini, known as Yousouf (or, here, Youssef: 1805–66), entered the French Army in Algiers in 1830. Fort-l'Empereur was a fortress three kilometres from Algiers; it was blown up by the Turks in 1830.
14. A type of seagull.
15. The 'grumblers' (*grognards*) were soldiers of Napoleon's Old Guard; the *brûle-gueule* (literally 'burn-gob') was a short pipe favoured by the *grognards*.
16. Alphonse de Lamartine (1790–1869), Romantic poet and politician.
17. Pierre Joseph Fau (1808–83), painter, pupil of Decamps.
18. Alexandre Decamps (*c*.1800–*c*.84) was the brother of the artist Alexandre Gabriel Decamps whom we have already met, and himself a critic.
19. Cephalus has a vision of his dog and its prey as turned to stone in Ovid's *Metamorphoses* VII, lines 790–1.
20. Alexandre Thierry (1803–58) was a doctor of liberal political opinions, and another friend of Dumas.
21. Corcelet's was another celebrated supplier of delicatessen in the Palais-Royal area of Paris.

22. Johann Gottlob Schneider and August Johann Roësel were eighteenth-century German naturalists.
23. Camille Flers (1802–68), landscape painter and representative of realist tendencies.
24. 'Munition bread' is the official name for hard tack or ship's biscuit.
25. 'I have spoken' (Latin).
26. Fénelon was the tutor of Louis de France, Duke of Burgundy and known as the Grand Dauphin as he was the heir apparent of his father Louis XIV, whom he predeceased in 1711; Catherine de Médicis turned a blind eye when her son, Henri III, surrounded himself with male favourites.
27. These examples of a self-indulgent and epicurean lifestyle are all taken from Greek and Roman antiquity, apart from Grimod de la Reynière (1758–1837), a renowned gastronome.
28. Antoinette Lalanne, Mme Saqui (1786–1866), a famous tightrope dancer.
29. A play full of effusive rhetoric, translated from a work by the German playwright Kotzebue and popular during the French Revolution.
30. 'Cush was the father of Nimrod, who grew to be a mighty warrior on the earth. He was a mighty hunter before the LORD; that is why it is said, "Like Nimrod, a mighty hunter before the LORD"' – Genesis 10: 8, 9
31. The Captain is from Marseilles, and Dumas occasionally gives him a strong Provençal accent, usually with overtones of exclamatory bravado. But since, most of the time, Pamphile speaks standard French, I have simply allowed him to drop into a somewhat nautical idiom.
32. An episode from the Apocrypha: see Tobit 6:5.
33. The bezoar (from the Persian *badzahar*, poison stone) is a stony concretion that forms in the stomach of certain animals: it was thought to neutralise poisons. Prince Camaralzaman is a character in the *Thousand and One Nights*.
34. Tigers are, of course, highly unusual – to say the least – in Africa.
35. Various legends linked Hercules to the south of France; strangling the Nemean lion was the first of his labours, and he wore its skin – which no arrow could pierce – thereafter.
36. Jean-Baptiste Gaspard Deburau (1796–1846) was the famous Pierrot of the Funambules Theatre. His meal was stolen by Harlequin in a *commedia dell'arte* routine.
37. The Minister of the Interior had, in 1806, been empowered to force every theatre to specialise in one genre: the Funambules was supposed to restrict itself to pantomime.
38. The former compiled – at some remove – biographies of the most famous philosophers of antiquity; Voltaire is celebrated for his mockery of the abstractions of philosophy, as in *Candide*, which makes particular fun of the language of causality adopted by Leibniz and his epigones.
39. A grotesque figure, small and fat, usually in porcelain, from the Far East.
40. These sons of the priestess of Hera in Argos showed their devotion to their mother by dragging her chariot to the temple themselves, when the two white bulls who were supposed to do so failed to turn up.
41. Villenave was a celebrated cutler and Désirabode was the King's dentist.
42. Pamphile actually says 'Son of the Sun'.

43. i.e. the usual ballast of heavy pieces of stone or iron.
44. See Numbers 13:23.
45. A nickname formed by metathesis.
46. The language of Occitanie, i.e. southern France.
47. 'Body of crime' (Latin).
48. 'To the city and the world' (Latin) – the blessing given from St Peter's balcony by the Pope.
49. The motto chosen by Jean-Jacques Rousseau: 'to risk [one's] life for the truth' (Latin), taken from Juvenal, *Satires* 4:91.
50. Saint Martha is supposed to have overcome the Tarasque, a dragon that was going around ravaging the area near Tarascon, in southern France, by sprinkling him with holy water and then leading him to Arles by the sash she had tied round his neck.
51. Enceladus was a giant with a hundred arms: together with other giants he rebelled against Zeus but was blasted by a thunderbolt and crushed under the weight of the whole island of Sicily.
52. The municipal guards were responsible for keeping order in Paris.
53. A generally conservative newspaper.
54. Joseph Exaudet (1710–62) was a violinist who composed, among other things, a celebrated minuet.
55. The Café Procope – still in existence in the Faubourg Saint-Germain of Paris – was a celebrated meeting place for the intelligentsia in the eighteenth century.
56. This was part of the traditional 'uniform' of the harlequin.
57. The artist Lysippus is supposed to have preserved the way Alexander the Great leaned his head slightly to the left.
58. A one-act comedy by Scribe and Xavier, performed for the first time in 1820. Jacques Charles Odry (1781–1853) was a celebrated comic actor.
59. Charles Edmé Vernet was another celebrated actor of the time who specialised in the roles of peasants, soldiers and fools.
60. A character in *The Bear and the Pasha*.
61. Like Harlequin, Colombine was a character in the *commedia dell'arte*.
62. The name of the pasha in *The Bear and the Pasha*.
63. Martin was a celebrated bear in the Jardin des Plantes.
64. In Virgil's *Eclogues*, the two shepherds take it in turn to sing.
65. Latona gave birth to Apollo and Artemis on a floating island known as Ortygia, which was then attached to the sea floor by four pillars and took the name of Delos.
66. These were the pleasure gardens of the Temple district in Paris, and masqueraders would process down from them on Ash Wednesday.
67. Not least because the Montmorency Falls, at 76m, are higher than Niagara.
68. These are both families of sedges.
69. A kind of rattlesnake.
70. The principal thoroughfare in Marseilles.
71. Andrew Jackson was elected President in 1828 and again in 1832.

72. Lucia Elizabeth Vestris (1797–1856) was a celebrated dancer and singing comedienne.
73. According to the Greek legend of Gyges, this would have made the ring's possessor invisible.
74. Even by Dumas's day, the phlogiston theory of combustion was obsolete.
75. Nicolas Toussaint Charlet (1792–1845) was a devotee of Napoleon whose big sideburns were widely celebrated.
76. A climactic moment in *La Maréchale d'Ancre,* a play by Alfred de Vigny (1797–1863).
77. Matthieu Laensberg (or Lansberg) was the supposed author of an almanac called the *Almanach de Liège*, which dated back to 1636 and was similar to *Old Moore's Almanac.*
78. i.e. Johannot. The novel mentioned was by Charles Nodier (1780–1844).
79. Before becoming Roman Emperor, Julian was made Governor of Gaul (*c.*354 AD).
80. Dominique François Jean Arago (1786–1853) was director of the Paris Observatory.
81. This seems to be an invented painting.
82. Ann Radcliffe (1764–1823), the British author of 'Gothic' novels.
83. In Chénier's play *Tibère.*
84. During the night of 4th August 1789, the Duke de Montmorency proposed the abolition of the nobility of France. Marie-Joseph-Paul-Roch-Yves-Gilbert du Motier, Marquis de La Fayette, was a French statesman who played an important part in the American and French Revolutions.
85. These were both chroniclers of the age of Joan of Arc.
86. The Montyon Prize was awarded to a poor but virtuous citizen; the honours lists awards were made every year in honour of rebels killed in the 1830 Revolution.
87. The first was a Parisian confectioner, the second a distiller.
88. There is a chapel dedicated to Our Lady in Guérande, near Nantes.
89. Latin: the golden mean prized by the poet Horace.
90. This character, from a play by Lesage (French writer, 1668–1747) first performed in 1709, became a byword for venality and corruption.
91. Karr was a novelist and satirical journalist, and friend of Dumas.

BIOGRAPHICAL NOTE

Alexandre Dumas was born in Villes-Cotterêts, France, in 1802. His father, a general in Napoleon's army, died when Dumas was only four years old, leaving the family impoverished.

In 1823 Dumas moved to Paris in order to find work. He was given a position with the Duc d'Orléans (later King Louis-Philippe), and supplemented his income by working in the theatre and in publishing. He began writing plays, eventually finding success with a production of his play *Henri III et sa Cour* [*Henry III and his Court*] in 1829. This he followed up with *La Tour de Nesle* [*The Tower of Nesle*] (1832), which is considered one of the great masterpieces of French melodrama. Alongside his plays, Dumas also penned novels and short stories; his output was prodigious and he produced some two hundred and fifty works. His historical novels were then, as now, his most popular creations, and he is recognised as playing an important role in the development of the genre. Among his most famous historical novels are *Les trois mousquetaires* [*The Three Musketeers*] (1844) and *Le Comte de Monte-Cristo* [*The Count of Monte Cristo*] (1844–5).

Dumas took considerable interest in the politics of his day, and was involved in the revolution of July 1830. In 1858 he travelled to Russia, and then, in 1860, to Italy, where he supported Garibaldi and the Italian Risorgimento. He lived an extravagant lifestyle, showering money on mistresses and friends, and soon found himself in considerable debt. He had married in 1840 – having previously fathered an illegitimate son, Alexandre Dumas *fils*, in 1824 – but he whittled away his wife's dowry so rapidly that the marriage proved short lived.

Dumas died from a stroke in December 1870. His son went on to become an author in his own right, but he refrained from his father's lifestyle of excess.

Andrew Brown studied at the University of Cambridge, where he taught French for many years. He now works as a freelance teacher and translator. He is the author of *Roland Barthes: The Figures of Writing* (OUP, 1993), and his translations include *Memoirs of a Madman* by Gustave Flaubert, *For a Night of Love* by Emile Zola, *The Jinx* by

Théophile Gautier, *Mademoiselle de Scudéri* by E.T.A. Hoffmann, *Theseus* by André Gide, *Incest* by Marquis de Sade, *The Ghost-seer* by Friedrich von Schiller, *Colonel Chabert* by Honoré de Balzac, *Memoirs of an Egotist* by Stendhal, *Butterball* by Guy de Maupassant and *With the Flow* by Joris-Karl Huysmans, all published by Hesperus Press.

SELECTED TITLES FROM HESPERUS PRESS

Author	*Title*	*Foreword writer*
Pedro Antonio de Alarcón	*The Three-Cornered Hat*	
Louisa May Alcott	*Behind a Mask*	Doris Lessing
Dante Alighieri	*New Life*	Louis de Bernières
Dante Alighieri	*The Divine Comedy: Inferno*	Ian Thomson
Edmondo de Amicis	*Constantinople*	Umberto Eco
Gabriele D'Annunzio	*The Book of the Virgins*	Tim Parks
Pietro Aretino	*The School of Whoredom*	Paul Bailey
Pietro Aretino	*The Secret Life of Nuns*	
Pietro Aretino	*The Secret Life of Wives*	Paul Bailey
Jane Austen	*Lady Susan*	
Jane Austen	*Lesley Castle*	Zoë Heller
Jane Austen	*Love and Friendship*	Fay Weldon
Honoré de Balzac	*Colonel Chabert*	A.N. Wilson
Charles Baudelaire	*On Wine and Hashish*	Margaret Drabble
Aphra Behn	*The Lover's Watch*	
Giovanni Boccaccio	*Life of Dante*	A.N. Wilson
Charlotte Brontë	*The Foundling*	
Charlotte Brontë	*The Green Dwarf*	Libby Purves
Charlotte Brontë	*The Secret*	Salley Vickers
Charlotte Brontë	*The Spell*	Nicola Barker
Emily Brontë	*Poems of Solitude*	Helen Dunmore
Giacomo Casanova	*The Duel*	Tim Parks
Miguel de Cervantes	*The Dialogue of the Dogs*	Ben Okri
Geoffrey Chaucer	*The Parliament of Birds*	
Anton Chekhov	*The Story of a Nobody*	Louis de Bernières
Anton Chekhov	*Three Years*	William Fiennes
Wilkie Collins	*The Frozen Deep*	
Wilkie Collins	*A Rogue's Life*	Peter Ackroyd
Wilkie Collins	*Who Killed Zebedee?*	Martin Jarvis

William Congreve	*Incognita*	Peter Ackroyd
Joseph Conrad	*Heart of Darkness*	A.N. Wilson
Joseph Conrad	*The Return*	Colm Tóibín
James Fenimore Cooper	*Autobiography of a Pocket Handkerchief*	Ruth Scurr
Daniel Defoe	*The King of Pirates*	Peter Ackroyd
Charles Dickens	*The Haunted House*	Peter Ackroyd
Charles Dickens	*A House to Let*	
Charles Dickens	*Mrs Lirriper*	Philip Hensher
Charles Dickens	*Mugby Junction*	Robert Macfarlane
Charles Dickens	*The Wreck of the Golden Mary*	Simon Callow
Emily Dickinson	*The Single Hound*	Andrew Motion
Fyodor Dostoevsky	*The Double*	Jeremy Dyson
Fyodor Dostoevsky	*The Gambler*	Jonathan Franzen
Fyodor Dostoevsky	*Notes from the Underground*	Will Self
Fyodor Dostoevsky	*Poor People*	Charlotte Hobson
Arthur Conan Doyle	*The Mystery of Cloomber*	
Arthur Conan Doyle	*The Tragedy of the Korosko*	Tony Robinson
Alexandre Dumas	*One Thousand and One Ghosts*	
Joseph von Eichendorff	*Life of a Good-for-nothing*	
George Eliot	*Amos Barton*	Matthew Sweet
George Eliot	*Mr Gilfil's Love Story*	
J. Meade Falkner	*The Lost Stradivarius*	Tom Paulin
Henry Fielding	*Jonathan Wild the Great*	Peter Ackroyd
Gustave Flaubert	*Memoirs of a Madman*	Germaine Greer
Gustave Flaubert	*November*	Nadine Gordimer
E.M. Forster	*Arctic Summer*	Anita Desai
Ugo Foscolo	*Last Letters of Jacopo Ortis*	Valerio Massimo Manfredi
Giuseppe Garibaldi	*My Life*	Tim Parks

Elizabeth Gaskell	*Lois the Witch*	Jenny Uglow
Theophile Gautier	*The Jinx*	Gilbert Adair
André Gide	*Theseus*	
Johann Wolfgang von Goethe	*The Man of Fifty*	A.S. Byatt
Nikolai Gogol	*The Squabble*	Patrick McCabe
Thomas Hardy	*Fellow-Townsmen*	Emma Tennant
L.P. Hartley	*Simonetta Perkins*	Margaret Drabble
Nathaniel Hawthorne	*Rappaccini's Daughter*	Simon Schama
E.T.A. Hoffmann	*Mademoiselle de Scudéri*	Gilbert Adair
Victor Hugo	*The Last Day of a Condemned Man*	Libby Purves
Joris-Karl Huysmans	*With the Flow*	Simon Callow
Henry James	*In the Cage*	Libby Purves
John Keats	*Fugitive Poems*	Andrew Motion
D.H. Lawrence	*Daughters of the Vicar*	Anita Desai
D.H. Lawrence	*The Fox*	Doris Lessing
Giacomo Leopardi	*Thoughts*	Edoardo Albinati
Mikhail Lermontov	*A Hero of Our Time*	Doris Lessing
Nikolai Leskov	*Lady Macbeth of Mtsensk*	Gilbert Adair
Jack London	*Before Adam*	
Niccolò Machiavelli	*Life of Castruccio Castracani*	Richard Overy
Xavier de Maistre	*A Journey Around my Room*	Alain de Botton
Edgar Lee Masters	*Spoon River Anthology*	Shena Mackay
Guy de Maupassant	*Butterball*	Germaine Greer
Lorenzino de' Medici	*Apology for a Murder*	Tim Parks
Herman Melville	*The Enchanted Isles*	Margaret Drabble
Prosper Mérimée	*Carmen*	Philip Pullman
Sir Thomas More	*The History of Richard III*	Sister Wendy Beckett
Sándor Petofi	*John the Valiant*	George Szirtes
Francis Petrarch	*My Secret Book*	Germaine Greer
Edgar Allan Poe	*Eureka*	Sir Patrick Moore

Alexander Pope	*Scriblerus*	Peter Ackroyd
Alexander Pope	*The Rape of the Lock and A Key to the Lock*	Peter Ackroyd
Antoine François Prévost	*Manon Lescaut*	Germaine Greer
Marcel Proust	*Pleasures and Days*	A.N. Wilson
Alexander Pushkin	*Dubrovsky*	Patrick Neate
Alexander Pushkin	*Ruslan and Lyudmila*	Colm Tóibín
François Rabelais	*Gargantua*	Paul Bailey
François Rabelais	*Pantagruel*	Paul Bailey
Christina Rossetti	*Commonplace*	Andrew Motion
Marquis de Sade	*Betrayal*	John Burnside
Marquis de Sade	*Incest*	JJanet Street-Porter
Saki	*A Shot in the Dark*	Jeremy Dyson
George Sand	*The Devil's Pool*	Victoria Glendinning
Friedrich von Schiller	*The Ghost-seer*	Martin Jarvis
Mary Shelley	*Transformation*	
Percy Bysshe Shelley	*Zastrozzi*	Germaine Greer
Stendhal	*Memoirs of an Egotist*	Doris Lessing
Robert Louis Stevenson	*Dr Jekyll and Mr Hyde*	Helen Dunmore
Theodor Storm	*The Lake of the Bees*	Alan Sillitoe
Italo Svevo	*A Perfect Hoax*	Tim Parks
Jonathan Swift	*Directions to Servants*	Colm Tóibín
W.M. Thackeray	*Rebecca and Rowena*	Matthew Sweet
Leo Tolstoy	*The Death of Ivan Ilyich*	Nadine Gordimer
Leo Tolstoy	*The Forged Coupon*	Andrew Miller
Leo Tolstoy	*Hadji Murat*	Colm Tóibín
Ivan Turgenev	*Faust*	Simon Callow
Mark Twain	*The Diary of Adam and Eve*	John Updike
Mark Twain	*Tom Sawyer, Detective*	
Jules Verne	*A Fantasy of Dr Ox*	Gilbert Adair
Leonardo da Vinci	*Prophecies*	Eraldo Affinati

Edith Wharton	*Sanctuary*	William Fiennes
Edith Wharton	*The Touchstone*	Salley Vickers
Oscar Wilde	*The Portrait of Mr W.H.*	Peter Ackroyd
Virginia Woolf	*Carlyle's House and Other Sketches*	Doris Lessing
Virginia Woolf	*Monday or Tuesday*	Scarlett Thomas
Virginia Woolf, Vanessa Bell with Thoby Stephen	*Hyde Park Gate News*	Hermione Lee
Emile Zola	*The Dream*	Tim Parks
Emile Zola	*For a Night of Love*	A.N. Wilson